THE NEW
NANNY

BOOKS BY L.G. DAVIS

THE NEW NANNY

L.G. DAVIS

bookouture

Published by Bookouture in 2023

An imprint of Storyfire Ltd.
Carmelite House
50 Victoria Embankment
London EC4Y 0DZ

www.bookouture.com

ISBN: 978-1-83790-470-9
eBook ISBN: 978-1-83790-469-3

ONE

CHRISTA

Not a single word.

It's been almost an hour since I landed in Salzburg, Austria. Hans, a short, heavyset man with a hooked nose and black, slicked-back hair, whom Robin and Paul Mayer sent to pick me up from the airport, still hasn't said a word to me.

I *did* make a few attempts at conversation, but he only responded with nods.

When we met in the arrivals hall, there had been no real reason for us to communicate, since he simply held up a sign with my name on it, and I willingly followed him to the waiting midnight-blue Mercedes with silk-lined leather seats and the faint smell of expensive cigars.

I'm not the type to make chit-chat, but it feels like the silence is stretching on forever. I had assumed he didn't understand English, yet he hasn't said anything in German either. If he did, I doubt I would understand much, but at least he could try.

We should arrive in the small, hilly town of Ruddel in about fifteen minutes or so, but Hans makes no attempt to break the uncomfortable silence.

Giving in, I turn my attention to the view outside the window and my gaze is met by a charming landscape of rolling hills and vibrant peaks stretching up into the infinite, azure sky. Austria is a stunning country, but instead of appreciating its beauty, my mind drifts to Robin Mayer and her family: my future employers.

I met Robin when she was in a state of disarray, four months ago, dark circles around her eyes and tears filling them as she told me how she had lost a baby six months before and was unable to care for her family and home by herself. She needed help, and I felt sorry for her.

When the Mayers asked me to accompany them abroad to their villa in Austria during the summer break, I didn't hesitate to say yes. I'd been working for another family on the same street, but this was an opportunity I couldn't turn down. Not in a million years.

At the sound of Hans coughing, my attention snaps from my inner thoughts and my eyes land on a cluster of terracotta rooftops tucked away between the jagged mountain peaks. Ruddel—the town I had been obsessed with reading about online. I'd even seen a photo of the Mayer villa, courtesy of Google Maps.

The sun shines on the small town, illuminating the deserted streets and casting long shadows. At 8 a.m., the narrow, cobble-stone streets are almost devoid of life, except for a few people readying their shops and restaurants for the day ahead. A church bell tolls, its deep sound ringing through the sleepy town.

The quiet late-June morning is almost magical, giving me a sense of what life must be like here. We drive past the town square, which is adorned by a bronze statue of a woman on a pedestal in the center of a cobblestone circle. The church in the next block has a tall clock tower and, behind it, rows of grapevines stretch out for miles and miles with the sun peeking through their leaves.

As I follow the winding path through the trees, the Mayer residence comes into view. Surrounded by lush green trees and hills, the sun glints off the many windows. Its white walls stand out against the lush green foliage, a vision of beauty with cascades of vibrant bougainvillea adorning them. Two granite columns frame the white marble steps that lead up to the entrance. An enormous fountain in the courtyard shoots water into the sky, while a statue of a woman stands in its center, her arms raised as if in greeting.

I push the button to activate the window, and a rush of fresh air floods into the car. The smell of wet soil and the sweet aroma of summer florals blend together, creating an even more serene atmosphere. I can't help but feel a sense of familiarity as I take in the scene. My throat closes up with emotion as it hits me that this is where I'm going to be living for an entire summer. Even Google Maps couldn't do it justice.

Hans opens my door, and I step out of the luxurious car and gaze in awe at the building. As he unloads my suitcase from the trunk, I become mesmerized by the garden outside. It's like a vivid painting, with its beaming summer blossoms sprawling out like a rainbow rug. Even though there's no one outside to welcome me, a thrill of expectation still courses through me.

I offer to help Hans with the bags, but he declines, carrying them up the steps. I follow behind, listening for any sounds coming from the other side of the large mahogany door.

At last it's opened and I come face-to-face with the boy I'm here for. My heart glows with joy at the sight of him standing there, his amber eyes peeking out from beneath his honey-blond curls.

He's wearing a sky-blue shirt with tan cargo shorts that hang just above his knees. For a teenager, he looks clean and well put together. It doesn't matter that rather than a smile, his lips are pressed into a thin line or that his expression is unreadable. There's time enough for us to get to know each other.

"Wyatt..." I whisper, almost breathless. Without thinking, I draw him into a hug. "It's so nice to see you again."

He smells like fresh hay on a summer day, the scent familiar and comforting.

"Hi," he mumbles, then stiffens in my arms before pulling away.

I don't blame him. Even though we met before in New York, and I had a short conversation with him, we're still strangers, I guess.

As I step into the grand, marble hallway with a big chandelier dangling overhead, I'm met by the morning light streaming in through the window, painting the room in a soft, golden hue. Then I spot Robin, Wyatt's mother, meandering down the curved staircase, one step at a time. Every movement of her body seems to pain her. It's apparent that she has difficulty getting out of bed these days and that's why I'm here—to take care of everything so she doesn't have to. She and her family arrived in Austria less than a week ago, and since I still had some things to take care of back home, we agreed that I would come a few days after them.

A small grin splits her face as she spies me standing in the hall. "Christa, you're here! Come on in." She moves toward me and places both hands on my shoulders, squeezing them gently before dropping them back to her sides. Her perfume reminds me of lilies in the springtime, and I feel a wave of calm wash over me. "I'm glad you made it here safely."

"Thank you," I reply, returning her smile. I glance beyond her at Wyatt, who is standing in front of a large stone fireplace, fiddling with the hem of his shirt.

Robin says something to the driver in German and he picks up my luggage from the floor where he had deposited it. He heads upstairs, probably to take them to my room.

Then she throws her son a look. "Wyatt, you should be more polite to our guest."

"I was." Wyatt's expression is unreadable as he wanders off. It seems the fact he said "hi" was enough for him.

"I hope your flight was uneventful, Christa," Robin says, ignoring her son's behavior, though her neck is flushed red. She meets my gaze and gives me an embarrassed smile.

Her large eyes are a deep brown, and they remind me of treacle as they glimmer with unshed tears. Her skin is too pale for the summer, as if she has been trapped inside a windowless room for a long time. Though not a classic beauty, her glossy, raven hair is beautiful in an ethereal way. It cascades around her shoulders like a mantle protecting her from the outside world, the tips highlighted with a hint of gold.

What really stood out to me when I met her is that unlike most of the middle-aged women on her street back in the US, she isn't a stick figure and seems to be comfortable in her body. I'm the same way. I've never felt the need to diet in my thirty-three years and I won't start now—my curves are just fine.

"It was wonderful, thank you," I reply, my voice dripping with sincerity. "I'm really looking forward to being here and helping you out."

She pulls in a deep breath, takes my hand in hers. "I'm very thankful for your help. It means a lot to me and the whole family. And welcome to Austria. I'm sorry about Wyatt's behavior just now. I noticed he was quite rude. He has been troublesome lately... he barely speaks to us in full sentences anymore."

Even though she's smiling, her body language exudes sorrow. Her shoulders are slumped forward, and heavy shadows still lurk beneath her eyes just as they did when we first met.

I'm not surprised. The grief of losing a child is an immeasurable burden—one that can be carried for eternity.

"It's all right." I give her a knowing smile. "He's just a teenage boy. They're like that sometimes."

"I suppose so. But sometimes..." She blows out a breath and throws her hands in the air. "Oh, it doesn't matter. I would love to give you a tour once you're settled. You must be exhausted. I haven't planned on having you help with anything until tomorrow so you can sort your things out and get your bearings."

"Not at all." It's hard to contain my excitement at getting to know Wyatt and helping him loosen up. The sooner I get comfortable in this place, the better. In fact, I'm so energized that I could start working right away.

Just as we're standing there, Robin's husband, Paul Mayer, comes down the stairs and I swallow hard. His dark-gray eyes are hard as steel and his thin lips are pressed together firmly.

Like his wife, he's not exactly striking. He's balding and stocky, with a scowl that rarely leaves his face. But the clothes he wears are expensive, and that subtly reveals his power and influence. His dark suit seems to be tailored to fit his frame to perfection, and he's wearing a tie with a ruby pin that glints in the light. His presence fills the room with a silent, ominous energy.

Robin told me that while she's a US citizen, Paul is Austrian and this is his family home. They met while he was studying in New York, and they eventually got married, but they only lived in Austria for about two years in total. At my interview, he had made it rather obvious that he was not in favor of hiring me or anyone else for this job, but I was able to prove my worthiness in the end.

"Christa," he says without smiling and comes to stand in front of me, arm outstretched.

I give his hand a squeeze as I shake it, but he doesn't return the gesture, quickly pulling away almost as soon as our palms meet. I can tell he still isn't convinced that they made the right decision by hiring me. But is it *my* presence here that he doesn't want, or just the presence of someone in general?

"Excuse me," he says, glancing at his wife, "I've got some work to do." With that, he walks away.

An icy chill runs down my spine. There's something about Paul that makes me nervous. I'd go as far as saying that the man makes me feel a little uneasy. I'm not exactly sure why.

"I'm sorry about that," Robin says when her husband nods and walks off. Though she doesn't spell out what she's sorry for, we both know.

It's going to be hard to do my job and take care of Wyatt if Paul disapproves of me, but I'm determined to show my value. Hopefully, with time, he will come around and accept me as a part of their family, and Wyatt and I will become friends.

I'm here now. I've made it through the door, and nothing or no one will make me go away. Paul Mayer just has to learn to live with it.

TWO

CHRISTA

Robin's footsteps echo through the foyer as she leads the way from one wing to the other. While she tells me the history of the house and the people who've lived in it over the years, we pass through two kitchens, two libraries, and several large bedrooms and bathrooms. Then we arrive in the drawing room, a majestic space with high ceilings and tall windows. A white grand piano sits against one wall and a few pieces of antique furniture are scattered around the room, but most are covered in plastic. Robin tells me about the artwork on the walls and the family stories that go along with it, told to her by Paul, who grew up here.

We spend a good amount of time walking around, exploring the different parts of the house, and enjoying the stillness of the place. Finally, we venture out into the garden, where the sun shines brightly, and a cool breeze brushes against my face.

The garden is teeming with life—birds chirp in the trees, butterflies hover around colorful flowers, and fat bumblebees buzz over the fragrant rose bushes. Robin explains how each tree and flower had been planted strategically to add to the beauty of the estate.

Back in the house we arrive in a dark hallway where she stops and leans against a wall.

"Sorry." She wipes the sweat from her brow. "I keep forgetting how big this place is." Her voice has grown hoarse from describing everything to me. "Do you mind if we continue tomorrow? It's just that I get tired very quickly lately."

"No problem at all. Please, go and get some rest. I can show myself around later." I pause. "If that's okay."

"Of course it's okay. It's so kind of you to understand. But before I leave you, we need to have a little chat first." I raise an eyebrow as she shakes her head. "I mean, we need to talk about what you're going to be doing around here. Unless you want to unpack first."

"No. I'm really not tired. I can do all that later."

"All right then. Let's go to the kitchen."

I follow her to the most beautiful black-and-white kitchen I have ever stepped into. The counters are made of white quartz marble and the appliances are chrome and state of the art. Cabinets are covered in brushed nickel hardware and glass cabinet doors. I feel as if I'm in a dream as I wander around the spacious room. The air is completely scentless, as if nobody ever cooks in here. With all the money they have, I bet they order in every day and the kitchen only serves as a showpiece, a work of art. It's the kind of kitchen one would feel afraid to spill anything in.

Peering through the tall windows, I marvel at the glorious mountain range that stretches longingly toward the sky, adorned with vibrant edelweiss. It's as if I've stepped into a postcard.

Most people would feel incredibly lucky to be in my position right now. I'm just so grateful that I was chosen for this job instead of someone else.

"Now," Robin says as she sits down at a kitchen island that's big enough to seat a small village. A thick, black folder rests in the middle. She removes a page from it and slides it toward me.

"Let's talk about your job here. I'm sure you must have many questions about what we need from you."

My gaze runs down the list on the piece of paper, which continues to the next side. Normal things for a housekeeper to do—dusting, sweeping, mopping... nothing I can't handle. I'm a clean freak by nature anyway, one of the many things I inherited from my childhood. I never thought that one day I would be grateful for the way I was raised. This house is large and daunting, but if anyone can handle the task of cleaning it, it's me. I'm up for the challenge.

"I hope it's not too much for you to do in addition to cooking and looking after Wyatt." She claps her hands in front of her. "The good news is, you don't have to worry about cleaning the other wing of the house since it's not occupied at the moment. But this side of the house is still going to be a very big job."

"I can handle it." I place both hands on the piece of paper and smile. "It won't be a problem at all."

"Great. That's good to hear." She wraps a lock of hair around her finger, her expression thoughtful. "When it comes to your daily work structure, you can start with breakfast, then tidy up the kitchen before getting to the bigger cleaning jobs. You can decide what works for you and what hours you want to spend on each task, as long as it all gets done by the end of the day." As she speaks, she twirls her wedding band around her finger. "When it comes to meals, unless I say otherwise, I'd like all mine served in my room. Paul is not much of a breakfast person and he eats out a lot, so you don't have to worry much about him. Lunch should be ready by noon, and dinner by seven. Does that sound doable?"

I nod, committing the schedule to memory. "It should be no problem. I can make sure everything gets done in a timely manner. Just let me know if there are any changes or special instructions. I'm sure I can handle it."

There's no way I will complain about anything. It's all a

small price to pay for being here. Besides, caring for a fifteen year old is not like looking after a baby or a toddler—Wyatt is able to do most things himself.

"That's great. I was worried for a moment because I know how much work is involved. In the past, when my mother-in-law was healthy enough to live here, she hired *two* housekeepers just to get everything taken care of."

I smile. "Don't worry at all. I've done worse."

She has no idea just how much worse I've had to do before. But that's not something she has to know. My life has to remain private.

Robin knots her fingers together, her expression growing solemn. "About Wyatt... He can be hard to handle, and he hasn't been talking much lately. Our relationship is complicated." She sighs. "I just... I guess I need someone to just be around, make sure he's all right. Does that sound reasonable?"

"Yes, yes of course it does."

"Sometimes I feel like I'm failing at being a mom and wife," Robin mumbles, her gaze on her folded hands. "I just can't seem to manage taking care of my home and family. It's not that I don't want to..."

"You don't need to explain," I say quickly. "Losing a child... it must be devastating. I can't even start to imagine how you feel. I'm really sorry you had to go through that."

My words feel inadequate, and I wish I could do more than just offer trite sympathy. The grief in her eyes is raw and palpable, as if her loss is a living, breathing thing inside of her.

She nods. "Only someone who has been through it would understand, I suppose." She blows out a breath and puts on a brave smile. "I'm so glad you're here, Christa. It was hard to find someone who was willing to come with us to Austria." She sighs. "Okay, back to Wyatt." She leans forward. "He's perfectly capable of taking care of himself, but he still needs guidance and oversight, like all teens do. His mood and behavior can be... unpredictable. And please don't take offense if he doesn't say much to you. He tends to speak in short bursts and gives curt answers. He takes being a sulky teenager to another level." She pauses to stare into space, as if deep in thought, before bringing her attention back to me. "Like I said, just be there when he needs you. Nothing complicated."

"That won't be enough," a voice booms from the door.

When I turn around, Paul strides into the kitchen, his face still hard and emotionless.

He clears his throat. "For a while now, Wyatt hasn't communicated with us unless he has had to. I'm hoping you can use your expertise in child psychology to figure out what the problem is. Have daily or weekly sessions with him. Find out what's going on."

Feeling uncomfortable because my experience in child psychology was faked on my resume, I look from him to Robin. "Sessions? What do you mean?"

Robin looks just as confused as I am as she twists her wedding band around her finger again.

"Therapy sessions," he explains. "But do not reveal to him what you're doing. I want him to feel like he can talk to you openly, without feeling like he's talking to a therapist."

Robin stands up abruptly. "Paul, I don't believe this is the right thing to do. We can't make Wyatt talk if he doesn't want to and I certainly don't want to lie to him."

I inhale deeply. "I'm quite all right with it, though," I say, before they can continue their disagreement. It shouldn't be too difficult. I've been wanting to get to know Wyatt better ever since we met.

"Excellent." Paul rubs his hands together. "I guess you are the right person for the job after all."

He leaves the room again, and I turn my attention back to Robin. "Thank you again for the trust you've placed in me. I'm pleased to be here, and it would be a privilege to look after your home and family. I have a lot of experience with children, and I will do my best to make Wyatt feel comfortable. I'll also make sure not to push him too hard. You just focus on getting better."

She smiles, but it looks forced this time. "As my husband said, you're the right person for the job."

"Thank you." I push back my shoulders. "So, what do you want me to start with?"

"You aren't too tired? You have a long journey behind you, and you must be struggling with jet lag."

"Not at all." I chuckle, even though her words trigger the exhaustion behind my eyes. I blink several times and inhale. "I like to think that I have more energy than most people. I'm ready to get started as soon as possible."

Robin picks up the folder, hugging it to her body. "That may be the case, but don't forget that you still have some unpacking to do. Why don't you do that and, if you're still up to it, you can do a little tidying." She glances sheepishly over her shoulder at the overflowing sink, her expression one of apology. "I'm sorry I couldn't get to those dishes."

"Don't be sorry. I'll go upstairs and unpack, then I'll take care of all of it." I pause. "If you need anything, anything at all, just let me know."

She chuckles. "Looks like you're going to have two children to look after, because I really feel like one right now."

"As I said—"

"You have more energy than most," she finishes for me and we both laugh. Then her hand goes to her chest. "Goodness! I've shown you a few rooms in this house, but not yours. Are you ready to see it?"

I get to my feet. "I'd love to see it."

My room is bigger and more luxurious than any other room I have stayed in. It's a tall, airy space with one wall of windows that look out over the mountains. In the middle of the room is a huge bed with a woven-looking blanket on it and rich-looking crisp, white sheets, which seem softer than anything I have ever slept in before. Six large pillows are stacked against the upholstered headboard.

"You have your own bathroom." Robin opens the door on one end of the room. "I hope you like it."

"It's beautiful." I come to join her at the door, taking in the huge walk-in rain shower. Everything is gray-and-white marble with patches of gold here and there. Instead of a home, this feels like a hotel I've come to vacation in.

"If there's anything else you need, just let me know. We want you to be comfortable here."

"Thank you. I already feel at home," I say. "Be careful, I might never want to leave."

She laughs. "Perfect. I hope you don't mind, but I think it's time for me to have a little lie down. I feel so exhausted that one would think I climbed up a mountain."

"I don't mind at all."

As Robin closes the door, I notice something and call her back.

"Hmm... there's no key in the lock," I say when she opens the door again. "Do you happen to know where it is?"

She gives a disappointed sigh and presses her hand over her heart. "Oh no. Has another one gone missing? That's too bad. This house is old and many of the keys are lost or have been misplaced. But don't worry, no one else has access to this room. Your privacy is guaranteed."

Even though it still bothers me that someone could easily enter the room unexpectedly, I trust Robin's words and thank her for her assurance, but I have another question.

"Are there any fun places I can take Wyatt to, to keep him occupied?"

She turns around slowly and her gaze meets mine before

she shakes her head. "I'd rather he stay here," she says. "He has everything he needs. Just be sure he doesn't watch too much TV. His father prefers him to read. This getaway is meant to be a retreat for him; a place for him to escape the stress of the outside world, and recharge before school starts again in the fall."

I frown. "You don't want him to go out?"

"Only if he absolutely must." Her lips curl into a smile, but her words are firm and pointed, driving her message home.

"Okay, I understand. I'll see you soon."

After Robin leaves, I stare at the suitcase for a while, pondering her words. I can't comprehend why they would want to keep a young boy from leaving the house. It seems cruel to me. I suppose I'm going to have to figure out ways to keep him busy so he doesn't feel like he's missing out on anything.

After I have unpacked my main suitcase, I shift my attention toward my backpack, searching for my phone charger. I reach inside one of its side pockets and feel something there. A piece of paper.

I pick out the paper and unfold it, revealing two German words written in black ink.

Sei vorsichtig

Since the words mean nothing to me, I put the note aside for now and continue unpacking.

As it's my first day with them, Robin asked me not to cook dinner and she ordered in tuna pizza from a pizzeria in the village, even though she and Paul did not eat with us.

Sitting alone with Wyatt in the dining room is almost excruciating because he barely says a word to me. It's the first time I'm in charge of a fifteen year old, and I have no idea how to connect with him. Younger kids are easier to impress. All one has to do is make a few jokes, give a few goofy faces, then watch their eyes light up.

"Wyatt"—I put down my slice—"what types of movies do you like? Maybe we could watch one together sometime."

He looks up at me and smiles a little before shaking his head. "Nah, it's okay."

I nod and think of another topic. "Forget movies. What kind of music do you like?" I ask, thinking it's a safe question.

He lifts and drops his shoulders. "I don't know. Whatever." He bites into his pizza and chews without meeting my eyes.

Not about to give up yet, I take a moment to think, racking my brain for something that might get us talking. What are teenage boys interested in? My mind answers instantly and I straighten up.

"Hey!" I lean forward. "Do you like to play games? Video games, board games, card games... other games?"

This time his eyes light up and he nods. "Yeah, I like those."

I smile triumphantly and my heart lightens. Maybe I can handle this. "So why don't we play a game after dinner. What do you say?"

He looks at me, saying nothing for a few seconds, then he nods. "Sure, why not?"

Relieved that he's speaking in full sentences with me, unlike with his parents, I lean back, smiling. I'm glad I persevered. Now I'm looking forward to our game night.

"What types of games do you like?" I ask and bite into my slice of pizza.

Wyatt scratches his chin and thinks for a few seconds. "Maybe we could play chess?" he suggests.

I can sense that his guard is still up, but at least he's talking and almost smiling now.

"Chess? That's great! I don't know how to play it, but I've always wanted to learn. Maybe you can teach me. I have to warn you though. I'm not a quick learner. It could take me a while," I admit, trying to make him laugh.

He reaches for another pizza, "No problem. I can help you."

I sense a shift in the atmosphere, like he's finally starting to warm up to me. "Thanks, Wyatt, I'm looking forward to it. Should we start after dinner? We could play right here." I gesture to the dining table, feeling a rush of relief and excitement that I was able to break through his walls, if only a little bit. I'm determined to keep the momentum going, though I don't want to seem too eager. The last thing I want is to chase him away.

He nods. "Yeah, that sounds cool. I'll get the chessboard ready." No longer interested in food, he pushes his plate away and stands up to go get the game.

While he's gone, I quickly clean up, anticipation building within me.

Wyatt soon returns with the chessboard and sets it up on the table. He shows me the basics of the game, explaining the rules and teaching me some strategies.

Reaching for a piece, he looks me in the eye. "Your king is in danger; what are you going to do?"

I move a piece to block the attack, then I smile at him. "Was that the right move?" I ask.

He laughs and claps lightly, apparently impressed by my move. "You've got potential, Christa."

By the time we're done, it's almost ten, which means we have been playing for over two hours. During the game I learned a few things about Wyatt. He's very smart and makes quick decisions, and he has a great sense of humor that comes out at the most unexpected times. He's also quite a good listener.

But he's a strange boy, too. Even though he's only fifteen, there's a maturity about him that's very adult-like in an almost eerie way.

"You know"—I smile despite exhaustion setting in—"if you want to, we can keep playing tomorrow. And I'll try to beat you. I'm getting better."

Wyatt tips his head back and lets out a low laugh. "Okay, I'll bring my 'A' game." He eyes me for a few seconds. "You're a quick learner," he says with a smile that brightens his brown eyes.

I laugh. "I'm still learning. But it's been fun."

What he doesn't know is that I'm actually a great chess player and have been playing since I was a child. But I just smile, feeling very happy that he accepted me.

"I'm going to bed," he says, picking up the chess pieces.

"Goodnight, Wyatt." Stretching out my arms to relieve tension, I watch him walk to the door and I can't help but feel a new sense of hope.

His eyes meet mine, and the softness in them is unmistakable. "Good night, Christa."

I fight the urge to hug him and instead just smile again.

After sitting alone in the dining room for a long time, thinking about Wyatt and the connection we made, I get up and head upstairs to my room. I close the door behind me, throw open the closet and reach for my backpack. It's empty since I unpacked everything. Except for one thing.

I take out the note I found in my backpack hours ago. I didn't think much of it then, but now my intuition is telling me to give it another read, to try to understand the meaning of the words.

I open the piece of paper and flatten it on my knee, then I reach for my phone and go online. I quickly search for a translator and type in the two words. With each letter I type, my intestines feel as though they're being twisted into a knot, and my fingers are trembling slightly.

Sei vorsichtig

Before I hit the blue translate button, I take a deep breath as if I need courage. For what, I have no idea. And then the translation appears. It's still on the small screen, but inside my head it's flashing like a neon light.

Be careful

Frowning, I hold the note in my hands, tracing the German words with my finger. The letters had been written in haste, so much so that the ink is smudged in some places.

I think of how it could have ended up in my backpack—wedged deep into the side pocket as if someone wanted to make sure it stayed in place and didn't fall out. Why? What could someone possibly want to warn me about? Could the note have ended up in my backpack by mistake?

Be careful. I repeat the words again in my head and a chill runs down my spine. It makes no sense at all. I shake my head. There's no way it was meant for me. And yet, I can't quite make myself throw it away.

I open one of the bedside drawers and drop the note inside. I can't help but think back to Hans, who drove me home from the airport. He was unable to verbally communicate with me, and he didn't even crack a smile. Sometimes a smile or the lack of it can speak louder than words. Is that why my subconscious is screaming at me to listen to the message?

I wonder if he was the one who left me the note. After all, he was the last person to touch my bags until I unpacked them.

THREE

CHRISTA

A jarring and insistent sound reverberates off the walls of the villa, a ringing that's reminiscent of an old-fashioned landline phone. Taking a pause from slicing the watermelon on the chopping board in front of me, I listen intently, trying to locate where the sound is coming from as I strain to hear it.

During my three days living with the Mayers, I've explored a good deal of the villa, and I haven't seen a landline phone anywhere, not even in Paul's home office, where he spends most of his time working. Curious, I set down the knife and make my way to the source of the noise, my feet padding softly on the wooden flooring.

The sound seems to be coming from the other wing. I pause at the foot of the stairs, waiting to see if either Paul or Robin will come out to answer it. Both of them are home, but there's no sound at all, not even footsteps making their way down the corridor.

Am I the only one hearing the ringing? Or is it part of my job to answer the calls?

As the sound persists, I make my way to the empty wing of the villa, down silent hallways, the sound growing louder as I approach a plain-looking door that stands halfway open. It's one of the guest rooms Robin showed me during her tour. She had mentioned that it used to be her mother-in-law Lena's bedroom before she was relocated to the nursing home.

The heavy scents of potpourri and air freshener are overpowering. On the walls are alternating patterns of pink roses and white daisies in a floral wallpaper. A white lace curtain hangs from the window, giving the room a soft and feminine feel. The oak bed, polished to a high sheen, is covered in a floral bedspread, its intricate pattern of blues and greens bringing a touch of color to the otherwise faded room.

All the furniture in this wing of the villa is draped in clear plastic, except in this room. Instead it's all covered by a film of dust. Maybe Lena asked for her room to stay the way she had left it, hoping to return to it.

Paul and Robin probably didn't come to answer the phone because they think it's someone calling for Lena, who's not here. Perhaps they can't be bothered to pass on a message. But from what I heard from Robin, it's been a while since Lena fell very ill and, after leaving the hospital, never returned to this house. Wouldn't people who know her also be aware of this by now?

I step inside and immediately I notice an old-fashioned, pale-yellow rotary dial phone on the bedside table, with its phone number written on a laminated card next to it. Perhaps Lena was afraid that old age would rob her of the ability to remember her number.

I pick up the phone. "Hello," I say hesitantly.

There's no response except for heavy breathing echoing through the receiver as the line crackles with static.

"Who is this?" I ask and nervously lick my lips, tension creeping up my spine as the breathing grows louder. Since reading the note left in my backpack, I've been a little on edge. I try again. "Is anybody there? Can you hear me?"

Finally, the caller says a single word, a name.

"Christa," the person on the other end whispers. Then the phone goes dead.

I set the receiver down, my spine tingling with dread.

There are so many things wrong with what just happened. I've only been working here for three days, and everyone who knows me back in New York has my cell-phone number. And they wouldn't have this number since I don't even know it myself.

I try to shake off the fear and uncertainty I feel and leave the room, clicking the door closed behind me.

As soon as I step out, I spot Robin coming down the hall. Her eyes widen when she notices me standing in the hallway outside of Lena's room.

"Christa, are you okay? What were you doing in there?" she asks, her voice probing.

I point a finger to the door. "The phone was ringing and I answered it, but there was nobody on the other end..."

Robin's face turns pale. "How strange—I can see why you're so unsettled." She pauses. "I'm surprised that phone is plugged in. No one has used it in years." She walks into the room and, within a few seconds, the phone is unplugged. Then she turns to me. "You mentioned that there was no one on the phone when you answered. Did the person speak at all?"

I purse my lips and nod. "They whispered something, but I... I didn't catch it. I'm not sure if it was a man or a woman."

Robin's face clouds over and she looks away for a moment, her eyes distant when she looks back at me and offers a weak smile. "I'm sure the call was probably for Lena." She pauses and meets my gaze with a stern one. "It would be best if you stayed away from this side of the house, all right?"

I nod and walk away, still feeling uneasy. Maybe I'm just on edge because of what I did to get this job, secretly afraid that if Paul and Robin find out they would let me go. There's no way I heard my name. I'm just being silly, and I have to stop before I ruin everything.

After dinner, during another game of chess with Wyatt, I make a conscious decision not to dwell on the mysterious phone call and focus on him and the game instead. Soon enough, the events of the day are a distant memory.

"Hey, Wyatt," I say as I make a move on the board. "I noticed that you have a PlayStation. What's your favorite game?"

He seems to tense up a bit before replying. "*Bloodcore*. It's a very intense game with fantastic graphic design. It requires a lot of skill and strategy. Why do you ask?"

I'm a bit taken aback by his response and the way his body language changed when I asked the question. I've heard about *Bloodcore* and know it's not recommended for a fifteen year old because of all the violence and gore.

"Isn't that a little morbid for someone your age?"

I don't know much about gaming, but I came across one of his gaming magazines in the living room and three of the games were circled, including *Bloodcore*. I thought talking about games he enjoys playing would be a great conversation starter, so I did some research on the internet to learn more.

"Maybe," he responds, "but it's also a lot of fun."

"And your parents are okay with you playing it?"

"I don't talk to them about it," he replies with a shrug, "but I'm smart enough to know what I can handle." He's trying to sound independent and mature, but between the words I sense something else. It's in this moment I realize how sad and lonely Wyatt feels, despite his tough exterior.

I say nothing more as I watch him play, but my heart aches. Robin and Paul are obviously not very involved in his life, and I feel a deep sense of sadness for him. Robin mentioned that

Wyatt doesn't talk to them much; maybe it's because they don't talk to him much either. I've only been living with them for three days and have already noticed they barely spend any time with him. I hope my presence can give him some kind of companionship and help him feel a little less lonely.

Without thinking, I reach out a hand and give his shoulder a comforting squeeze. "You know, if you ever need someone to talk to... I'm here."

I feel him tense and then relax slightly. He looks up from the board and meets my gaze before looking down again. "Your queen is in trouble," he says with a smirk.

I laugh and shake my head. "So it is," I respond, before returning my attention to the board. As I do, a warmth spreads throughout my chest, knowing I helped him, even if it was only a small gesture.

We play a few more rounds and the tension slowly fades away. When we wrap up the game, I ask him what his favorite food is.

"Spaghetti, hamburgers, and apple crumble."

"That's good because I make a mean apple crumble."

He lets out a small laugh. "Maybe one day I'll get to try it."

I smile and ruffle his hair. "Whenever you're ready."

"I'm always ready for apple crumble." He stands up and starts walking away, but then turns back to me with a smile. "Thanks for the game." He yawns loudly.

"Any time," I reply with a nod before he disappears through the door.

After giving the kitchen a good cleaning, I'm heading upstairs when I notice a light coming from the living room. I know it can't be Robin or Paul because they always watch TV in their bedroom.

When I peek around the corner, I find Wyatt on the couch, his eyes closed while an action movie is playing. Hugging a cushion to his body, he looks like a little boy in need of a hug.

I consider waking him, but instead I turn off the TV and take a blanket from the hall closet, tucking it around him. He stirs but doesn't wake. Then I sit on the couch next to him, watching him sleep peacefully, desperate to reach out and push the curls back from his forehead. But what I did is already enough. I hope he can feel that he isn't alone and that I'm here for him.

I'm dozing off when I feel something warm lean against me. I open my eyes just enough to see that it's Wyatt, sleeping with his head on my shoulder, his breathing even and his face peaceful. My heart flutters and I close my eyes. We stay like that for a while, until he finally opens his eyes, and looks at me with surprise.

"I fell asleep." He yawns and moves away quickly.

"Yeah, you did. It seems like you needed a little rest."

"Sorry for..." He blushes and looks away.

"Not a problem, buddy." I tap him on the arm. "Time for bed."

He nods, standing up, and thanks me before he leaves.

FOUR

ROBIN

It's 5.20 a.m., and she's already awake, and so am I thanks to my insomnia. I squint at the screen of my iPad and watch her wander out of the room and down the hallway toward the stairs.

For five days in a row, Christa has been waking up no later than 5 a.m., and she always starts the day with an early-morning walk. It does not bother me that much, but it sure baffles me. Who gets up that early when they don't have to? If I had the choice and had no responsibilities, I would stay in bed all day. Most people would do anything to stay snoozing, hitting the alarm clock over and over. But not Christa.

I slide out of bed and cross to the window in time to see her making her way down the dirt road that leads to the river running behind the house.

I hear the sheets rustle as Paul wakes up as well. I don't look at him until he's standing beside me, scratching the top of his head.

"Do you still think it's a good idea she's here?" he asks, yawning.

My fists clench tightly, my nails digging deep into my skin as I face my husband. "I don't think you realize just how much work there is to be done around here. So, yes, I do still stand by my decision to hire her." My voice quivers with emotion. "I thought you had made peace with this."

During Christa's interview, Paul had shown up early from work and pulled me aside. He'd asked if it was really necessary for us to have a nanny for a fifteen-year-old child. He felt it was absurd. Since he did not have the decency to lower his voice, and Christa heard the entire conversation, she'd quickly told us that in addition to being a nanny, she was prepared to take on any household chores. I liked the idea immediately and changed the role to that of a family assistant, a job that would combine the nanny and housemaid responsibilities. But apparently that still wasn't enough for Paul.

I brush past my husband and return to the bed, climbing back under the covers, my iPad next to me. "At least we don't have to find a housekeeper. Christa does the job of several people for a fraction of the cost." I glance at the window again. "And we didn't have to hire someone from the village."

"I really don't get why we didn't. I'm sure it would have been cheaper."

"I can't believe you're saying that." I push the words through clenched teeth. "Especially after what happened last time. I'm sure people are already gossiping about us as we speak."

"I don't understand what the problem is, Robin." Paul comes to sit on the edge of the bed. "Does this have to do with my mother? Or what happened seven years ago? People forget. They move on with their lives. I'm sure the rumors have died down."

"Some people are strong enough to forget, Paul." I swallow the hard lump in my throat. "But not everyone."

He glares at me, his jaw clenched tight. "How long is it going to take for you to leave the past behind?"

I stare into his eyes for a long moment before tears fill mine.

"I don't know," I murmur, my voice breaking. "I might never get over it. If it weren't for you dragging us back here, I wouldn't have come. I told you—"

"My mother is lying on her deathbed right now. Her last wish is for us to be here until—"

"Until she dies. I know." I cross my arms. "It's just so hard being back here. The memories of betrayal are still fresh."

I am aware of why we have returned to Ruddel, and it has nothing to do with Paul's love for his mother. I know all too well how much hatred he carries for the woman who had always preferred his dead brother, Fritz, to him, and made no effort to conceal it.

When both Fritz and their father died in a car accident, Lena's anguish caused her to place the blame on Paul, since he had been the one driving. She needed someone to blame to ease her pain. Paul was twenty-two at the time, and unable to cope with his mother's resentment, on top of struggling with the loss of his father and brother. He left Austria to complete his studies in New York.

When he met and married me, six years later, Lena was not invited to the wedding. A year after we were married, Paul was appointed CEO of his family's wine-making empire because his mother had decided to step down. She was diagnosed with breast cancer and wanted to focus on her health. Wanting to be by his mother's side despite their tense relationship, Paul and I relocated to Ruddel.

The first thing my mother-in-law asked me when we met was why I wasn't pregnant yet. Twelve months, she argued, was more than enough time for a woman to conceive.

Lena survived the cancer, but in the two years we lived in Ruddel she continually compared Paul to his dead brother and mostly ignored me, as if I wasn't even there. Eventually, I no longer felt I belonged in my new home, although I did feel sympathy for the older woman and her plight.

When I sank into a deep depression, Paul made the decision to move us back to New York. He was able to manage the business remotely, returning to Ruddel for necessary meetings and tasks.

Due to the irreparable rift between Paul and his mother, when Wyatt came into our lives, a year after we left Austria, the only contact we had was to send her photos of her grandson each year for her birthday. As much as I wanted to spite the old woman, I still felt pity for her and was afraid of further damaging Paul's fragile relationship with his mother.

When Paul found out Lena's cancer had returned, and that it was terminal, he still felt heartbroken by the news. He'd kept Wyatt, who was now eight, from his grandmother, not wanting her behavior to affect him or for him to witness her mood swings and cutting remarks, but the new diagnosis changed everything. If she was dying, even after everything she'd done, Paul felt he had to be with her. He didn't want to regret any of his actions if the worst happened. So we packed up our belongings and came back for the summer of 2015. I only agreed to accompany him when I heard that Lena was staying in a nursing home and not at the house with us. Even when the woman was unwell, she was unpleasant to be around.

When we left Ruddel again, after that summer had ended, our lives were changed forever, and no one, even Lena, has set foot in the house again since that summer... until now.

As I stare at my husband, I wish I had refused to come this time and instead stayed back in New York to prevent old wounds from being ripped open.

Paul grunts with rage. "It's been seven years since we were all here, Robin. I know you didn't want to come back, but we had to." He bunches his fingers into fists until his knuckles turn white. "My mother is not perfect, but she's a frail, old woman now. She can't hurt you anymore. Maybe we should leave the past behind and make amends before it's too late." His voice rises with anger, as if daring me to disagree.

I chuckle and shake my head. "You think I'm stupid, don't you? You're not here because you want to make peace with her."

"What's that supposed to mean?"

"It means I heard you speak to her over the phone. I heard what your mother said to you. I know she used your inheritance as leverage to force you to come home. She threatened to disown you and give all her wealth to charities of her choosing." I draw in a deep breath and shut my eyes, forcing myself to breathe. As I open them again, I allow a tiny smile to curl my lips. "You're here because you don't want to lose your inheritance, not because you want to make peace."

Paul blinks, the truth in my words sinking in. He hangs his head, ashamed. "You're right. It's not the only reason I wanted to come back, but I certainly don't want us to lose everything." He blows out a breath. "It might do you good to make peace with the past—we can't turn back the clock."

Without giving me a chance to respond, he leaves.

On my iPad, I watch him head to the office, where he will spend most of the day, except for the one hour that he will visit his mother at the hospital... alone. I wish I could have told him that some things can be forgiven, but they can never be forgotten. And some actions can never be undone. That's why it was a big mistake to come back here.

Less than ten minutes after Paul leaves the room, he pokes his head through the door again, his expression serious. "Robin, I'm getting rid of some of the cameras today. You need to stop watching people like a hawk. The cameras outside are staying, but the ones inside are going. Surveillance is for security purposes, not for invading people's privacy."

I nod. "Fine. Do what you want."

When he's gone again, I leave the bed and return to the

window. From here I can see the river, the sparkle of the water as the early-morning sun hits it. I squint my eyes, and in the distance I spot a dark figure. I've only ever seen Christa in black clothes.

But then I see something else, another person near her, someone in what looks to be a red sweater. My stomach twists as I watch them. Christa is talking to one of the locals. Something I've been trying to avoid.

I need to keep my eyes open, to stay vigilant. I have to watch her to make sure she doesn't speak to the wrong people, hear the rumors. One word said by the wrong person at the wrong time could destroy everything.

As cruel as it makes me feel, I make a wish for Lena to die sooner rather than later, so we can get the hell out of this place.

FIVE
CHRISTA

When I open my eyes, the clock reads 5:05. This has been my wake-up time since I was ten years old. Many children are able to stay asleep, snuggling with their stuffed animals and trying to get a few extra winks, but this isn't something I ever had the privilege of doing.

This habit has become so deeply rooted in me, that I don't even require an alarm clock to wake up. When I was a child, alarm clocks were forbidden, and I've never used one as an adult either. At thirty-three, I continue waking up early, even when I don't have to. As much as I hate it sometimes, it's something I'm incapable of changing, and I'll probably be doing it until the day I draw my last breath.

I look out my window and watch the sun slowly make its ascent into the sky. It's a soft pink and orange glow that signals a new day, filled with possibility and hope. The mountains, the trees, the tall grass all welcome it, a promise that everything is going to be okay.

Feeling wide awake, I swing my legs out of bed and enter the bathroom. For a split second, my hand lingers on the hot water button in the shower. One press of a finger and the warm water would wash over me. But I don't do it. I go for the cold, just like I always do. I punish my body like I've done for many years. Because this is another of many habits I can't seem to shake.

Some people take cold showers because they want to feel invigorated. For me, it's different. It's like a penance, something I need to do in order to prove that I'm still in control, something that keeps me grounded and keeps me going, no matter how much my body screams in resistance. I welcome the cold water, the chill running through my veins like liquid ice. It slides off my body, taking with it any doubt and negative thoughts that are lingering in my mind.

Whatever is left, I wash it off with soap and a washcloth, scrubbing my skin raw until it almost hurts. Once my skin and hair are completely rid of dirt and debris, I step out of the shower stall. A pleasant aroma of vanilla and lemon fills the air, emanating from the shower gel I used. I take a deep breath, allowing the scent to drift toward my nose.

Through the window, I watch the mountains reaching into the sky as they always do. They look so majestic and strong, and I feel as though they're giving me strength, telling me that whatever I went through in the past, I will be okay.

Wrapping a fluffy, warm towel around my body, I give myself the permission to be cozy before I head out. Then I get dressed. Choosing an outfit is never a difficult task for me as I always wear black, eliminating the need to consider which colors go together. It's a simple and effective process that means I'm ready to face the day in no time. Today, I opt for my favorites: black tights and a black tank top, and a black sweater to ward off the morning chill.

Before I know it, it's 5:20 a.m. and I'm walking out the door to go for a stroll or a jog. I won't decide until I'm outside. Choice is a luxury I never take for granted.

I come to a halt in front of Wyatt's door. I think he's snoring, but I'm not sure I'm hearing right. I move away from the door and head down the stairs, thinking of the hours we've spent together since I've been here. Paul asked me to help him open up, but what he doesn't know is that Wyatt is already wide open, just not in their presence.

One thing I noticed that's as clear as day is the fact that he always seems rather uncomfortable around them, maybe even afraid. Just yesterday he was talking normally, but when his father stepped into the kitchen, he suddenly became distant. Seeing the disconnect between the two of them, I couldn't help but feel sad. Before I had applied for the job, they seemed like a typical, contented family, but it was clearly a facade. Wyatt and his parents have not shared a single meal together since my arrival, and they don't spend more than a few minutes together in the same room each day. It's almost as if they try to avoid each other.

Robin eats all her meals in the bedroom. Paul is not a break-fast person, and he's never in the house for lunch since that's the time he visits his mother at the hospital. For dinner, when he's home, he reheats the food I leave for him in the refrigerator.

As soon as I open the front door, a gentle breeze blows around me, carrying with it the crisp smell of roses and magnolia. After leaving the drive, I make my way down a dirt road toward the river.

Since I discovered it the day after I arrived, I have been going there every morning. I love the sound of the water as it runs downstream from high above the rocks to low in the shallow middle. The reflection of the early-morning sun as it touches the surface takes my breath away. As long as I remain on shore, I can enjoy the sight.

I listen to the sound of my sneaker soles crunching against small stones, the birds singing in the nearby trees, which send their whispers through the wind as it brushes my ears. This is nature in its untainted form.

Standing at the edge of the river, I gaze down into the clear water and admire the smooth stones beneath.

I'm in my own zone when I sense someone watching me.

I look to my left to confirm my suspicions. Sure enough, there is someone in the distance, silhouetted against the sun. My heart leaps with excitement as I make my way over to meet the stranger. It's the first time I've seen anyone in this area so early in the day and my first opportunity to talk to someone outside of the Mayer family.

It takes me around five minutes to reach him but as soon as he sees me, he looks up. He's tall, with broad shoulders, and he's holding a fishing rod. He must have come to catch fish while the river is still calm. He welcomes my presence with a smile that reveals very white teeth hidden behind a thick, gray beard and I smile back.

"*Guten Morgen.*" My German is limited, but the best way to a local's heart is to speak at least a few words of their language.

"*Guten Morgen.*" He nods, and his smile widens even more. "*Wohnen Sie in der nähe?*" he asks.

But that's where my German ends and confusion starts. I should have practiced more before coming to Austria. I tried learning on a language app, but, in my opinion, German is a hard language to learn, and it took me a while to catch on, so I gave up.

"*Entschuldigen Sie bitte. Sprechen Sie Englisch?*" I finally manage to ask, my embarrassment obvious.

"Yes, of course. I speak some English," he says. His tone is pleasant and laced with humor.

"Oh, that's good." I'm relieved that we will be able to communicate without hindrance. Maybe I'll make a new friend today.

"I just asked if you live nearby," he tries again.

"Yes. Yes, I do. For a while at least." I lower myself onto a large rock that's jutting out of the soil. "I'm in Ruddel for work."

"Ah!" He rubs his beard with his free hand. "Very exciting. Do you work in the village?"

I shake my head and point behind me at the Mayers's villa that's visible in the distance. "Up there."

The man follows my gaze and I see him stiffen, just as Wyatt did the day his father walked in during breakfast. "You work for the Mayer family?" His tone is no longer friendly or pleasant.

"Yes. I'm here to work as their housekeeper and nanny. I do both." I pause. "Do you live around here?"

"Oh, I see." He turns away and tugs on his fishing rod. His reply is curt and to the point. "Nice meeting you."

I stand up, puzzled by the sudden change in his demeanor. "I'm sorry... Um... Is something wrong?"

"I need to continue my fishing. Enjoy your day." He follows that up with something else in German that I don't understand. His face has taken on a different expression, one that's hard and unreadable, as though a curtain has fallen at the end of a performance.

I frown, not understanding exactly what's going on here. "I don't mind chatting. The family is still sleeping and—"

"Sorry, miss. I need silence to fish." He doesn't even look at me.

I get the message. Something I said or did has clearly rubbed him the wrong way, cutting our brief conversation short. I'm basically being dismissed.

"Of course," I reply, trying to mask my disappointment. "I'm sorry to have disturbed you."

I proceed to my usual spot by the river, intending to stay there a while. But after a couple of minutes, I change my mind. On my way toward the house, I replay the conversation in my mind, wondering what had caused it to end so abruptly. As I close in on the villa, I look up and see Robin at their bedroom window, staring out like she has done the last couple days. A shiver runs through me. What is she doing? Keeping an eye on me? But why?

SIX

CHRISTA

I open the front door to find Robin lingering near the staircase, an unusual occurrence since she rarely comes downstairs before noon, unless she has somewhere to be. As she requested, I usually bring her meals up to her bedroom every day, which has enough room for a separate sitting area. But it's too early for breakfast.

"Good morning." I manage a smile, despite the feeling of unease spreading through my stomach. "Would you like me to make you an early breakfast?"

"Who were you talking to at the river?" she deflects, not answering my question.

"I bumped into a local... a fisherman. It was just the two of us at the river, so I went over to say hi. It was nice talking to someone else who isn't a Mayer."

My feeble attempt at a joke to lighten the mood goes unnoticed by Robin. She doesn't crack a smile. Instead, she rakes her fingers through her disorderly hair and crosses her arms. "What did he say to you? Anything interesting?"

I can sense the tension in her voice.

"Not much," I respond honestly, puzzled by her reaction. "We didn't talk for long."

"What do you mean?"

I want to ask her why she's interrogating me, but I stay quiet and just say, "We said hello, but before we could take the conversation further, it all stopped. It was really weird."

"I see," Robin responds before striding into the kitchen.

I trail after her, feeling increasingly uncomfortable. "Robin, is everything all right?" I ask as she stands by the window, her back to me.

She turns and takes a seat at the island, her hands fidgeting with the tabletop. Although she has the means to maintain neat and perfect manicures, her nails are bitten down to the quick.

"Christa," she exhales. "You should probably know that the people around here are... odd."

"In what way?" I pull out a chair at the island and sit. "The man seemed nice at the start."

She shrugs. "There are just strange people around here, that's all. If I were you, I would keep a distance. That's why I stay home and hardly invite anyone over."

"But isn't that lonely?" I immediately regret my words, inwardly cringing.

"No, not for us," she answers without missing a beat. "We're here for peace and quiet, far away from all the hustle and bustle. We've still got each other for conversation, so it's not like we're completely isolated."

Her words reach my ears and I understand their meaning, but she's wrong. I have never met more lonely people. They don't even spend time together.

"I would actually like to get to know the locals. I find it exciting to see new places and to get to know new people."

"That's not a good idea." Her tone hardens as she lifts her hand to her mouth. She's about to chew on a nail, but stops herself. "You can't trust anyone in this town. The gossip here is like wildfire and, before you know it, you're the latest topic."

"I guess that's true of every small town, isn't it?" I say. What happened here? Did she have a disagreement with someone and since then doesn't want to talk to the locals? But what does that have to do with me? "So, you're saying I shouldn't speak to anyone at all?"

How is that even realistic? Unless I stay cooped up in the villa, I will come across someone, and I do not intend on ignoring them.

"I wouldn't advise it. I know it sounds silly, but I can't help but be wary of the people in this town. I'm sure they mean no harm, but I'd rather stay here in our own little world. I hope you feel comfortable in this house and have everything you need."

"Yes, yes, of course," I lie. Her words are really starting to get to me. Is she implying I'd spread rumors and go around town blabbing about the family's private matters? It's clear she doesn't trust me, and I'm offended by her lack of faith. But it's best not to make a scene, so I keep my thoughts to myself.

"Great." Clearly satisfied with my response, Robin stands up from the island and waddles to the door, her hips swaying from side to side. In the doorway she turns to face me again. "Christa, you've been doing a really good job here and I would love for you to continue. Instead of focusing on the locals, there's a lot to be done in this big house, wouldn't you agree?" She puts a finger to her lips in thought. "I'd love an omelet on toast and some fruit for breakfast. Can you handle that?"

"Absolutely," I say in a low voice, still feeling insulted by what she just said to me.

"Excellent. Bring it up in an hour, though. It's way too early for a meal now."

She exits the kitchen. As she fades away, I can only speculate what made her so negative toward the locals. I'm also perplexed as to why she believes chatting with the townspeople would have an impact on my work. I'm perfectly aware of my responsibilities and there's no way I would put my job in jeopardy, not after all the effort I put in to get it. And not with everything I have on the line.

At first, I thought her words were a veiled warning that if I was too chatty, I would forfeit my job. But, surely, that can't be what she meant. The mere thought of it leaves a sour aftertaste in my mouth. Something about the way she spoke to me triggered something inside, a feeling of discomfort. It wasn't only her words, but also her expression and body language. Up until now, she's been kind and mostly quiet, but today I saw a different side to her, one that made me think back to the note I found in my backpack.

I'm starting to question if I should be on guard. It's illogical because although I can sense something off about her and Paul, they seem like normal people. I'm on edge, torn between listening to subtle warnings and having faith in my seemingly harmless employers. How can I trust this feeling inside me when it makes no logical sense?

My mind is playing tricks on me and driving me crazy. The note has to have been a mistake. It definitely wasn't meant for me. Robin and Paul are just people who like to keep to themselves, who enjoy the peace of their remote villa in the mountains. There's no crime against that.

SEVEN

CHRISTA

I decide to spend the day cleaning the villa from top to bottom. It's the only way I'm able to distract myself from the dark thoughts and the myriad of emotions and questions clouding my mind.

But before I get to work, I join Wyatt for breakfast, which is always a joy. While some kids love variety in their meals, Wyatt eats the same breakfast every day: an omelet and toast, which he washes down with a glass of fresh orange juice. He has a specific way of eating his omelet, making sure to cut it into small, uniform pieces before he takes a single bite. I've tried offering him something different for breakfast, but he always refuses.

He's a strange boy in many ways, but I always look forward to the time we spend together when neither Paul or Robin are around, which is often. Sometimes it feels as if it's just the two of us living in the house, even with Robin upstairs in her bedroom.

As soon as we're done having breakfast, I head to the laundry room and load the washing machine with sheets and towels. I begin my cleaning session by dusting the baseboards and lamps in all the rooms that are in use; I vacuum the rugs and clean the cabinet doors, light switches, and fan blades; then I mop the floors, shampoo the carpets, shine the mirrors. I scrub until my fingers throb. But it doesn't help calm my thoughts. The words on the stupid note still linger in the back of my mind, like an annoying song stuck on repeat, and I can't help but feel a sense of dread, anxiousness, and suspicion that I'm missing something huge. Mostly I worry about Wyatt. At the very least his parents neglect him.

I'm standing at the mantle in the library, running a dust cloth over the brass picture frames, when I notice that none of the photos are of Paul and his family. Staring out of each frame is another woman with the same dark-gray eyes as him and a nose that is slightly upturned. In some of the photos she's with a baby that could be Paul, but I'm not sure. In many of them she's photographed with a teenage boy, who resembles Paul but cannot be him because, instead of blond hair, his is jet black, and he has a birthmark on his chin. As I look closer, I notice that it's the same boy next to the woman in every photo. I realize they were taken over many years as he looks to be in his early twenties in the last frame.

Robin had mentioned that Paul had an older brother who died in his twenties. It dawns on me that if the boy is the brother, then the woman must be Paul's mother. But why are there no photos of Paul, Robin, or Wyatt?

A wall above the leather couch by the window is also covered in family portraits, but none with the three of them in it. It's clear that Paul's brother was his mother's favorite. I guess she never accepted Paul's wife and son either. And yet Paul is the one left behind to care for a parent that doesn't care for him. I feel especially sad for Wyatt—it must hurt to have a grand-mother who never dotes on him.

Ignoring their family issues, I get back to cleaning and only stop at midday. As I trudge up the stairs to check on Wyatt, I spot Paul in the hallway. Since we hardly see each other, I never really know what to say to him.

He sees me and walks over, dressed in khaki trousers, a beige shirt, and white loafers. "I've been meaning to ask, how are the therapy sessions going with Wyatt?" His face is unreadable as he waits for me to answer. "It's been a few days and I haven't noticed an improvement in his behavior. He's still barely speaking to us."

I hesitate. I want to tell him that Wyatt is a normal teenager, and that I've never had any issues communicating with him, but would he feel insulted by that? I decide to play it safe.

"We're getting there," I reply and hold my breath.

He glances at his wristwatch, then back at me with furrowed brows. "Do you have any idea what's causing him to be so reclusive?"

I shake my head. "I believe it's just a typical teenage phase."

He squints as he considers my words. "So in other words, from the perspective of someone who studied child psychology, you think this is just temporary... a passing phase?" He looks unconvinced. "Even if it's been going on for years?"

My stomach twists at his inquiry. "That's my opinion of it, yes. I do think it's part of adolescence and I'm sure he'll come out the other side eventually."

Paul nods once, as if he's processing it, then he walks away without another word. Less than a minute later, he announces that he's going to visit his mother, then he's out the front door.

It's strange that Robin never accompanies him to the hospital. He's taken Wyatt twice this week, but Robin hasn't left the house since I got here.

After catching my breath, I head over to Wyatt's room and knock. "Are you okay?" I ask the boy when he tells me to enter. "Do you need anything?"

He shakes his head and goes back to playing a game on his PlayStation, his curls bobbing on his forehead. It troubles me that he often plays rather violent games. When I brought it up with Robin, she looked disturbed by it, but she quickly brushed it off and moved on to another topic. I hate to think that Wyatt finds comfort in violence. I can't help but wonder what he's thinking and what he's feeling. No matter how much time I spend with him, he still seems so alone.

My heart feeling heavy for him, I close the door and make my way to his bed, sitting down on the edge next to him. "I'm going to start making lunch. Do you have anything in mind that we can do together after we eat?"

For a second he looks up, his honey-brown eyes shining. "There's a stable in the village. Can we go and look at the horses?"

"Can you ride?" I ask.

He shakes his head and sighs. "My mom promised to send me to lessons, but it never happened."

"Maybe you should ask her again... remind her."

"It's a waste of time. I already asked and she keeps finding some excuse to avoid it. She won't even let me go look at them."

Sensing his disappointment, I feel the urge to help. "Let me ask her," I offer. "She must not have realized how much you want it."

"Don't bother." He shrugs and his eyes return to the game he's playing.

He obviously doesn't believe I can get through to Robin. I have doubts myself, especially after she had made it clear that she doesn't want Wyatt going out of the house. It's a shame because horse therapy is one of the best treatments for children and teens with anxiety issues to help them feel more grounded and connected. I stay next to him, wanting to protect this child from any kind of pain, any kind of rejection.

"Have you asked your dad about the horses?"

He scoffs. "And disturb his precious work? Besides, it's not like he cares what I do or what I want. Not anymore."

"I'm sure that's not true, Wyatt. He's just very busy."

"It is." He looks up again. "When I was younger, it was different. He was different. He used to take me to all sorts of places, even the ice-skating rink. Now he's just like her. He doesn't care about me."

"Oh, sweety, I'm sure your mom loves you very much." I squeeze his hand and it's almost as if the boy's pain is seeping out of him and transferring to me.

"No she doesn't," he scoffs. "She doesn't do jack for me, not after what happ—" He stops himself from continuing.

"After what happened, Wyatt?" I place a reassuring hand on his shoulder. "You can talk to me. You can trust me."

EIGHT

CHRISTA

"Just forget it," Wyatt says. "It's not important." He folds his arms across his chest, then drops them again, perhaps thinking the action rude. "Do you like working here?" he asks suddenly, changing the subject.

"Yeah," I stutter, taken aback by his question. I want to push him to tell me what he stopped himself from saying, but it's obvious he's upset, and I feel so sorry for him. When he's sad his eyes take on a vacant stare, as if there's nothing left behind them but a cold void, so I decide to take his cue and move on. "I love hanging out with you," I say.

"Y... yeah, it's cool having you here," he says. "To have someone to talk to."

"I'm glad you feel that way." I can't help the smile that curls my lips as I reach out and put an arm around his shoulder, giving him a squeeze. He doesn't pull away, but I do because I don't want to overstay my welcome.

"Look, I'll go and prepare lunch, then I'll talk to your mom about you coming with me to the village. I could just say we're going for a walk." I wink and get to my feet.

After leaving Wyatt's room, I head to the master bedroom and knock. I hear a faint "come in" and enter.

An hour ago, Robin had asked me to clean this room and when I was done, everything was perfect: the bed was made, the wooden floor was glistening, and all the dust had been wiped up. Now the space is a mess again. It amazes me just how untidy a person can make a room within a short amount of time. The sheets are rumpled around Robin and crumpled newspapers and tissues litter the floor and bed; there are also a total of four glasses on the nightstands since she's not a fan of using a glass twice.

Without asking her, and fuming inside, I start picking up things from the floor, including a bra. It's a struggle to keep my annoyance hidden from her.

"Do you need something?" she asks.

I remember why I'm here. Holding onto a piece of newspaper in my hand, I force a smile. "Yes. I just... I know you said it's best to avoid the village and locals, but I think it would really be nice if Wyatt and I have our next therapy session in the village. We could talk while walking around the shops and tourist attractions."

"No," she says fast and firm. "I told you that I don't want him..." She pauses. "*We* don't want him to go to the village."

"I'm sorry, but I don't understand why not. It could really help him warm up."

"Wyatt is *my* son and I know what's best for him. It should be clear by now that I want him to stay in the house, and on these grounds. If he leaves, it must be with us, his parents. I think the therapy sessions are a waste of time; if he doesn't want to speak, he shouldn't be made to."

I clench my jaw and suppress a sigh, feeling my face heat up with anger. I want to yell, to let out the tension boiling beneath my skin. Why would they want a teenage boy to stay cooped up in this gilded cage? It's starting to feel like a prison. Even for me.

But the sternness in her gaze warns me against pushing my luck.

"Yes, ma'am," I say and make to leave.

Suddenly, she calls out for me and I freeze, turning around slowly.

"Paul won't be needing his office today. Feel free to use it for your therapy session."

I nod and leave the room, my fingers twitching with the urge to slam the door shut, but I manage to close it gently. I wish I could go back in there and give her a piece of my mind, but I can't. I have no choice but to respect the rules in this house.

Instead of going to the village after lunch, Wyatt and I settle down in the home office, which has leather sofas, dark wood paneling, and bookcases filled to the brim with hundreds of books—all under a spectacular crystal chandelier. An antique desk sits in the middle of the room, and a wall of windows lets in natural light from the garden outside. But the atmosphere is still stuffy and oppressive.

Wyatt and I sit down on one of the plush rugs with a glass coffee table between us as we get ready to play a game of Monopoly. There's no way I'll make him feel like he's in a therapy session. I haven't even told him about his father's request to get him to open up.

We play quietly. Wyatt is focused and intense, concentrating on his properties, but he casually throws out jokes and comments that make me laugh. His interactions with me are spontaneous and easy, a side of him his parents obviously don't get to see often.

"So," I say, counting my money, "describe your perfect day."

He frowns at me for a second but then starts talking. "It would be with my friends. Just us, no parents. We'd go camping and maybe kayaking in the lakes." He nods. "We'd definitely do lots of outdoor activities all day. Then at night, we'd relax by a campfire, telling each other ghost stories."

He's about to say something more, but the door opens and Robin is standing in the doorway, still in her pajamas late in the afternoon. In an instant I notice how his shoulders cave in and his eyes take on a wild, distant look that wasn't there a few minutes ago. The moment Robin moves, taking one step then another into the room, I can almost see him shrinking into himself. It's very rare for them to be in the same room, and there's so much tension it's almost too stifling to bear.

"What are you two up to?" Robin asks, her eyes boring into mine.

"Just playing Monopoly and talking," I reply.

Wyatt stares at the floor.

"Talking, huh? What about?" Robin's eyes never leave mine.

I shrug. "Oh, nothing, just ordinary things."

"That sounds like fun. Feel free to continue." She says nothing more as she settles into one of the armchairs and watches us.

I try to pick up my conversation with Wyatt, changing the discussion to more mundane topics, but he's unresponsive. I can tell his entire mood has shifted. The bright, easygoing boy is gone, replaced by a sullen introvert who fills the room with oppressive silence. His eyes keep drifting from the Monopoly board to Robin and I can see that his hands are slightly shaking.

Is he afraid of Robin? I wonder. *Should I be as well?* I think of the note: *Be careful.*

NINE

CHRISTA

The next afternoon, I'm inside the pantry searching for sugar to make apple crumble because Wyatt begged me for it. I made it on the second day after arriving in Ruddel and he's obsessed with it. But from the looks of it, the sugar is finished. So I run up the stairs to speak to Robin.

As soon as I enter, she slides what looks like an ultrasound photo under a book on the coffee table, a photo of the baby she never got to hold in her arms.

My heart aches for her, and I quickly look away out of respect. As a woman, I feel her pain deep down to my core. Losing a child is something no woman should have to go through. It's a sorrow that can never be removed, just eased by time, or not at all.

Unable to stop myself, and seeing a chance to make a connection and build trust, I walk over to her and lightly hug her, letting her know that I am here for her and she doesn't need to feel alone in her pain. If I were in her shoes, that's what I would want. I don't know what to say, but sometimes actions can speak louder than words.

I let go and whisper, "I'm sorry." Tears fill my eyes and I

blink them away. "I can come back later." I want to give her back the time to spend with the memories of her lost baby.

"No," she says, her voice cracking with emotions. She looks a little embarrassed. "What can I do for you?" Her voice is so different from the one I heard yesterday; the warm and gentle tone is back. Maybe it's because of the hug we just shared. "Is everything okay?" she asks with a tiny smile that teases the corners of her lips.

Even though she's still in her pajamas, she's not in bed this time but is sitting on a white couch by the window, cradling a striped beige-and-white couch cushion.

"Yes." I force a smile. "Everything is fine. I just need to go to the village to get some sugar and a few more apples. We've run out and I want to make apple crumble for dessert tonight."

Her face hardens again, the transformation so quick it's like a light switch has been flipped. Her eyes are now deep, dark wells. "Do you have to make it today?"

I nod. "Wyatt really wants me to. He liked the one I made the other day."

She gets off the couch and pulls the curtains further apart. "If you wait, Paul could bring you the ingredients. He's arriving before lunch tomorrow. Make a list of everything else you might need."

Paul left last night for a business trip, but I have no intention of waiting for him to return. Robin doesn't offer to get the sugar herself. She's really going to every length to avoid being among people. Whatever is going on with her is deeper than I could probably imagine.

"I'd rather make the crumble today. Wyatt is so excited about it."

She settles back down and crosses her legs, her eyes focusing out the window. "But how will you make it to the village? Paul has the car."

There's another car on the property as well as a number of

bicycles in the shed. But I don't mention this since she already knows.

"I don't mind walking. It should take no more than thirty minutes. I've walked farther than that before, and it's a nice day."

She can't stop me from going out. I need to clear my head. And the fact that she's so adamant that I should not talk to the locals makes me want to do it even more. In fact, that's exactly what I plan to do. I actually don't need her permission to leave the house, and if I have to buy the groceries myself, I will. Anything to make Wyatt happy.

Robin tries harder to get me not to go, including reminding me of chores that need to be done around the house, but I tell her everything is done. I've cleaned, cooked, washed more laundry, and completed everything else that needed doing.

Finally, she gives in and says, "Fine. Go buy what you need. But be back soon."

"Do you think I could use one of the bikes in the shed?" There's no harm in asking. The worst she can say is no.

"Right, I forgot about those. Hmm... sure."

Before I leave the house, I tell Wyatt I'm going out for a bit. The disappointment on his face at not being able to come with me is heartbreaking. I assure him I will be back before he knows it with all the ingredients for the crumble. That puts a smile on his face, which makes me feel relieved.

I lean in closer and whisper, "Don't worry, we will go out together one of these days. I just have to convince your parents."

"Cool," he whispers.

I find it rather strange that a fifteen-year-old boy would not even try to sneak out of the house. It's not as if the doors are locked. But I guess it's just one of those things that make Wyatt weirdly unique. Or maybe he doesn't have any friends in town and can't be bothered to go out on his own.

I'm walking down the hallway upstairs on my way to get my

purse when I pass Paul and Robin's room and hear the sound of crying from the other side of the door. For a moment I stop and stand in front of the door, wondering if I should enter, whether I should offer Robin comfort. She's hurting, and, on one hand, I understand her behavior is the only way she knows how to stay in control when everything is falling apart. But, on the other hand, I feel Wyatt's pain; he's hurting too and needs someone to be on his side.

In my bedroom, I'm suddenly lonely and desperate for an outside connection. I close the door, pick up my phone, and call Emily, my best friend and ex-roommate. She's a therapist and might be able to help me navigate this situation. Sometimes it takes someone from the outside to put things into perspective, and having a good listener to talk to can really help process emotions.

Emily and I grew up in neighboring towns in Kentucky, and have known each other practically our entire lives. Even when we left our hometown, we stayed close and she's always been like a sister to me, the one person who understands me better than anyone else in the world.

Unlike me, though, she has carved out a pretty little life for herself. She graduated in psychology, found love, got married, had a daughter, and now works as a therapist for women in abusive relationships. Throughout my life she has always pushed me to become more than I thought I was capable of, even though I often felt like I was stuck. She understood my struggles even when no one else did, probably because she was aware of the scars I carried from my childhood.

When she picks up, her voice is groggy from sleep—it's early morning in New York—but she sounds excited to hear from me. "Hello, stranger," she says, yawning. "I knew you couldn't just let me know that you arrived safely, without filling me in on everything else that's going on over there in *The Sound of Music* country."

I snicker at the thought. "To be honest, it's not as thrilling as you might guess. Em, this family is odd."

"How so?"

I take a deep breath. I'd already filled in Emily on the job and the family before I left, and she knows what I knew then, so I launch right into what I have discovered since.

"For starters, Robin—the mom—won't let Wyatt leave the house. He's fifteen and I can't even take him on errands or a stroll in the village. That's where the stores are."

"That's strange. Any idea why?"

"I have no idea. She also acted strangely when I told her I talked to one of the locals. I went out for a walk the other day, and I met a fisherman. I later told her about it, and she warned me to stay away from the townspeople. Apparently, they're full of gossip."

"Is there any particular gossip she's trying to avoid, maybe?"

I pause for a moment, reflecting on it. "Your guess is as good as mine. I suppose I'm about to find out."

"How will you do that if you're not allowed to leave the house?"

"*I'm* allowed to leave the house, silly. I'm an adult. But Wyatt is the one who's not allowed to leave the grounds."

"That's totally unhealthy for a teenage boy."

"I know. But I'm working on it. He's so sad most of the time and he seems... sometimes I think he's scared of them."

"Of his parents? Have you discussed it with Robin? It might help to talk to her and get an idea of the root cause of the issue. It could be a simple misunderstanding, or it could be something more involved."

"I want to, but she's really going through a lot and I don't want to be pushy. I think she'll come around eventually. I'm trying to be patient. I'm still building up our relationship, so I don't want to press the issue too hard. I wouldn't want to upset her even more."

"I see what you mean," Emily says. "It could be that, since she lost a baby, she's become more protective and doesn't want Wyatt leaving the house for fear of something happening to him. If that's the case, then it will likely take more time and patience to get her to open up and discuss it. Or it could be something else entirely. It's impossible to know without talking to her and getting to the bottom of it."

"You could be right about her being protective." It had definitely been a good idea to call Emily. "I'm just glad I'm here to look after him, you know. There's another thing I've noticed. Even though he's different around me, happy even, he's so withdrawn around them, a completely different boy."

"Have you noticed any signs of them harming him in some way?"

"Aside from keeping him here like a prisoner, I haven't seen any signs that point to them harming him physically. But what they're doing could be considered mental abuse, don't you think?"

"Definitely. Isolation and control can be just as damaging as physical abuse, sometimes even more so." Emily takes a deep breath and continues, "If you're able to build up a good relationship with Wyatt, it's possible you could get him to tell you what's going on. Encourage open dialogue between the two of you. Give positive reinforcement when he talks to you and make sure to keep the conversations light and encouraging. Eventually he might open up." She pauses. "If you find any more evidence that they are hurting this child, you have to do something about it. You may need to contact the authorities, Christa. Do not attempt to handle it on your own."

TEN

CHRISTA

At 3 p.m. the village is alive with movement. Bicycle bells jingle as their riders weave their way through the throngs of people, some with shopping bags, others sitting at outdoor cafés, enjoying conversations and a warm cup of coffee or tea, while the smell of freshly baked pastries wafting from the nearby bakery tempts those along the sidewalks. Tourists wander around with cameras in hand, admiring the small town's colorful buildings and lush green surroundings. At the center of the village, the farmer's market bustles with energy.

After parking my bike at a nearby rack, I make my way to the market, marveling at the vibrant stalls packed with local artisans' handmade jewelry, pottery, and textiles. I come across a group of boys of about six or seven running around the market square, laughing out loud as they play a game of tag in the sunshine. Stopping to stare, I imagine that Wyatt was one of them when he was younger.

As I turn a corner, shopkeepers and vendors call out loudly, offering their wares, but I decline with a wave and a smile. After my short stroll, I get my bike again to head to the grocery store.

Since I noticed only two grocery stores while walking

around, I go for the larger one of the two, located between a bank and a furniture store. The building is a structure of concrete and wood, and the windows display bags of freshly harvested potatoes, sprawling apples, and other fresh produce. Though a bit worn-down, it's still elegant in its own way.

The first thing I smell when I enter is a mixture of fresh coffee, baked bread, and a faint fragrance of herbs and spices. The warmly lit interiors are filled with locals bustling about, and I greet a few of them in the hopes that one of them will strike up a conversation with me. As friendly as they all seem, none go any further than a "*Guten Tag*".

Even though I only came for a handful of groceries, I remain in the store for a little longer, walking down the bright aisles, admiring the interior, which boasts wooden floors, open shelving, and old mason jars filled with pickled vegetables. Being inside the store somehow makes me feel connected to the town and its people. I can't help but be appreciative of the feeling, a sense of belonging. I feel sad for the child at home who is being denied this. He needs other people to talk to; he needs more than what's inside the walls of his home to explore.

"Good afternoon," I say to a woman who walks past me, followed by two girls. It's only when she turns to look at me that I realize that I spoke in English and not German.

She looks at me and smiles. "Good afternoon to you," she responds in perfect English and stops walking, her smile bright and welcoming. With a perfectly round curly Afro puff on the top of her head, and eyes that seem to beam with laughter and kindness, she exudes a presence in the store that cannot be missed.

"You speak English?" I ask, my heart lifting. I won't have to go through my limited German in search of the right words to say.

"A little," she says, then she puts a hand on top of one of her little girls' heads. The girls each have two curly Afro puffs on both sides of their heads, and large, brown eyes. They must be twins because they're identical.

"You sound American," the woman says.

"Yes, I am," I reply.

We start talking about the weather, the town, and even about the food in the store. After a few minutes, I prepare myself to bring up the topic of why I came to Ruddel in the first place, even though I'm a bit worried I might get the same reaction I got from the fisherman at the river.

Unfortunately, a man down the aisle calls for the woman and the girls.

"I have to go. My husband is waiting for us," she says and wishes me a pleasant stay in Ruddel before she walks off, the wheels of her shopping cart squeaking as they roll against the polished wooden floor.

It's almost 4 p.m. when I find what I need, including more apples, with the help of the little dictionary I brought with me to help translate the labels on the products. Even though Robin had not wanted me to come to the store initially, she still added a few more things to my list. Finally, I head to the cash register. As the woman behind the counter rings up my items, she says something to me in German that I do not understand. It sounds like a question so I shake my head. After that she scans all my items and I pay. Then she pushes them to one side, and moves on to the next customer.

"Can I have a bag please?" I ask.

She shoots me a death stare, then pushes up her glasses and says something else in German, the annoyance dripping from her voice.

"I'm sorry," I say in English. "I don't speak German."

One of the men in line behind me pulls a bag from a hook on one of the shelves and hands it to me. He's very handsome and very tall. His blue eyes twinkle in the fluorescent lights of the store, and he has an infectious smile. But I can't stop staring at his hair, which is full and black as midnight, the strands falling carelessly across his forehead.

"*Danke,*" I say to him.

The woman scans the bag and holds out her hand for the payment. I guess the question she had asked me earlier, and to which I replied with a "no" was whether I needed a bag.

My cheeks warm with embarrassment, I pack my groceries and leave the store. Outside, I'm making my way to the bike rack when a thump from the ground below my grocery bag stops me in my tracks.

I look at my feet in time to see my groceries scattered at my feet, and the green apples rolling away in all directions.

Crap.

I hurry to gather some of them up, but there's a gaping hole at the bottom of my bag so I can't put them back in.

"Do you need help?" a man's voice says from behind me in English.

I look up to see the customer who had handed me the bag in the store.

"Yes, that would be nice, thank you so much," I say.

Together we run after my groceries, though most of the eggs cannot be saved.

"I'm sorry." He picks up the drenched carton of eggs.

"No, it's fine. Thank you so much for your help." I watch as he takes it to a nearby bin and comes back to me.

All my groceries are at our feet since there's no other bag to put them in, and I won't be able to carry them all in my arms.

"Wait here," he says, holding up his hand and then he hurries off.

Less than a minute later he's back with another plastic bag, which he fills with my groceries. He won't let me help. As I watch him, I notice a few gray hairs on his temples that seem to only be visible in the sunlight. He must be only a few years older than me—five, tops. When he's done packing my groceries, he looks up with a smile that curls one corner of his lips.

Something flutters inside my belly, but I ignore the sensation. Yet this is my chance, my chance to strike up a proper conversation with someone.

"Thank again," I say to him, though I don't make a move to leave.

"You're very welcome." He glances back at the grocery store before returning his gaze to mine. "Are you new in town?"

"Yes, I just started working for a family here... the Mayer family," I say, pleased he decided to make conversation. I watch his face carefully for a reaction, any reaction, but I see none. Or maybe I do, a brief shift in his eyes? But I can't be sure because even if it was there it was quick, too quick for me to notice.

"That's interesting. I thought you were a tourist."

"No... well, I might as well be. I'm only staying here for about three months. I'm sort of an au pair."

"For which family, did you say?" he asks. "Everyone knows everyone around here."

"The Mayers," I say. "Do you know them?"

"Ah!" His Adam's apple bobs as he swallows hard. "The wine family? I definitely know them. How long have you been in town?"

"A little over a week."

"Okay, and how do you like our little town so far?"

"It's beautiful, but I'm still getting used to everything. I haven't been about much."

"You'll feel right at home. People here are very friendly."

"I'm sure they are." As I say the words, I remember the fisherman, hoping he was an exception.

"Well, I have to leave, but if you need a friend in town, someone to show you around, give me a call." He digs into his pocket and pulls out a piece of paper and a pen. He jots something down on the paper and hands it to me.

I look down at it, then smile up at him. "I'm sure I *will* need a friend around here. Thank you so much."

"No problem. Just give me a call if you ever feel lost in this small town. My name is James, by the way."

"I'm Christa." I reach out my hand to shake his. "It's nice to meet someone else who speaks English."

He chuckles and squeezes my hand. "I'm actually half British, but my father is from here. So this is kind of my hometown, and once upon a time, I actually taught German to tourists. That's how I made my money during the summer holidays."

"That sounds like fun." I pause, wondering if maybe I should start taking German lessons at some point. It would definitely help me make friends.

After an awkward silence, I thank him again and we say goodbye. But when I'm walking away, he calls my name, and I spin around to face him.

"I know we just met," he says, "but are you by any chance free for a coffee tomorrow evening around six?"

Surprised by the question, I hesitate for a moment, then I nod with a smile.

ELEVEN

CHRISTA

It's Tuesday, five days since James and I arranged to meet. But that didn't happen, and nor were we able to meet the days after that. Whenever we've tried, Robin has come up with last-minute urgent chores she wanted done.

I have a right to days off, but she kept rearranging my schedule to suit her needs. The two days I did manage to get off, James was out of town, so we couldn't meet up, which is a shame because I've been unable to get him out of my head and I'm really looking forward to seeing him again.

I could, of course, meet him in the evening after work on some days during the week, but I don't want anything to interfere with my bonding time with Wyatt. I know how much he always looks forward to playing chess with me after dinner. It has become our thing.

This morning, as I bring up Robin's breakfast, I find her asleep, but when I put the breakfast tray on the coffee table she wakes and sits up in bed.

Instead of leaving her room immediately, I say, "Robin, if it's all right with you, I'd like to take tomorrow afternoon off instead of on the weekend. I have some personal errands to run in the village."

She says nothing. No reaction whatsoever. Then she finally gets out of bed and comes to pick up the glass of orange juice, raising it to her lips. She takes her time drinking while eyeing me over the rim of the glass.

"I'm not feeling well," she says, her voice weak. "My headaches are getting worse, and Paul will be at the company office this week. I would prefer to have someone here to keep an eye on Wyatt. I'd appreciate it if you keep to your regular schedule and take your time off on the weekend."

The irony of her statement does not escape me, considering it's she who disrupts my schedule. As I think over her words, a thought strikes me.

"What if Wyatt comes with me? This way you can rest and not worry about him. We'd be back in no time." I pass her a gentle smile, hoping she will see it as my way of caring for her.

With a sigh, she reaches for a grape and pops it into her mouth. "Christa, you know how we feel about Wyatt going out."

"Yes, I do know. But that boy is miserable being here all day."

"I don't want to have that discussion again. Wyatt is perfectly fine. He has everything he needs right under this roof."

I want to say more, but I'm afraid this could turn into an argument. I still have to protect my job, so I nod and walk to the door. But before stepping out, I meet her gaze.

"Robin, going forward, I need more reliability with my scheduling to be able to manage my own tasks." I close the door softly, leaving her to process the information.

Since coming to Austria, I've been doing my job diligently, going beyond what's asked of me, being her nurse, Wyatt's nanny, and everything else she needs me to be. I'm not complaining, because it's such a joy caring for Wyatt, and I plan on always being here for him, but I also need to make connections outside of this house, to make friends and to find opportunities for Wyatt to do the same.

As soon as the door clicks shut, something crashes to the floor, or did Robin throw the tray at the wall?

"What's going on?" Wyatt asks, appearing from his room.

I shrug and we both stand there listening to more things breaking on the other side.

"Should we go and finish the puzzle we started last night?" I whisper. I need to take him away, to keep him from hearing his mother's pain, being traumatized by it.

He nods. He was excited when I gifted him the thousand-piece puzzle, which is an image of New York by night with all the buildings lit up.

Together we head downstairs, and once we sit down at the dining table, he looks at me and cocks his head to the side. "Is my mom okay?"

"She's... she's not feeling well." I guess that's half of the truth. But what if that's not enough for him? Picking up a puzzle piece, I take the opportunity to be more honest with him. Maybe the only way through this is to make him understand exactly what Robin is going through.

"Wyatt, your mom losing the baby was a really hard thing for her to go through. She might not be able to cope with her emotions right now, but it's important to remember that she needs time to heal, and it's okay for her to be sad about it."

He slides a piece into an open slot and, without looking at me, he says, "She never has much to say to me." He's speaking as if he doesn't care, but I catch a slight quiver in his voice. It's strange for him to say those words given that Robin claims he's the one who doesn't say much to them.

"I'm so sorry, Wyatt," I whisper. "She's depressed right now. It doesn't have anything to do with you, okay?" I reach out to touch his arm. "Some people just struggle more with things than others. It doesn't mean that she loves you any less or doesn't care about you. While she heals, you have me... and your father."

"My father?" He lets out a bitter laugh. "I never see him. He's always working. Even when he's home, he's not."

He's right. Paul is hardly ever home; when he is around, he's locked up in the office. I can count on my hands the times I've heard him talking to Wyatt.

What I do get to hear a lot are the fights between him and Robin that seem to be increasing every day. They do it behind closed doors, thinking no one will hear them, but even if I don't hear the exact words sometimes, I know they're ugly. They argue more than they talk to each other normally.

"Wyatt, are you happy?" I push, needing to know more about his situation, his feelings.

"I'm happy that you're here," he says.

I smile, my heart glowing from the inside out. "So am I. I'm happy to be here with you." Happy that, with everything that he's endured, Wyatt is finding comfort in my presence here.

For the next few minutes we continue our puzzle in companionable silence. And then, just as she's been doing almost every time Wyatt and I sit down for our "sessions", Robin appears in the dining room. The days and times are written on a piece of paper she keeps in their bedroom on the nightstand.

It's obvious she's been crying because her face is swollen and red. She looks at us for a moment, then looks away, busying herself with something on the sideboard before taking a seat at the dining table.

As usual, our conversation dies and Wyatt focuses instead on the puzzle, not even looking up at Robin.

"Are the two of you having a good time?" she asks finally.

Wyatt pauses, holding a piece in midair, yet saying nothing.

"Yes," I say, but there's a hard tone to my voice, even though I try my best to hide it.

After a few minutes, Wyatt and I change the subject and talk about ordinary things like the weather, school, and Wyatt's friends back home. Our conversation must be so boring that Robin stands again and leaves the room. Wyatt visibly relaxes, his shoulders slumping and his facial expression lightening. I can tell it really bothers him when she's around.

"I know she doesn't love me," he says quietly, painfully.

My head snaps back, his words hitting me hard. "What makes you think that, Wyatt? She's your mother."

"Yes," he says, "but she's never said that to me."

"That's really sad. I'm sorry." My heart aches for him, for all the moments of love he's been denied over the years. "You're such a good kid and she's lucky to have you. I'm sure she cares about you."

He chuckles. "She has a funny way of showing it."

"Don't forget that she's hurting right now."

"I know she lost her baby. I guess she doesn't care about anyone else that's left behind." He smiles sadly and goes back to his puzzle. "It doesn't matter, anyway. I don't care. I'm just the adopted child. I guess I should be grateful that I have a roof over my head."

I know that Wyatt is adopted because Robin was open to me about it, but hearing it from him, and seeing the pain of rejection in his eyes, is hard to bear.

"Wyatt... I'm so sorry you were separated from your birth family. But your parents wouldn't have adopted you if they didn't love you."

He doesn't reply, instead allowing the silence to fill the air around us.

When we leave the room, my heart is heavy and I wish I could take his pain away.

After he disappears into his bedroom, I go to mine and see

that I have a missed call from James, which I immediately return.

"Hi," I say when he picks up.

"Hi there, tourist." His voice is laced with humor. "Are we still on for tomorrow?"

"I'm sorry, but I won't be able to make it tomorrow either."

"Oh, I see." I can hear a hint of disappointment in his voice.

"I need to take care of Wyatt. Robin... his mother has migraines."

The truth is, after seeing Wyatt so upset, I don't want to leave him alone.

"Really? It kind of sounds like she just doesn't want you to go out."

"No, she really is unwell." I pause. "But we'll meet up soon, I promise. I'll make sure of it."

"I hope so. But no pressure. You do what you have to do to keep the royal family of Ruddel happy. But you have the right to go out, Christa. You're not a slave."

"Yes, yes, I know. It's just that Robin is going through so much, and I want to help out as much as I can until she gets back on her feet. Then I'll have a bit more flexibility."

"Well, I look forward to seeing each other again."

"I do too, James."

TWELVE

CHRISTA

Two days after talking to Robin, I'm finally meeting up with James. Since he hardly has time during the day on weekdays, I have made an exception and agreed to meet him in the evening, and I'd plan in some extra time for Wyatt tomorrow for our game of chess.

To my surprise, over breakfast, Robin tells me to take one of the cars.

Since early this morning she has been a different and much nicer person, which is unexpected considering that late last night when I'd gone downstairs for a glass of water I'd overheard her and Paul arguing.

I didn't hear everything they were saying, but I *do* know that shortly after I returned to my bedroom, the argument escalated and she left the house. I watched her from my window as she made her way down the path outside, headed for the river, I assumed.

They must have patched things since then because this morning she and Paul were pretty pleasant to each other, and even to Wyatt. And both joined us for breakfast, which was even more of a shocker.

As I pull away from the house, my eyes on the road ahead, the mountains on both sides of me, I wonder what the argument last night was about. I have a feeling they were arguing about me, that whether hiring me was the wrong decision.

"Just admit that we made a mistake," was thrown around a few times by Paul, but I didn't eavesdrop long enough to hear Robin's response. Given that my room is just down the hall from theirs, if one of them had opened the door, I wouldn't have had enough time to make an escape. I could also have interpreted things wrong and they are just a normal couple who were having a normal disagreement.

When I make it to the village, the sun is just setting, the burn of light sinking into the trees and brightening the sky for a few long moments before disappearing. The majority of the locals in town have already gone home; the people on the streets are mostly tourists.

James suggested we meet at Messer, a steak restaurant. As I find parking in a tight space, I'm suddenly nervous about seeing him again even though we've talked a lot over the past few days like old friends. I wrap my favorite purple pashmina scarf—a gift from Emily—around my shoulders to keep away the evening breeze and exit the car. On my way to the restaurant, I pass an old man with a walking stick, and he nods toward me, mumbling a hello before continuing on.

I open the door to the restaurant and am surprised by the retro vibe inside—plush green furniture, vintage photos, and soft jazz playing in the background. There are also candles lit around the room, adding a romantic ambience to the place. The smells of steak, grilled vegetables, and spices mingle with the scent of candles burning. I ask a waitress to escort me to a table in the back, and James arrives about fifteen minutes later.

"I'm so sorry for being late," he says. "I took a nap and totally missed the alarm." Without missing a beat, he kisses me on the cheek and it doesn't feel awkward at all.

"You took a nap in the late afternoon?"

"I sure did. Naps are holy to me." He pulls out a chair for himself. "Trust me, you should try them."

"Okay, I promise to give them a try."

"Good. You won't regret it." He pauses. "It's nice to see you again, Christa. How have you been?"

"Busy." I chuckle. "I'm sorry we couldn't meet before today."

"That's all right. Me being out of town didn't help much either, did it? I'm an architect and I'm currently working on a project in Vienna that requires me to be there quite a bit. I guess we were both busy."

"You can say that again," I say. "Robin, my boss, has been very overwhelmed. She's working through some things at the moment and I'm trying to help out as much as I can."

He dips his head to the side. "What kinds of things?"

Even though I didn't plan on telling him anything personal about my employers, he seems like a good person, someone I could be friends with. "She lost a baby last year, and she's still pretty depressed."

He nods and buries both hands into his hair. "Wow! That's a lot to deal with. But it must be hard for you too. It can't be easy to see someone in that kind of pain. It must be even harder seeing that she doesn't want you to go out and take a break." He pauses. "To be honest, I never thought she'd let you out." He waves over a waitress. "Are you up for something to eat or just a drink?" he asks as the waitress arrives at our table with her notepad.

"I wouldn't mind a bite to eat. I haven't eaten much all day."

"Great. Neither have I since I was napping away the day."

We both order steaks with mashed potatoes. For drinks, James orders an entire bottle of water since he apparently doesn't drink anything else. I order a large glass of Almdudler, a popular Austrian carbonated soft drink. We talk a bit about our day, then I decide to ask him questions before he does it to me.

"So, what do you do when you're not napping?" I ask. "You mentioned that you used to teach tourists German. Do you still do that sometimes?"

"Only when I'm short on cash." He laughs out loud. "No, I'm actually too busy for that. I really enjoyed it though."

"Busy being an architect?" I accept my drink from the waitress and take a sip. "I can't imagine there's too much work for you around here. Is that why you have to travel a lot?"

"You're right about that. My clients are spread out across the country. Before meeting you, I was actually away from Ruddel for a while. I returned a few weeks ago. But I do have a house and family here."

"Oh, really? Why were you away?"

He shakes his head and pours himself a glass of fizzy water. "It's a long story. Maybe I'll tell you all about it one day." He takes a gulp of water from his glass. "How about you? Have you always worked as a—"

"No. I studied child psychology. But after the second semester, I discovered I didn't want to work in the field, so I chose to be a nanny instead. Since quitting my studies, that's what I've been doing."

"You must love children a lot," he remarks as he takes another sip.

"I do more than love them. I care for them deeply and try to give them the support they need. Not all parents can provide that. I just want to make sure the kids feel safe and secure."

He nods in understanding. "That's very noble of you. And you're right about some parents' failure to look after their own kids. It's a good thing there are people like you willing to help out."

A smile curls my lips. "I really enjoy taking care of Wyatt especially."

"I can see that," he says, his gaze on my face.

"Really? How?"

"In the way your eyes lit up when you spoke about him just now. What makes him so special?"

"I don't know. There's just something about him that makes me want to be there for him, to protect him."

"How old is this special boy you talk of?"

"Wyatt is fifteen."

"Did you say fifteen?" He leans back with a smirk. "You're babysitting a fifteen year old?"

"I wouldn't exactly call it that," I reply with a laugh. "I'm more like a friend to him. We spend time together doing things like playing games or talking. Since his mother is not able to be there for him right now, I'm trying to be a support system for him."

"That's really great of you," he says, his expression changing to one of admiration. "It's nice to see someone so dedicated to helping others."

"Oh come on," I joke, "you don't have to lay it on that thick!"

He laughs and shakes his head. "No, I really mean it. You're an inspiration to me."

"Thank you. That means a lot," I say, feeling my cheeks grow warm. I take a sip of my drink, avoiding his gaze because compliments make me a little uncomfortable.

We continue with small talk until the waitress returns with our steaks and sets them in front of us. We both eagerly dig in. The food is delicious, the steak cooked to perfection; only the center is rare and tender, while the outer edges provide a pleasant resistance. The sauce is pungent and spicy, with just the right amount of sweetness, and the garlic mashed potatoes are creamy and buttery, which balances out the sauce.

Once we have finished indulging, James leans back in his chair with his arms crossed. "By the way, many people have a lot to say about your employers. It's no wonder they want to keep you locked up in their villa."

"Really? What do people say about them?"

He runs a hand through his hair. "Let's see... where to begin?"

"Anywhere," I say, trying to hide how eager I am to hear someone else's opinion on the family.

James edges closer as though he wants to whisper something to me over the sound of the folk music floating in the air around us. "I heard that seven years ago when they came here to be with Paul's mom, they hired a local nanny from the village to look after their son. Not long after she began working for them, she vanished."

"What do you mean by vanished?"

He shrugs. "One day she was there, and the next, she was gone."

"How could she just disappear?"

"Nobody knows."

"So she was never found?"

"No. It's been seven years now and it's unlikely she ever will be."

As I process his words, a chill passes over my body and I try to shake it away. "What do you think happened to her?"

"Everyone thinks that family did something to her. The police were involved. The entire Mayer family, including the old woman, were questioned, but no evidence was found to prove that they had anything to do with the nanny's disappearance." He takes a large gulp of his water. "I'm not surprised they didn't find anything, to be honest. They didn't want to."

"What do you mean?"

"The Mayer family is the wealthiest family in this town. Their wine empire and the bars and restaurants they own in Ruddel and around the country have made them a powerful presence here. They have the power to make sure the police can't or won't find any evidence against them."

I sit there, stunned. I never even considered that Robin and Paul could be involved in something like this, connected to a crime. As I take it all in, the food starts to turn in my stomach.

"James, what do you personally think they did to the nanny?"

"My guess is they got rid of her."

"Got rid of her? But how?"

"No one just disappears into thin air. Honestly, I think they killed her. That's why I wanted to meet you. You need to be careful, Christa. You could be next."

THIRTEEN

CHRISTA

When I get to the villa around 8 p.m., I'm still shaken by what James told me about the Mayer family, and I can't stop thinking about the creepy phone call I answered three days after moving in. Was that some kind of warning, like the note that told me to be careful? I'm more convinced than ever now that the message was meant for me. That driver wanted to let me know that Paul and Robin could be dangerous.

Prior to hearing the rumor, I ran a lot of scenarios in my mind as to what the couple could be hiding, but nothing came close to the possibility that they could be responsible for someone's disappearance... or murder. Someone who worked for them just as I am.

When I park the car outside the massive property and reach for the door handle, I notice that my hands are shaking slightly. After hearing what I just heard, any sane person would go in there, pack their bags, and leave.

But I can't do that. Even if I wanted to, it's not an option.

Maybe James is wrong about Robin and Paul. What if this nanny just left town of her own accord? For all we know, she's living a new life someplace else. It happens often enough that someone just ups and leaves their old life to start afresh. But according to James, many people in Ruddel believe the Mayers are guilty of something. Could they all be wrong?

I take a few deep breaths, trying to calm my jagged nerves, to still my racing heart. It doesn't work. I finally get out of the car, the evening breeze brushing against my skin that's now covered in goose pimples brought on by fear and anxiety. How will I be able to go on pretending I don't know their secret? How will I ever be able to look Robin in the eye again? It would be so easy to just walk away and fly back home. But that's out of the question.

With my heart in my throat, I take a few shaky steps toward the stairs leading up to the front door. Before I can reach the door or pull out my key, it's flung open and Robin is standing in front of me. It's almost as if she's been waiting for me to arrive.

My stomach turns as she puts on a smile, pretending that everything is all right. She looks pale, her eyes wild, her hair even more disheveled than usual. The smile does absolutely nothing for her.

"Christa," she says, breathless as she lets me into the house. "Did you have a lovely time?"

I walk inside and turn to her. "It was interesting," I say simply. "Very interesting, in fact."

"Really?" Robin closes the door and starts chewing on a nail that's barely there. "Where did you go? What did you do?"

The questions again. But now I understand her. I understand that they are coming from a dark and potentially dangerous place.

I study the woman in front of me carefully, wondering whether she could be capable of murder. In my eyes, she just looks like a broken woman. Instead of answering her right away, I head to the kitchen for a glass of water because my throat is so dry that I'm finding it hard to swallow. Robin follows right behind me, her house slippers shuffling on the kitchen tiles.

"Are you okay, Christa?" she asks behind me. "Did something happen while you were out?"

I don't respond until I'm done gulping down almost half the glass of water. "I'm just not feeling well," I say, which is partly true. I feel sick to my stomach.

"Did you eat something that doesn't agree with you?" Her voice is becoming more anxious by the second. "What did you eat? Who did you—"

"I met up with a friend actually."

Robin moves to the island and holds the edge with both hands. Even from where I'm standing by the sink, I can see her cheeks turn pink. "Oh! Who... who did you see? I didn't know you had friends in Ruddel."

"Yes, you're right," I say, biting my tongue. "I don't have friends here. But I had dinner with someone I met recently. Maybe we'll end up being friends."

I want to confront her, to try to pull a confession out of her. But I can't say anything that's on my mind without putting my job at risk. I need to be here for Wyatt, especially after what I now know.

"I see. Well, I apologize for my curiosity. I've always been a rather curious person. I guess it's in my nature." She turns away from me, hiding the truth buried in her eyes.

At that moment, Wyatt appears in the doorway of the kitchen, but the second he sees his mother, he disappears again. He tries as much as he can to avoid being in the same room as her. I really need to talk to Robin again about allowing me to take him out of this house without upsetting her.

I take a deep breath and say the first thing that comes to mind. "Robin, I know we talked about this before, but I was wondering if you would reconsider letting me take Wyatt to the village. I know he's kind of a loner, but I think getting out would be good for him."

Robin's expression shifts immediately and she says, "I

understand your concerns and I can see why you think it would be a good idea, but there's nothing in the village for him. He doesn't even have friends around here."

"Maybe it's time for him to make some," I reply with a forced smile.

She purses her lips and sighs. "That's not necessary since we're only here for the summer. And he seems content enough to me. All he wants to do is play video games and watch movies all the time anyway."

"But is that healthy?" Realizing I might be pushing too hard, I immediately try to tone it down a bit. "Look, I just thought maybe he can meet some other kids, you know? It could be good for him to socialize a bit instead of staring at a screen all day."

Robin takes a moment to think before responding. "Well, the population in this town is mostly older people, and there aren't many children his age, so I don't want him being disappointed," she says, her voice softening.

"Sure, but maybe a walk in the village now and then would be enough for him." I keep my voice as calm as I can manage. "I would certainly enjoy the company."

"I'll... I'll think about it." She parts her lips then presses them together again. Then without another word to me, she walks out of the kitchen. I listen to her footsteps making their way along the hall and up the stairs.

Air gushes out of my lungs and I lean against the sink. This time it's me clutching the edge, trying to hold on, trying to hold myself together as the words I wish I could have said burn holes in my throat.

After composing myself, I head to my room to call James.

"Thanks for meeting up with me," he says when he picks up. "I had a nice time."

I close the door and head to the bathroom before saying anything else. "Thank you for telling me... those things."

"You're welcome. If you're working for them, you deserve to know the truth."

"And you're really convinced the rumors are true?"

"I am. So what are you going to do? Will you quit and go back to the States?"

"I'm not sure what to do, to be honest. Right now I'm just a bit in shock."

"If it's true what everyone is saying, you might not be safe in that house."

"I know, but I can't leave. I need to be here for Wyatt. He needs me. And I don't believe the rumors."

"Okay." He sighs. "Maybe it's not such a bad idea for you to stay."

"What do you mean?"

"I mean that seven years ago the police weren't able to find any evidence that your employers are responsible for Eva's disappearance. Maybe you can. You are on the inside. Maybe you could give this town the answers it needs."

I lean against the closed bathroom door and close my eyes. "Eva?" I swallow hard. "That was her name?"

"Yes," he replies. "I never really knew her, but after all these years, there are still a few flyers about her disappearance on some of the village's bulletin boards."

Knowing her name changes everything. Instead of just a nanny, she's a person, someone else's child. But I'm still finding it hard to believe that the Mayers would be involved in her disappearance. Despite their peculiar behavior and strained relationships, to think they could be guilty of murder is too much. It would take someone who's pure evil to do something like that.

FOURTEEN
CHRISTA

It's 2 a.m. and, as far as I know, I'm the only one still up. My attempts to relax are futile. I can't seem to quiet my thoughts, and my heart is beating out of my chest. Even with my eyes shut, my mind is flooded with questions that I don't have answers to.

I lay in the dark, my ears alert to every sound in the house, the slight creaks and moans that come with an old building at rest. Feeling suddenly so overwhelmed, I fling my feet out of bed and sit on the edge, my eyes closed as I try to focus on my breath and to still my racing mind. Inhaling deeply and then exhaling in a rush, I open my eyes and wait for them to adjust to the darkness.

After a few more unsuccessful attempts at trying to sleep, I get out of bed and pad over to the door in my bare feet. I venture out into the hallway and come to a halt in front of Wyatt's room. I linger there for a short moment before walking back to my bedroom, feeling as if I had just completed a marathon after all the energy I had put into walking only a few steps.

I'm not sure what else to do, so I pick up the phone and dial

Emily's number. It must be 8 p.m. in New York, so I know she'll be awake. I'm not sure how much to tell her about the situation, but talking to her about anything would make me feel better.

She answers on the third ring. "It must be pretty late over there," she says.

"Yeah, it's two a.m., but I can't sleep. What are you up to?"

"I just picked Sandy up from a birthday party. I'm about to put on a movie. What are you doing up at this hour?" she asks, worry tinging her voice.

"I need to tell you something."

"Christa, is everything okay? You sound out of breath. Has something happened?"

I inhale and settle back into bed, pressing the phone to my ear as I speak in a hushed voice. "I heard some news about the Mayers that's messing with my head." I recount my conversation with James to her.

When I'm finished speaking, there's a long pause on the other end of the line.

"Listen, Christa. You've got to get out of there. Don't let the same thing happen to you."

I massage the back of my neck, feeling the strain from the conversation. "I can't. You know that."

She's quiet for a moment. "But it sounds like a risky place to be. How can you guarantee your safety?"

"I'll be fine. I plan on being here until we return to New York in September, then I'll think of what to do next."

"I don't know," she says, her voice flat. "I think you're making a mistake. I think you need to let go. This is not healthy."

"How could you even ask that of me?" Tears prick the backs of my eyes. "You know how hard it's been for me."

Emily's voice is firm as she says, "Yes, I do." And then she continues, "But I don't want anything to happen to you. You're my priority."

"I know, but so far there's no proof that what I heard about them is really true."

"So you think it's just nasty gossip?" She still doesn't sound convinced. "I'm really freaking out over here. I'm worried about you."

"I honestly don't know if it's true," I admit.

"That's the issue." She releases a loud sigh. "It could be."

"There isn't any evidence to back it up. Maybe I could find some... I'm just... I'm really scared for Wyatt."

We stay quiet for a while before she speaks again, her tone still anxious. "I'm not telling you what to do in this situation. But please, be careful. If at any point you feel like you are in danger, get out of there immediately. Can you promise me that?"

I give her the assurance she needs to hear, even though I know it's unlikely that I'll keep the promise. I'm worried about Wyatt more than myself, and I refuse to leave him.

An hour after we end the call, I finally fall into a dreamless sleep.

Even though I went to bed late, I still wake up at five, just like I always do. I want to go outside, to go for a jog in the fresh air, but my muscles are sore, and I fear for Wyatt's safety if I leave. Even though I tried to convince myself that his parents would never harm him, their child, I'm not certain. He could be in danger.

Last night, when James sent me a text to ask when we can meet again, I couldn't give him a definite answer because it will be hard to leave Wyatt alone with Robin. As long as I'm not a hundred percent sure he's safe, my job is to shield him as best I can, even if it means I never get to go out again.

I take an ice-cold shower, allowing the water to numb me, feeling my skin stiffen and goosebumps rising on my arms and the rest of my body. As droplets of freezing water drip down my hair and face, I silently count to twenty before turning off the faucet. Afterward, I remain motionless in the shower cubicle, shivering, but not only from the cold.

Shortly before six o'clock, I creep out of my room and head downstairs. On my way to the ground floor, I catch a whiff of fried bacon and eggs. I find Robin in the kitchen making breakfast. An array of ingredients are spread across the counter and three plates have been laid out on the kitchen island.

"Good morning, Christa," she says in a cheery voice.

When she turns around, I'm astonished by her appearance. Instead of one of her pajama sets, she's wearing a light-gray cardigan over whitewashed jeans. She has put on some makeup as well, giving her face a youthful appearance, and her hair is pulled back in a ponytail that accentuates the features of her face. Even her normally dull eyes have a little warmth to them.

"Good morning," I say and approach the island, gesturing to the dishes. "You didn't have to do all this."

"Oh, I just wanted to surprise you and Wyatt with breakfast," she explains, a hint of pink creeping into her cheeks. "And I thought it would be nice if we all ate together. Unfortunately, Paul is already out of the house, so it'll just be the three of us." She reaches for a dish towel and wipes her hands, then she comes to the island, pulling out a stool for me. "Please, have a seat. I'd like to talk to you about something."

"Okay." I drop into my seat as she sits in the one next to me.

"I wanted to talk about our conversation yesterday." Her eyes are on the dishcloth in her hands. "I thought about it all night and agree with you that it would be good for Wyatt to socialize more. It's just that I'm so protective of my son. The thing is, when he's not around me, I get anxious. And he's not that familiar with this town. He was eight when we were last here."

I nod. "I fully understand, Robin, but I think keeping him in the house all day is making him miserable, and you really don't have to worry about him. He won't be alone out there. I'll be there and I'll take good care of him."

"You're right. I'm just being silly."

Although I wish she would also own up to not having shown Wyatt the love and attention he deserves, I'm surprised she's admitting to being wrong.

This is a start.

"How can I help?" I ask. "What do you want me to do?"

"I want you to take him out today. Drive him to the bookstore to get some German language books. His father doesn't have much time to teach him and I only speak a basic level of it. I thought it might be a good idea for you to learn with him."

"But I don't speak German." I'm surprised she would even suggest that.

"I know." Her throaty chuckle catches me off guard and I can't help but smile back. "But maybe you can learn with him. You could make it part of your... sessions."

"Yes, I like that." I smile at her. "I think that's a good idea."

It doesn't matter what she wants me to do as long as it means getting the boy out of the house and into a public space surrounded by other people. If I have to learn German to make that happen, so be it.

But I'm also confused. If she's now allowing Wyatt to get out of the house, to risk hearing rumors about his family, could it mean that James and the others in town were wrong about her and Paul being dangerous?

Or is this some kind of game she's playing with me?

FIFTEEN

CHRISTA

As soon as we leave the house and Wyatt and I get into Robin's car, a wide grin splits my face and my heart lightens. I'm still shocked that Robin allowed Wyatt to come out with me. I can see her standing at the window, watching us, but it doesn't bother me.

"How are you feeling?" I ask Wyatt as I back the car away from the house. "Excited to be out?"

"It's awesome." He rubs his hands together. "So, where are we going?"

"Your mother said I should take you to the bookstore. Apparently, we should get some German books. She wants us to learn the language together."

"Come on, that's boring," he says. "I'm not interested in learning German."

"But your father... he's Austrian, and learning a new language is never a waste of time. You never know when you might need it."

"Trust me, as soon as I'm eighteen, I'm never coming to Austria again."

"German is spoken in lots of countries, you know," I remind

him, laughing. "Maybe one day you'll find yourself in a place that speaks it, and you'll be grateful to know it."

"Can we do something else?" he pleads, ignoring what I just said. "I want to have fun. My mom doesn't need to know."

I glance at him, then back at the road ahead. "Wyatt, I can't tell your mother I'm taking you to the bookstore only to take you somewhere else." I tighten my grip on the wheel. "You know what? How about we do both?"

"Great idea." He grins at me. "If you don't tell, I won't."

"Okay, perfect. So, what is it you really want to do?"

"I'd love to go see the horses."

"Sure, we can do that. I think I know where one of the stables are." I've passed the place before, and I know it's located on the outskirts of town.

During the drive, the atmosphere in the car turns even lighter and more cheerful. Wyatt talks about his favorite video games, all of them too violent, and I share the few funny stories I have from my childhood. During lulls in our conversation, he keeps his eyes focused on the outdoors, humming a tune under his breath, as if this is the first time he's ever been outside. It's understandable. He's been trapped in that house for two weeks, forbidden to leave. Outside the walls of the villa, he seems so different, more carefree and alive, that it's hard to believe he's the same person.

I turn on the radio and together we sing along to an ABBA song.

"You know what?" he says, laughing. "I wouldn't sing out loud if I were you."

"What's that supposed to mean?" I know full well what he means. Let's just say that some people are blessed with a voice, and others are not. I'm one of the latter.

"Do you really want me to say it?"

"No." I swat his arm. "You're the only person I'd dare sing around, trust me."

"Good," he says and we continue to sing, creating an out-of-tune duet that's weirdly beautiful, to my ears at least.

I glance at Wyatt and my heart skips a beat as a bubble of joy expands in my chest. If I had the power to freeze time, I would do it, to stay in this moment a little longer. I'm grateful for the gift of today, for the opportunity to bond with him like I had planned to from the day I accepted this job. I'm grateful for the opportunity to give this boy a real chance at experiencing something close to normalcy.

We reach the village, and cruise around for a bit, taking it all in before we drive to the stable. We pass the church, the bakery, one primary school, a kindergarten with a sunflower garden, and the cemetery. We finally make it to our destination and get out of the car. The smell of fresh hay and horse manure is familiar to me since I grew up on a farm.

Inside the stable, horses are lazily grazing in the wide and open field, and a few foals are frolicking around in the sunshine. I'm enchanted by the breathtaking sight of the majestic animals.

I turn to Wyatt with a serious expression. "Are you sure you won't tell Rob—your mother about this?"

"I won't, I swear." He takes a deep breath and releases all the tension he's been holding in, as if it's his first breath of fresh air ever. He stretches his arms up into the sky, like a butterfly coming out of its cocoon.

He looks so happy, so at peace, and for a moment I just watch him enjoying his freedom. And then we start walking toward the stables, watching as one of the caretakers grins as he offers an apple to a horse, a black-and-white mare.

Wyatt's enthusiasm grows as we near the horses. His face lights up when he takes in all the smells and sounds of the animals. When the caretaker feeding the mare sees us, he comes in our direction and calls out a hello.

Wyatt and I respond to the greeting in German, but when he says more, we look at each other in confusion.

"See why we have to learn German?" I whisper to Wyatt.

He cringes and nods.

Fortunately, the language barrier doesn't stop the man, who resembles Santa Claus, from letting Wyatt enjoy himself. He takes him to the horses, allowing him to pet them and offer them treats before leading him to a small, white-chestnut filly with a black mane and tail. She nuzzles his hand and gently pushes her muzzle against his chest. I sit on a bench close to the stall and watch him talking to the horse like someone who knows it.

After a few minutes, the caretaker says something to Wyatt with the help of hand gestures, and even from a distance I can see Wyatt's face brighten.

He looks in my direction, then runs up to me. "Can I have a quick ride? He's letting me."

"What? How... how did you understand him?"

"I heard him say *'reiten'*, which means ride. I do know a few German words, you know."

I get to my feet. "I'm not sure that's a good idea, Wyatt."

We came here without Robin and Paul knowing. If something happens to him, it's not going to be good.

"Come on! Just a few minutes. I won't be gone long, I promise."

Wyatt's eyes plead with me and I finally relent. I sigh, still not sure if this is a good idea, but I can tell that he really wants to do this.

"But you don't know how to ride." I gaze past him at the man, who nods his head.

"He'll teach me."

"Did he tell you how much it will cost?"

Wyatt shakes his head. "I'm sure it's not much."

"Wait a minute," I say and make my way to the caretaker. "How much?" I ask in English.

Since he doesn't understand, I point to Wyatt, the horse, then rub my forefinger and thumb together.

The instructor smiles and gives me a thumbs-up. Then he picks up a stick and writes the number thirty on the ground. "*Dreißig Euro.*"

When he looks up, I tap at my watch, wanting to know the number of minutes Wyatt would get at that price.

He writes another thirty on the ground.

It's going to cost thirty euros for a thirty-minute riding lesson, and I don't mind paying it if it will make Wyatt happy.

"Okay." I turn back to Wyatt. "Thirty minutes, that's all. And you have to promise me you'll listen to the instructor as much as you can and be careful, okay?"

"I will," he says and turns back to the man, who helps him up into the saddle. His eyes sparkle with joy and excitement as he gets adjusted to the horse and begins to ride, following the instructions of his new teacher.

To my surprise, he's not a complete beginner. After a few moments, he's able to trot the horse around the circle and follow the instructor's commands like a pro. He has an easy way with the horse, coaxing it to cooperate with simple commands. The loud neighing of the horse almost drowns out Wyatt's laughter, but it's clear to see how much he's enjoying himself.

When their time is up, Wyatt and the instructor come back to where I'm waiting. Wyatt carefully dismounts the horse and hands the reins to the instructor before turning back to me with a huge grin on his face.

"Thank you, Christa. That was awesome."

"I didn't know you could already ride," I say, still amazed.

"One of my friends back home has a horse. He taught me how to ride a little. It's the best thing in the world." His face grows serious. "Please don't tell my mom. She doesn't know."

I give his arm a reassuring squeeze. "I promise."

"Can we come here again some other time?"

"We'll see." First, I have to make sure Wyatt will really keep our daily activities to himself because if Robin finds out, she might never let him out again.

We get into the car and this time we drive to the bookstore, where we won't be spending much time since we stayed at the stable longer than I thought we would. The bookstore is tiny, just one room with a few shelves of books, most of them about Ruddel, cooking, and German lessons. Wyatt looks around excitedly at the titles. He chooses a book filled with pictures of horses.

I take the book from him and look down at it. "I'll get this one for you, but the rest have to be German language books, okay?"

"Sure. Thanks." He takes the book from me and flips open the cover.

I'm leafing through a cookbook when a woman wearing a blue dress and thick glasses touches my arm. She has a name tag that reads "Ida".

"It's nice to see you again," she says in English.

"What do you mean?" I take a step back while Wyatt watches on with a curious expression on his face.

"I remember you from a few years ago."

"I don't understand." I shake my head. "I'm new in town."

The redhead squints her small round eyes. "I'm very good with faces and I do remember you. You came in here looking for a German dictionary and asked for some directions. It's quite a while back, but I remember you very well." She dips her head to one side. "The color of your eyes is quite unique and it stayed with me. My mother was here that day and I remember her saying that mixture of green and blue reminded her of the sea shortly before it storms."

My stomach drops and my heart starts racing. I'm not sure how to respond. Wyatt looks up at me with knitted brows. Though he looks confused, he says nothing.

Finally, I manage to say, "I'm sorry, I'm sure you're mistaken. I've never been here before."

Ida's kind smile is replaced with a look of confusion before she shakes her head and takes a step back. "It's all right. I'm sure I'm mistaken. Sorry to bother you."

As soon as she leaves, I choose two random books and we head for the checkout counter, where Ida rings up our purchases without meeting my eyes.

Once we're back in the car, Wyatt looks at me with narrowed eyes. "What was that all about? You were in Ruddel before?"

"No," I say with a chuckle. "Of course not, Wyatt. You know this is my first time here."

"But that woman seemed really convinced she'd seen you before."

"She's just confused. Now, how about some hot chocolate before we head back home?"

"To prison, you mean?" He laughs. "Hot chocolate sounds good."

"Great," I say through my tight throat.

The entire time we're at the café, Wyatt is talking nonstop, but I barely hear what he's saying because I'm still thinking about the woman in the blue dress.

When we finally arrive at the house, Robin is waiting with a torrent of questions, but I brush them off until she finally quits.

At the end of the day, when I'm alone in my room, anxiety sweeps through me, and my heart starts to race until I feel hot all over, so hot that I take my second cold shower of the day.

This time, I stay under the jet of freezing water for much longer, until my skin numbs and my head cools enough for me to crawl into bed and try to put the strange encounter at the bookstore out of my mind.

SIXTEEN
CHRISTA

Within two weeks, Wyatt and I have gone out on three more occasions, and each time I've taken him to the stables to interact with the horses. How could I deny him something that makes him so happy?

Neither of us has told Robin or Paul about our forbidden excursions. Every time we return home, I let her ask all the questions, but I give her only filtered answers. So does Wyatt. As far as she's concerned, when Wyatt and I are not home listening to German audiobooks or reading German books, we go to the bookstore and spend hours there.

She still reminds me from time to time to stay away from local gossip. But the important thing is that Wyatt is still safe, with me. And the more time we spend together the more he trusts me.

I also need Robin and Paul to keep trusting me until I can find something on them, if there's even anything to find.

Today, we've just left the stables and are about to enter our favorite coffee shop for some hot chocolate when we run into James, who's walking out of the church nearby. At first, he seems surprised to see us, but after a moment, he smiles and comes over to greet us.

"How exciting to bump into you two." He stretches out his hand toward Wyatt. "You must be Wyatt. I've heard a lot about you."

"And you must be James," Wyatt says with a warm smile as he squeezes my friend's hand.

Wyatt has heard a lot about James as well since I told him he's my only friend in town. I never asked him not to tell his parents about James, but he kept it to himself anyway. Now that we're allowed out regularly it probably matters less if Robin knows I'm speaking to people from town. She seems to be respecting my decisions a little more, which is a good thing because I cannot allow her trust in me to waver.

I look up at the church. "Were you sending a few prayers to the man upstairs?" I ask.

"Yeah." He pushes his hands into his pockets. "Just trying to be a good Christian man."

I raise an eyebrow. "Who would've thought?"

"I know, right? But guess what? My father was actually a pastor in this church."

"Oh, that's exciting." I never pegged James to be a religious kind of person, but I do respect him for being faithful to his faith. It gives him depth of character.

Even though we have only met up once since our dinner, we still talk on the phone sometimes. He told me that he has a sister who also lives in Ruddel, that their parents died in a car accident when they were young, and they were then raised by their grandmother. He also told me that he lived in London for a few years before coming to settle in Austria.

"Where are you two headed?" he asks, patting Wyatt's head as if he knows him.

"We're about to stop somewhere for some hot chocolate, then we're headed home."

"I wish we could stay longer in town," Wyatt murmurs under his breath.

"How about I treat you to lunch?" James asks. "I know a great grill restaurant."

"That would be fun," Wyatt says before I have a chance to reject the offer.

"I don't think it's a good idea," I say to Wyatt. "Your mother will be expecting us." The longest we've ever been out is around two hours, and if we get close to that, Robin starts calling and asking where we are and when we'll be coming home.

"I understand," James says. "How about another time? If you let me know next time you're in the village, I can join you."

I can almost feel Wyatt physically deflate next to me with disappointment.

"Yes, we can do that. That's a good idea." I slide my arm through Wyatt's. "Next Wednesday at twelve?"

Wednesdays are our session days, and we're now allowed to spend them outdoors on the grounds or in the village. Even when we're learning German together, I always insist we do it by the river. So far, Robin has agreed without complaint, but I know that if we're on the grounds, she watches us from the many windows of the villa.

"It's a date," James says with a mock salute.

* * *

As promised, the next week we do meet James for lunch, and afterward we take a quick stroll through the village. When we walk past the bookstore, I see her again, the woman with the thick glasses. She's standing outside, smoking a cigarette, and staring straight at me. Her gaze is so intense, so full of recognition, that it feels as if she's seeing right through me.

"Um... hi," I say, my voice coming out a little too high and strained.

"Hello," she replies, looking at me curiously, her eyes lingering a little too long on my face.

James also greets her in German and we walk on.

"When we were at the bookstore, that woman said she'd seen Christa before, years ago," Wyatt says to James.

James eyes me with a quizzical expression.

I gulp and force a smile. "I think she was just confused. She must've mistaken me for someone else."

That seems to satisfy him, and he doesn't question me anymore. But when I look back at the woman, I can still feel her piercing gaze following me.

James accompanies us to the stables; while Wyatt helps the caretakers with the horses in exchange for a free ride, James and I sit a distance away, alone, enjoying each other's company.

"I know I keep asking you this," James says, "but are you being careful around the Mayers? I still find it hard to believe that you decided to stay."

"Yes, but I can't just quit and leave. I know you feel I'm in danger, but if that's the case, so is Wyatt."

I take a deep breath and let it out slowly before pushing my hands into my hair. "I've always told myself that they'd never be a risk to their own child, but perhaps you're right. It wouldn't be the first time parents have hurt their children. I hate not knowing if they really did something to that woman. The not knowing part is the worst."

At that moment, a loud whinny rings out from the stables. Wyatt is laughing, and we can hear him talking to one of the horses. James and I both laugh, too, my worries quickly forgotten for now. We sit in silence for a few minutes and watch Wyatt and the animals.

"I know what you mean," James says finally, continuing our conversation as if there had never been an interruption. "It's a horrible feeling to not know what the truth is. But everyone thinks they killed the nanny. That's why I'm so scared for you."

"So am I." I tip my head back and gaze up at the sky, the warmth of the sun touching my face before I look down again. "The only way for me to be at ease is to find out the truth. I need some kind of proof, but it's not easy for me to snoop around with Robin being home all the time. I did try, though, to find something... anything that would prove they had something to do with Eva's disappearance, but I found nothing." I pause to kick some dirt around, making a light indentation in the soil. "Maybe there's nothing to find. I mean, Robin lets us out of the house now. She doesn't seem afraid anymore that we'll hear rumors about them. Either way, I'll keep looking. I need to get to the bottom of this."

"Secrets have a way of coming out eventually. If they are hiding something, sooner or later, they will let their guard down. She's probably only letting you out because it would be against the law to keep you and Wyatt from leaving the property. It doesn't necessarily mean she's okay with it."

"Maybe you're right." I squint at Wyatt in the distance. He's now riding Judith, his favorite mare, and his legs swing freely, like a marionette in the breeze. He looks content, and I wish more than anything that he could stay that way forever.

"He seems like a good kid," James says next to me. "And it's clear that he likes you a lot."

I smile. "The feeling is very mutual."

"I like you a lot too," he adds.

I turn to him with a frown.

"Don't look so surprised," he says. "Why do you think I keep looking for excuses to spend time with you?"

"I don't know. I keep thinking maybe you're just a little bored. There's not much to do around here."

He laughs and rubs his stubbly chin. "That's partly the reason, but I really do like you, Christa."

"The feeling is mutual in this case as well." As I look into his eyes, I feel a flutter inside my belly, something I haven't felt for a long while. I've dated on and off the past few years, but every time it got serious, I pushed away. I pushed away because I was afraid of letting my guard down, becoming vulnerable enough to get hurt, and to be rejected. Most of the men I dated were never interested in friendship first. So this is different with James. We're starting off as friends and growing into more. But how long until I push him away?

"I'd really like to take you out to dinner again sometime," he continues.

"I know," I say. "It's just that I'm still not comfortable with leaving Wyatt alone at home."

"Look, I don't think you should worry about him. They may be responsible for what happened to Eva, but they wouldn't hurt their own son, would they?"

"I don't know." I tuck my hands under my armpits. "I really don't know what to believe at this point. It's best not to find out, so I'll stay by Wyatt just to make sure he's safe."

"Yeah, I understand." With that, the conversation comes to an abrupt halt and James excuses himself. "I should get back to my place. I have a few things I need to take care of."

His facial expression tells me it's just an excuse to get away. He has probably realized that he has no chance with me.

But I'm wrong. A few hours later, late at night and long after everyone has gone to bed, he calls to let me know he's outside. I find his car parked a distance away from the villa, and when I get in I notice he has brought a whole dinner to share with me in the backseat of his car.

"I thought that since you couldn't get away, I'd bring you dinner."

"How very thoughtful of you! Thank you. This all looks delicious." Even though I've already eaten dinner, my mouth waters as I take in the salami pizza, ribs, and freshly baked bread.

"I baked the bread myself. That's why I had to leave you at the stables." He breaks off a piece of bread and hands it to me.

"Seriously?" I raise an eyebrow and bite into it. "This is really good."

"Thanks. I learned from the best. My mother was a baker."

"So your father was a pastor and your mother was a baker?"

"Exactly. And I was her little helper."

"Wow." I bite into the succulent bread again. "I have to say you have graduated from helper to master baker."

"Well, thank you. That means a lot." He picks up a slice of pizza.

We continue eating in silence and then, just as I'm reaching for another piece of bread, our hands brush. I gasp as a jolt of electricity surges through me and I feel my cheeks flush. His eyes meet mine, and in that moment time stops.

No words are exchanged, but our heads move closer, drawn together by an invisible force. Suddenly our mouths are pressing against each other. My heart swells, and warmth floods my body as our lips move in perfect sync.

I came to Austria for work, and starting a romance with James, or anyone else for that matter, might not be a good idea. But being in his arms feels so good. So I pretend it is a good idea.

"I wish I didn't have to go," he says. "I wish I could steal you for a few more hours."

"I'd like that," I say, the words coming from my mouth before I can even think about it.

"We should definitely do this again, then."

"Yes, we should."

"Christa, I'd love to spend more time with you, but I fully understand that you're worried about Wyatt being around his parents. Can I make a proposal?"

I dip my head to the side. "Sure."

"Since you and Wyatt are learning German together, why don't I teach you?" He clears his throat. "I can come here, once a week, or you two can come to my place. There are also some beautiful parks around Ruddel. It would give you something to look forward to. And it would be free of charge, of course."

"That sounds perfect." A smile creeps up my face. "Alternatively, we could be meeting at the bookstore or a library. That way, I wouldn't have to ask Robin for permission."

"Of course, we could, but wouldn't you want to be in a more comfortable place instead of a stuffy old library? My place would be much better for that. I have a nice couch, and I also happen to have some relevant books from my teaching days."

"That's true." My mind starts to wander, imagining myself in his home. The thought of us alone makes my heart flutter. "I suppose that would be better. But I need to talk to Robin first, to see if she's okay with it."

"That's perfectly fine, darling." He tucks a strand of my hair behind my ear and kisses the tip of my nose.

When he looks deep into my eyes, my pulse quickens.

"Thanks so much for dinner," I whisper, my cheeks flushed. "It was a really lovely surprise."

"I'm glad you enjoyed it. I hope we'll get to spend more alone time together again soon."

"We will. I promise."

SEVENTEEN

CHRISTA

A day after James and I had our late-night rendezvous, I broach the subject with Robin when I bring breakfast to her room.

"Robin, I wanted to talk to you about something." Anxiety swirls at the pit of my stomach. I wait for her to respond before continuing, but as soon as the words leave my mouth, her eyes darken with suspicion. If she says no, I will still be able to meet James in a public place, but I really want to be in his home. One's personal space can typically reveal a lot about a person, and I am very curious to see what he's like from within his domain.

"What would you like to talk about?" Her voice is emotionless.

I take a deep breath and tell her about James's offer. I explain that it would be a great opportunity for Wyatt. I leave out any mention of me and James being anything more than friends, not wanting to make her suspicious.

She narrows her eyes. "How do you know this man? Is he from around here?"

I take a breath to come up with a lie that might help speed

things along. "He's actually from Vienna, but he's spending a couple of weeks in Ruddel."

"So you don't really know him?"

"I do," I lie. "We've been friends since before I came here. Long-distance friends. When he heard I was coming to Ruddel, he decided to visit."

As soon as the lie comes out, I realize my mistake. Ruddel is a small town and the Mayers are known here. What if Robin knows him?

Robin's eyes narrow even more until they look like slits. "Just friends and nothing more?"

My face turns ablaze with embarrassment. "Just friends, yes." I suddenly feel like a teenager being interrogated by her parents. "He has experience in teaching German to tourists. I really think this would be good for Wyatt. Please think about it."

"What's his name?"

I freeze and bite into my lower lip, wondering if I should tell her the truth or keep up the lie. Then I decide that any more lies could end up backfiring, so I tell her the truth. "James."

It's a common enough name and judging from Robin's face, she doesn't seem to recognize it. She lets out a long sigh before finally saying, "Let me think about it."

"Of course." I'm glad that she hasn't said no immediately.

But before I leave the room, she gives me a stern warning. "For now, I want you to keep Wyatt away from this James person. You're the only person I trust with my son."

"I will," I say with a stiff smile, wondering if she knows that Wyatt and I have been secretly meeting James.

After leaving the room, I feel relieved that Robin is at least considering James's offer. Now all I need to do is wait and see what she decides. Until then, I won't mention anything to Wyatt. There's no point in getting his hopes up when there's still a chance Robin could say no.

. . .

For the first time since arriving to work for the Mayers, over a month ago, we all have dinner together. Paul is home and out of his office for once, to join me, Wyatt, and his wife at the dining table. Instead of me preparing dinner, Robin ordered Chinese food, which is a nice change. During the meal, there's little talk and I can feel the tension in the air.

In the past, before I found out Robin and Paul could be responsible for a murder, I would have looked forward to the prospect of eating with the whole family, expecting it to be a pleasant experience; this time, however, I'm nervous. I feel like Robin, whose eyes never leave my face, can sense that I'm withholding something from them.

Wyatt seems to be just as uncomfortable as I am and still seems afraid of his parents. His posture is stiff, and he doesn't speak much, only answering with a brief yes or no when spoken to. His gaze is firmly affixed to his plate throughout dinner. I feel pity for him, knowing the inner turmoil he must be facing.

"Wyatt," Paul finally says, breaking the awkward silence, "have you been enjoying going to the village with Christa? Your mother says you've been going to the bookstore a lot."

I stiffen. What if Paul knows that we have been spending time with James and that I've been taking Wyatt to the stables without their permission? What if someone saw us? Is this dinner more than just sharing a meal? I'm getting the feeling it could be an interrogation. My stomach rolls. If they find out what I've been up to, they could fire me on the spot, and that would prevent me from getting to the truth.

Wyatt gives me a quick glance, then returns his gaze to his plate.

Please don't tell them.

To my relief, he nods and mumbles his agreement, then goes back to eating.

Paul tries harder to get him to talk, but Wyatt doesn't react much. The boy is so disconnected from his parents that it hurts to watch them together. The conversation soon drifts away from Wyatt and our excursions and silence returns as everyone finishes eating.

As soon as the plates are empty, I push back my chair to clear the table, but before I'm able to get to my feet, Robin speaks up. Her voice is soft, yet it holds a note of authority.

"Christa," she says, "we'd like to speak to you in private, if you don't mind. Don't worry, it won't take long." She turns to Wyatt. "Why don't you go read a book in your room?"

Wyatt almost runs out of the room, eager to be free from the oppressive atmosphere.

My heart stops and fear creeps over my body. My first thought is that I've been found out, that they know the extreme lengths I went to in order to get this job.

When I applied for the position, I told them I had studied child psychology, but I left out the part where I never finished my studies. To make myself sound more qualified, I presented them with a fake degree. I was determined to get the job, whatever the cost.

Robin studies me for a moment, then smiles. "No need to look so worried. We just wanted to talk about our expectations of you, and make sure we're all on the same page."

"Sure." I relax a bit, relieved that my secret is still safe. But what exactly do they want to discuss?

Paul continues, "Robin tells me you have a friend who offered to give you and Wyatt German lessons?"

"Yes," I manage to say. "He's very kind to offer his time, and he won't be charging anything."

"Apparently he used to be a German teacher," Robin says to her husband.

"I see." Paul pauses to wipe his lips with a napkin. "We'd like Wyatt to take advantage of this opportunity, but we want to make sure that if he does do this, he's supervised at all times. No wandering off with your friend or anything like that. And do not leave him in the company of anyone else."

"Of course," I say. "I promise to keep an eye on him."

Anger boils inside my veins. The way they control the boy's life is wrong. But I keep my feelings to myself. All I can do right now is offer my assurances that I will continue to keep him trapped in the bubble they have created for him, a bubble that without me in it would probably suffocate him. No, I will never let that happen.

"We also want to meet this tutor first," Robin adds. "Invite him to come to the house tomorrow afternoon."

I swallow hard and nod. Hopefully, James won't mind. And I hope they won't recognize him as a local. The conversation lasts a few more minutes. When it ends, I release a breath I didn't know I was holding and leave the table.

After cleaning up the kitchen, I go to say goodnight to Wyatt and tell him the good news, that he will have permission to get out of the house more. I'm just too excited to keep it to myself.

"I'm going to propose twice a week. One of those days, you can do whatever you want, okay?" I put a finger to my lips. "Our little secret."

"Anything?"

"Well, within reason. And as long as you don't tell—"

"I won't, I promise." His face lights up, and I know that he would do anything for more freedom. He throws himself into my arms and gives me a warm hug. "Thank you, Christa."

"You're welcome, honey." I tighten my arms around him.

Wyatt smiles when he lets go of me, and it's such a relief to see the joy on his face. No matter what his parents may do, he will always have me. I will do whatever it takes to make sure he's safe and taken care of. He deserves happiness, and I will make sure he gets it.

When I step out of his room, I wipe away the tears that have started to escape my eyes. Tears I could not let him see.

When I call James to let him know, he's extremely excited at the prospect of getting to spend more time with me. He doesn't even mind coming over to meet Robin and Paul, as long as it ends up giving him more access to me and Wyatt. I'm touched that despite not knowing me for long, he's clearly invested in trying to protect me and, in turn, Wyatt. No man has ever gone to such lengths to look out for me and it helps to break down the walls around my heart a bit, but there's still a long way to go.

EIGHTEEN

CHRISTA

The next afternoon, when both Robin and Paul meet James, there are no signs at all that they know him from around town, which is a relief, but when we all take a seat in the library, I can't help but notice that James looks a little uncomfortable around them. The way he avoids their gaze, the way he fidgets when either of them speak, makes me think he's more than just a little apprehensive, as if he's holding himself back from telling them exactly what he thinks of them. But who wouldn't be uncomfortable in the presence of people rumored to have killed someone?

"Would you like something to drink?" Robin asks James, offering him a cup of herbal tea.

"No thank you," James says, his voice tight. He's still not making eye contact with either of them. I get the feeling that he doesn't want to stay any longer than necessary, and I can't say I blame him.

The tension in the room is palpable, but he eventually relaxes and makes the language lessons offer straight to them.

"I'm not asking for any payment. I enjoy teaching, and this seems like a great opportunity to help someone who needs it."

His voice wavers a bit, but he keeps talking. "My focus would be to teach him conversational basics, help with reading and writing, and also with grammar."

The whole thing sounds like an interview, but the atmosphere has shifted. There's still a thick air of suspicion and unease, but it's laced with something else: Gratitude and understanding.

Paul nods in agreement and his face creases into a smile. "We're very grateful for your help, James. And you're sure you don't want us to compensate you for your time somehow?"

"Not at all. As I said, I'm happy to do this, and it's a favor to my friend here."

His eyes meet mine, and it's like someone turns on a light inside my heart. I look away before Robin and Paul notice the flush on my cheeks.

"If that's the case," Paul continues, "then we accept your offer and we thank you for your generosity."

Relief washes over me, and I'm about to say thank you too, but James beats me to it. "It's really no problem. I'm happy to do it."

During the rest of the conversation, he plays along with everything I told Robin about him, including that he's just a visitor in Ruddel. Finally, he gets to his feet. "I'm afraid I have to get going now." His words sound genuine, but the guarded look on his face has returned and it makes me think he's still not entirely comfortable with being here.

"Of course," Robin says, standing as well. "Thank you for coming, James." She reaches out for a handshake, but James cleverly dodges it, pretending he didn't see it by quickly turning to me.

Unperturbed, Robin drops her hand again and moves to the door to open it for him.

As I lead James to the car, he slowly leans in to kiss me on the lips and I feel an electric current surge through me. Paralyzed by fear and anticipation, I barely manage to step back in time.

"We're friends, remember?" I nervously fold my arms across my chest. "I don't know if they will be on board if they knew you and I are—"

"Yeah?" He raises an eyebrow. "Exactly what are we?"

I don't know the answer to that question. Even though there's a clear connection between us and I find him extremely attractive, does kissing him once make him my boyfriend?

"It's complicated," I say, looking away.

"That's okay." He kisses me on the cheek instead and opens the door to his Nissan. "I understand. I'm simply happy to see you, even if it's only like this... for now." He winks and gets in.

* * *

The week passes by in a rush and it's already time for Wyatt's first outing with me and James, who invites us to his place for the first time. He lives in a cottage at the edge of the village, and I'm immediately charmed by the place and can see why he chose it. Entering it is like walking into a different world.

The interior is a musician's dream. The decor is vintage, eclectic, and rich in culture, from the wooden beams on the ceiling to the guitars and instruments hanging from the walls. The living room is decorated with old posters of iconic singers and beautiful vinyl records stacked against the wall.

Even the kitchen has musical notes on the white tiles.

"Wow," I breathe when he ushers us to the kitchen table, and Wyatt gawks at an electric guitar on the wall. "You never mentioned you were into music."

"You never asked." He pulls out a chair for me. "I used to be part of a small band when I was studying, but it was a long time ago. What can I get both of you to drink before we start the lesson? I have peach-and-lemon iced tea, coffee, and a bottle of red wine."

"Wine, please," Wyatt jokes and laughs when I shoot him a look. "Joking. Iced tea, please."

Watching them together, I can almost pretend we're a little family, something I have never allowed myself to have because my heart was locked away. But the thought of wishing it could be true presses against my chest like an actual weight, a heaviness I cannot shake. I'm thankful for this time with James and Wyatt, and part of me wishes it could last forever.

I'd be lying if I said I'm not falling for James, and I'm not sure if I'm ready for that. I worry that he might not like the person I really am, the woman beneath the mask. And he might not be able to handle my past if he knew about it. But I can't think about that now, so I just continue to enjoy the moment as it is without tainting it with regret or worry.

"Guess what, Wyatt?" James says when we're about to leave. "I have a nephew who doesn't live far from here. His name is Simon and he's sixteen, just a year older than you. He would really love to meet you."

Wyatt's eyes narrow at the thought of meeting a stranger, but he nods slowly. "Maybe," he says.

Even though Wyatt sometimes talks about his friends back in New York, I know he's an introvert at heart. To outsiders, he may seem aloof and unapproachable, but deep down he's a kind and gentle soul, and I hope Simon will see that.

"Hey"—James ruffles his hair—"it's just a suggestion. I promise you, he's cool. He's also a PlayStation fan, just like you, and he has loads of games you could both play."

"I guess," Wyatt says with a shrug. I can sense that a part of him is excited at the prospect of meeting a new friend, but he's still hesitating, which is understandable.

"We can talk about it some other time," I suggest. "You don't have to decide now."

"No," Wyatt interjects. "I don't mind meeting him."

"Great." James rubs his hands together. "Before you head back home, I could take you to meet him for a few minutes. And if you like each other, next time, you could spend some more time together at his house. If not, you never have to see each other again."

I told James that I wanted to find something for Wyatt to be doing on one of the days aside from German lessons, and I'm touched that he's suggesting this as a way to fill Wyatt's time. And while I'm still worried about Robin finding out, I think this would be good for him.

"That sounds like a great idea." I smile. "Let's do it."

"Yeah." Wyatt scratches the back of his neck. "We can go."

James's nephew and his sister only live ten minutes away by car. Wyatt and I leave our bikes at his house and he drives us the short distance. Simon and his parents are warm and friendly, and to both our surprise, after a few minutes of hesitation, Simon and Wyatt hit it off, talking and joking about video games and other teenage stuff like old friends. We only stay for twenty minutes, but it's long enough for Wyatt to click with Simon, and for us to feel comfortable with the arrangements for the two of them to get together again.

When we get back to James's house, Wyatt is beaming and I can't help but feel grateful for James's generosity. While Wyatt is playing at James's piano, I thank him and tell him how much this outing has meant to me.

"It was great to see Wyatt spending time with someone his age. Thank you."

"You really care about him, don't you?" James replies.

"Of course I do. I want him to be happy."

"Well, then this is the least I can do." He smiles, then closes the kitchen door. "Do you think maybe I could sneak another kiss?"

I don't answer, but he's close enough now that I can feel his warmth and smell his spicy cologne. I'm not sure if this is what I want right now, but he looks at me with such tenderness that my heart melts and I find myself leaning closer to him. And before I can think twice, his lips find mine. It's the kind of kiss I've been waiting for since the first time our lips touched. It's gentle, tender, and full of promise, and it makes me feel like I'm home.

When we pull away from each other, tears are streaming down my cheeks.

"My goodness, Christa, are you okay?" James wipes my cheek with his thumb.

I shake my head, unable to speak.

He takes me into his arms and I nestle into his chest. "Hey, it's okay. You're okay," he whispers into my hair.

Eventually, I pull away and wipe off the tears. "I'm scared, James... for me and Wyatt. I wish I could take my son and get as far away from this place as possible."

It's only when James's face turns red that it hits me what I've done... said. Panic washes over me and I wish I could erase the last few seconds of our conversation, but I can't.

He steps back and shoves his hands into his pockets, his eyes full of questions. "Your son? Wyatt is your son?"

I sigh and press a fist to my forehead. "Yes," I whisper. "He's mine." I pause and bite into my trembling bottom lip. "Look... I... we have to go."

"Wh—How? Wait, we need to talk. I'm coming over tonight. I'll park at the same spot as last time. Can you come out? Pretend you're going for a late-night walk or something?"

"Yes," I whisper, my throat tightening.

I've just exposed my secret. Now, there's no going back. What's going to happen now? What if James tells Robin and Paul my truth?

NINETEEN
CHRISTA

The night air sends a chill down my spine as I make my way toward James's car, my heart pounding so hard I hear it in my ears. Instead of talking in the car, I suggest driving to a diner in the village. Even though I hate to leave Wyatt, this is a conversation that requires a proper sit down, and the last thing I want is for Robin to hear me.

During the drive, my mind is filled with thoughts of Robin and Paul discovering I've gone out at 11 p.m. and later questioning me on why I didn't let them know beforehand. I remind myself that I'm an adult and that I'm allowed to come and go as I please.

We drive in complete silence, all the while my mind turning over and over the same question: what is James going to do with what he has just found out about me?

The diner is a typical Austrian joint, tucked inside an old cellar with porcelain tiles covering the walls. The decor looks like it hasn't been updated since the 1950s, and the lighting is dim, adding to my fearful mood.

The place is empty apart from a few old people sipping tea and talking quietly near the back. A waitress wearing a green and white dirndl—an Austrian traditional dress—warns us that they will be closing up in half an hour, but that's more than enough time for what I have to say.

We settle into a table in a corner, away from prying eyes. James orders a Radler and I order a glass of fizzy water, my throat dry like the desert sand. I find it strange that he's ordering beer since he told me once that he only drinks water. I guess my revelation has shocked him so much that he needs something stronger.

When the drinks come, he takes a swig of his beer, his eyes locked on mine. "Tell me what's going on," he says.

So, I do. I tell him only what I'm comfortable sharing. Some things are better kept hidden.

"Fifteen years ago, I gave birth to a baby boy. He was so perfect, but I wasn't okay. Depression left me unable to take care of him, so they took him away and forced me to go to a mental hospital for a few weeks. When I returned, they told me my son had died, but I refused to accept it. I just knew he was alive and they were lying to me."

"Why?" James's face is etched with concern as he leans closer, urging me to continue. "Why would they do something like that?"

"While I was sick, they called me crazy and warned that if I didn't pull myself together, they'd take my son away."

"Did they tell you what he died from?"

I press a scrunched-up napkin to my eyes. "They claimed it was Sudden Infant Death Syndrome, but I didn't believe them. Deep down in my gut I just knew that my baby was alive. I just knew—"

"Who are *they*, Christa? Who are these people?" James's eyes are coated with tears as well.

I glance back at him and blink as if seeing him for the first time. Then I drop my head. "It doesn't matter. What matters is that I found my son and I'm terrified of losing him again."

When I stop talking after almost saying too much, James says nothing for a while, and the room seems almost quiet, except for the sound of a coffee machine humming in the background. All other sounds have been drowned out by that of my heart thumping in my ears. James's face is unreadable, and I'm scared he'll run away and never talk to me again or, worse, threaten to tell Robin and Paul what I revealed to him.

Finally, he leans back in his chair and scrubs at his face with both hands. "So, Wyatt is adopted and Robin and Paul don't know you're his mother."

It's not a question, but I answer it anyway. "Yes. I was seventeen when I had him, and..." My voice is hoarse, my throat feels like I've swallowed sandpaper, and my hands shake as I talk. "When he was gone, I felt so empty. I had nothing left in me. I was numb, and I felt like I had failed as a mother. I spent years searching for him in every face I saw—" I trail off, unable to keep talking.

James reaches across the table and places his hand on top of mine, squeezing it warmly. "You didn't fail as a mother. You did everything you could to find him despite the odds."

"Thank you, James. That means so much." I let out a long breath, relieved that he's not judging me for failing to keep my baby with me. "When I found him again, I felt like the world had shifted, and suddenly, my life made sense again. I knew that I couldn't let him slip away again, so I stayed close." He doesn't need to know about how long I spent working at the old hospital where they told me he died, the paper trail I followed to an adoption agency in Lexington, and the adoption papers that led me to Wyatt.

He nods and takes a huge gulp of his drink. "So this is why you're so protective of him..." He seems lost in thought. "It's only a matter of time before someone finds out."

I know what he says is true, but I'm too afraid to do

anything about it, afraid that if I tell them the truth, I'd be driven away from my son, never to see him again.

"I just wanted to be close to him... to take care of him," I reply, feeling defeated. "But now..." My voice drifts off.

Looking after Wyatt is not a job for me. It's a privilege, a deep-rooted desire that fills my entire being. He's my son, and nothing is more important than being there for him, spending as much time as I can in his presence.

James leans back in his chair, his eyes on my face. "I kind of wondered why you were so obsessed with the boy and were terrified of leaving him alone." He runs a hand through his thick hair. "Why didn't you tell me before now? We are... were friends."

I purse my lips and bow my head in shame, tears stinging my eyes. "I couldn't," I choke out as fear claws at me from within. "I couldn't tell you, or anyone. It was too risky."

When the tears start flowing faster, James slides out of his chair and comes around to my side. He wraps his arms around me. As sobs rack my body, I cling to his chest for comfort.

"It's okay," he says softly, stroking my hair in reassurance. "We'll figure this out. You can trust me." He takes my hand in his and squeezes it tight.

My body relaxes for the first time in weeks as I lay my head on his chest, relieved that I can trust him with this secret. But still, fear lurks at the back of my mind that something could go wrong.

"I'm scared for my son, James."

"Don't be. We'll get him away from those people. What we need to do is prove that they're not fit to be parents... that they're murderers. That would make it easier for you to get back your son."

"Or maybe I should just—"

"No," he says, reading my mind. "They are his legal parents.

That would be considered kidnapping and who knows what else."

I nod, realizing he's right. The safest course of action is to prove they are unfit parents.

"I'll do whatever it takes," I whisper, more tears filling my eyes. "I can't let them hurt him."

"Don't worry." James pulls me closer. "You and me... we'll find a way to keep Wyatt safe. I promise. You just need to find evidence at the house and we'll figure out the rest."

My hope is restored, and for the first time in weeks, maybe even years, I feel in control. I can do this. We will find a way to get Wyatt back with me. He is my son. Mine and not Robin's.

I swallow against the lump in my throat and reach for a napkin to blow my nose. "I need to get back to the house."

"No, you can't. Not in this state. You need some time away from there. Spend the night with me," he says, wrapping his arm around my shoulders.

His grip is warm and secure, and it's exactly what I need right now. I nod and let myself relax into him, resting my head back on his chest. Then I pull away again, fear and worry returning.

"I can't leave Wyatt there alone with them. He's not safe."

"Christa"—James takes both my hands into his—"if they wanted to hurt him, they would have done so already. They're his parents. Not biologically, but legally. That means they have some responsibility over him. Just try to rest tonight, and tomorrow you can go back and search for more evidence."

I take a deep breath, trying to clear my head and focus on his words, to believe him. "You don't think they will take it out on him, if they find me gone?"

James chuckles in spite of himself. "They can't do that, my love. They don't know yet that you are his mother. Get some sleep away from that house, and I'll drive you back very early tomorrow morning."

I nod and he pulls me close again, and I feel his warmth envelop me. A few minutes later, he pays and we leave.

At his cottage, he wraps me in his strong embrace and kisses me passionately. His calloused hands ignite my skin, setting my body on fire, and I melt into him. As his kisses wash away the pain and troubles that weigh me down, I give myself completely to him, abandoning all my fears and worries. Forgetting the battle that lies ahead of me, I allow relentless pleasure to course through me.

It's almost 3 a.m. and still dark when I wake up in James's arms in a panic and beg him to take me back to the villa, guilt clawing at my stomach lining.

My steps quicken as I enter the house, only to find Robin in the dark living room with the TV on mute. The light from the television illuminates her face, revealing a mixture of sadness and despair. A comedy show is playing, but she doesn't look like she's in the mood to laugh. She's just sitting there in the dark, in complete silence, staring at the TV with a blank expression on her face.

The air is charged with tension and I can feel her eyes burning through me as I stand frozen like a criminal caught in the act. The question is, why is she here? Did she come down for a drink and decide to watch TV, or was she waiting for me? What if she saw me leave and get into James's car?

I quickly remember that what I do in my private time is none of her business. She's my employer, not my mother. I have nothing to be ashamed of.

"Hi, Robin"—I try to control the quiver in my voice—"you're up late." I'm a grown woman and I shouldn't be afraid of her, but I kind of am.

She flicks on the lamp next to her, chasing away the shadows and revealing more marks of stress on her face. "As are you, it seems." Her words come out like claws, scratching at the silence that follows them.

I glance toward the window and spot the curtains fluttering in the breeze, and instantly hear the chirping of crickets drifting in. They remind me of my childhood on the farm, but instead of bringing on a feeling of security, it only heightens my fear and apprehension. My throat tightens and my tongue feels like a leaden weight in my mouth. I need to keep calm. I can't let her suspect anything.

Robin looks away, and we don't speak for a few moments. The air around us feels heavy, like a wall of smoke choking me with every breath. I know I have to act fast. I force myself to look her in the eye.

"Yes, yes, I just went for a walk in the village." My pulse races as I search for an excuse. "It's nice outside, and I needed some fresh air." I wish I could think of a better reason, but that comes out first.

"At such an odd hour?" She glances at the clock on the wall, then she shifts her weight before taking a sip of water, or is it something stronger? "Well, I guess we all need a break sometimes." She takes another drink from her glass, her eyes still filled with suspicion.

I fake a yawn and move toward the door. "I guess it's time for me to call it a night. It's been an exhausting day."

Robin gives me a strained smile that doesn't reach her eyes. "Yes, I'm sure it has been." She stares at me intently before adding in a whisper, "Sleep well, Christa."

My throat clenches as her words hang in the air between us like an accusation.

"Sleep well," I whisper back before leaving the room. My pulse racing, I quietly take the stairs two at a time.

Right now I hate myself for being so weak in her presence, for acting like I have something to hide. I still don't know exactly how I'm going to do it, but I do know that Wyatt needs to be taken away from here as soon as possible. For both our sakes. Staying in this house is starting to suffocate me and I'm determined to break free from its invisible bars.

I text James from the bedroom and relay the short conversation I had with Robin. Instead of texting back, he calls and listens intently to what I have to say, exhaling a loud sigh once I'm done.

"Be really careful, Christa. You cannot let them suspect anything. We have to find evidence that they're unfit parents and then you can get Wyatt back safely."

As he says the words, I still remember the warmth of his embrace, the taste of his lips on mine, and the touch of his fingertips on my body. I needed that, and I think he did too.

"I know," I whisper. "Thank you for everything."

Even though it was hard to open up, it was a good idea to tell James that Wyatt is my son because now I have him on my side to help me. But I have to be careful from now on. I need to hide the rest of my past, so he doesn't change his mind about me.

TWENTY
CHRISTA

It's been two whole weeks since I confessed to James that Wyatt is my son. We've just returned home after our German lesson, followed by a short visit with Simon. While the two boys have been enjoying each other's company, I've been getting to know James better as we spend more time alone at his place, often in each other's arms. Revealing my secret has brought us even closer together.

Robin is in her bedroom, and I can hear from the other side that she seems to be on the phone. It's shortly before lunch, and before I head down to prepare it, I go to my room to change into my house clothes.

The moment I enter, I know something is different. The first thing I notice is the perfume in the air. Robin's signature white-lily perfume; it hangs in the air like a cloud. The day I arrived in the villa, it reminded me of a field of blossoms in the springtime, but now it makes my throat tighten and my stomach lurch.

She was inside my room, which, like all the other doors in the house, does not have a key.

I close the door and my gaze sweeps the entire space,

searching for signs of disturbance, but there's nothing. I feel like, if she was in the room, she was searching for something specific —but what? Everything seems to be in its place, yet a feeling of unease lingers, as if something was moved or shifted from its usual place.

My gaze shifts to the half-open nightstand drawers. My hands tremble as I frantically search through them, tossing aside loose change and old receipts, searching for anything that could incriminate me, even though I know I'm not that careless. My heart races as I slide the last drawer closed, relieved to find nothing that could get me into trouble. My relief only lasts until I enter the bathroom. One clear sign that someone was definitely in the room is that the towels in the bathroom are not folded in the intricate way I always do them. Whoever unfolded them has not had the patience or skill to refold them back to their original style.

A cold sense of suspicion and dread comes over me. It can't have been anyone else but Robin. I just feel it. But what do I do now that I know she has invaded my space? I can't possibly confront her. What if she tells me she knows the truth about me? Perhaps the best way to go about this is to ignore it and pretend I didn't notice anything. I'm pretty sure she will do the same.

On my way to the kitchen, I can hear that Robin is still on the phone, so I decide not to disturb her, but I bump into Paul in the kitchen. He's sitting at the island, drinking a glass of orange juice and reading a German language newspaper. He barely looks up when I enter.

"Hi, Paul," I say as I walk over to the refrigerator and grab the chicken wings I had thawed earlier.

He responds with a soft groan before looking up at me. "How were the German lessons today?" he asks.

I instantly tense up. Before he can detect my discomfort, I

force a smile. "Really well. I think Wyatt is making a lot of progress."

Paul glances at me and I spot a rare smile on his face, something I'm unaccustomed to. The man rarely smiles or talks to me in general.

"That's good news." His eyes remain on me, making my skin prickle at the weight of his gaze. "Christa, do you enjoy working here?" he inquires.

I take a deep breath and steady myself against the kitchen counter, expecting the worst. "What do you mean?"

"I'm just asking if you enjoy working here... for us."

"Yes, of course," I reply with a quick nod. "I'm grateful for the opportunity."

He leans forward and studies me. "Are you sure about that?" He pauses. "You don't seem too enthusiastic half the time, and definitely not happy."

"Oh, maybe it's because I don't usually show much emotion," I stammer, feeling anxious.

"Is that so? You were definitely more cheerful when we first met at the interview. I remember how excited you were to come to Austria."

"I still am," I assure him. "I'm just very busy and trying to stay focused on the job."

"You're doing a wonderful job," a voice from the doorway cuts in and I look to find Robin standing there. But her eyes are blank. "We're grateful for all the hard work you've been putting in, but sometimes I sense that you're missing home."

"No, not at all," I reply. "I'm having a lot of fun here and I'm really enjoying the work too."

"Regardless," Paul goes on, "we have decided that we should leave Austria before our original date of departure."

"Earlier?" My stomach drops. "Why?"

"I have many matters to take care of in the US, and we will

be taking my mother with us to continue her treatment there. So there's no point in us staying in Austria longer than necessary."

"When?" I lick my parched bottom lip. "When do you plan to leave?"

"When are *we all* leaving, you mean?" Robin asks, leaning against the doorframe.

"Yes, that's what I mean."

This cannot happen. They cannot leave before I find out what they did to that woman. I have to prove they're dangerous. I need to leave this country knowing that Wyatt is no longer going to be a part of their lives in the US.

"In one week," Paul says, then he stands, picking up his newspaper. "That should give all of us a little time to still enjoy ourselves here."

My throat tightens, rendering me unable to say anything else. But I force myself to speak. "All right," I murmur, feigning enthusiasm to prevent them from becoming suspicious. "Sounds like a plan."

I'm far from being okay with this new turn of events. I guess one week is better than nothing. All this means is that I need to get serious about this investigation, to find out what they're hiding as soon as possible.

"Great. I'll buy the flight tickets tonight," Robin says.

Later, when I tell James about it, he's just as devastated as I am, maybe even more so. "We can't let this happen," he exclaims.

"I don't know what we can do about it," I reply. "If they want to return to the US, there's really nothing I can do to prevent it. But I won't let them take my son away without knowing exactly what they're capable of."

"Exactly. We need to search more thoroughly for evidence," he says.

It's no surprise that I haven't found anything to prove Robin and Paul are dangerous. Even though she hasn't spoken to me much, Robin has been watching me like a hawk. Since the night I came home and found her waiting for me in the living room, I get the feeling that she no longer trusts me. I'm not sure if she ever really did.

I did my best to find clues. When I got the chance, especially while cleaning the house, I snuck into the garage and looked around, but all I found was a collection of old newspapers, some parts for a motorbike, and a few tools. One of the old local newspapers did feature Eva's face on the front page, and the article inside was written around the same time she disappeared. I memorized almost every word in the article, after I translated it from German to English.

> Eva Weber, 26, was reported missing nearly a month ago, when she left her parents' house to return to work with the Mayer family in Ruddel.
>
> There has been no information regarding her whereabouts since then. Police have been searching for her ever since, but have not been able to locate her.
>
> The Mayers denied seeing her after she left their house around 6 p.m. at the end of her shift.
>
> Her parents remain hopeful that she will be found alive. If you have any information, please contact the Ruddel police department at the following number.

I wish the article was enough evidence to link Robin and Paul to Eva's disappearance, but it's not a crime to hold on to an old newspaper. If anything, it could prove that they genuinely cared about her and wanted to keep up with the story.

I'm still in the dark when it comes to understanding what happened to Eva, but I'm determined to get to the bottom of it. All I can do now is stay alert.

Still on the phone to James, I close my eyes and flop onto

the pillows, and my hand automatically slips underneath out of habit. My fingers come into contact with a piece of paper that I pull out, my heart in my throat. A missing person flyer with the word *Vermisst*—missing—written in bold letters at the top. Below it, a picture of a stunning woman with black hair and very dark eyes stares out at me. Underneath it, her name stands out.

Eva Weber.

Last week when I was in town with Wyatt, I found it pasted to a pole in the middle of the street. Though worn by time, it's still readable. I'm not sure why I brought it home that day and hid it inside the mattress cover. I looked at it last night, but I'm pretty sure I had returned it to its hiding place before falling asleep. So how did it end up under my pillow? Someone must have left it there for me to find.

"James, I think they know." I stare at the piece of paper, which is trembling slightly in my hand. "I think they've figured out that I suspect them for Eva's disappearance. That's why they want us to leave."

James goes silent for a few seconds before responding. "That alone tells me that they're guilty. Why else would they want to leave Austria so suddenly?"

TWENTY-ONE

CHRISTA

The day after I'm told we're leaving Austria, both Robin and Paul are out of the house. Even though I did not ask their permission, I proposed to James that we should have a German lesson at the villa. The plan is to get him to help me with the search. With so little time left before we fly back home, I need his help.

"Where did they go?" James asks as he steps through the door. His eyes linger on my face for a moment longer before giving me a soft kiss on the lips.

"No idea," I reply with a shrug, feeling my cheeks heat up from his closeness. "They said they'd be back by lunchtime."

He glances at his phone. "It's ten, so that gives us around two hours. We better get started."

I glance at the stairs. "What will we do with Wyatt?"

I did tell Wyatt that James was coming over, and he was ecstatic. By now he knows that our German sessions are more of a leisure activity than actual lessons. The problem today is that there's no way for us to search the house without him becoming suspicious and asking questions. I wouldn't know what to say to him if he did. And I definitely wouldn't want to lie to him.

"Did you tell him yet?" James whispers. "I really think he's old enough to know the truth."

"I'm not sure. What if he says the wrong thing at the wrong time? What if at some point he's really upset with them and it slips?"

"You're right." He runs his fingers over his stubble. "I have an idea." He takes out his phone.

"What are you doing?"

"Since Wyatt and Simon can't spend time together today, how about arranging for them to have a video call or play a video game together?"

"Yeah, that's a good idea. That should keep him busy for a while."

And of course Wyatt is fully on board. So we set him up in his room and close the door. I made sure to bring him everything he needs, including his favorite snacks, so he wouldn't feel the need to come out of his room.

Satisfied that Wyatt is content, James and I head down to the basement to start looking.

Basements have a way of hiding secrets, and I hope this one is no exception. Myriad items are stacked along the walls —books with yellowed pages, framed photographs of family members, and a carefully arranged collection of porcelain figurines. An Austrian dirndl is draped across an old armchair, still bearing the faint scent of mothballs from years past. It's clear that these items once belonged to Paul's parents.

On one wall of the basement is a huge bookshelf that reaches all the way to the ceiling; it's filled with more books, mostly encyclopedias. James pulls out a few of them and pores over them, as if he expects something to jump out from between the pages.

"This is pointless," I say as I close a cardboard box filled with Christmas decorations. "We won't find anything here."

"You may be right," James rubs his chin. "What about their bedroom?"

"Their bedroom?" I wring my hands. "I'm not sure that's a good idea. What if they figure out someone was in there?" After all, it had not been hard for me to know someone had been in mine.

James takes me by the shoulders and turns me to face him. "Christa, this could be our only chance. We might never get the opportunity to search this place again."

"You're right," I say. "Let me just check on Wyatt to make sure he doesn't need anything."

As soon as I reach the top of the stairs, I know Wyatt is happy in his room. It's evident from his loud laughter. Instead of knocking on the door, I stand outside with a smile on my face. I love that he's happy and that I'm partly responsible for it.

When I turn away from his door, I spot James coming up the stairs, walking straight to Robin and Paul's door, which is only a few steps from the landing. I'm surprised that he knows where to go given that the villa has so many rooms.

Once inside, we look around everything. I'm actually more careful than Robin was because I'm sure to fold everything the way it was before, putting everything safely back in its place. The only useful thing we find is a cell phone in one of the drawers next to the king-size bed. A password is required to get inside, but that's not a problem for James.

He takes the phone from me and begins typing away at lightning speed. Within seconds, he's unlocked the device.

"How did you do that?" I ask, shocked.

"Let's just say I have a set of skills that come in handy in situations like this." James smirks at me. "Actually, one of my uncles owned a tech firm, so I picked up a few things from him."

"That's great. I'm impressed."

He doesn't respond because he's already searching through the phone.

After a few minutes, having found nothing useful, he quits. But before he returns it to the drawer, I take it from him.

"Let me try." Instead of reading through Robin's emails as James did, I check the notes app and every other app on the phone until I come across one named Journali. "I might have found something. Robin likes to journal and she has an app." I wave James over. "Wow!" I breathe as I scroll through folders. "There are years and years. There must be something in here."

"But we don't have time to read all the entries, so we have to choose."

"You're right." I decide to pick the folder labeled 2015, the year Eva went missing. Pulling out my phone, I take photos of as many entries as I can, including some from the last eighteen months. I'll read them all later. I exit the app and replace the phone in the drawer. "Do you really think she'd be careless enough to confess to a crime in her journals?"

"Sometimes when a person is carrying something really heavy, it helps to write it down," says James.

Before I can respond, we both hear Wyatt's door opening down the hall.

"We should get out of here," I whisper.

Thankfully, when we get to the landing, Wyatt is disappearing into the bathroom and I don't have to worry about him seeing us come out of the master bedroom. James runs down the stairs while I remain in the hallway, waiting for Wyatt to leave the bathroom to make sure he doesn't come looking for me.

When he comes out, he grins at me. "Hi, Christa."

"You done talking to Simon?" I ask.

"Nope." He walks back toward his room. "We're playing online games. Can we please have more time?"

"Sure, go ahead."

As soon as his door closes, the sound of a car engine hits my ears and my heart jumps to my throat. I run to the window and it's them. They're back way before the time they said they would return. I run to James to warn him.

By the time Paul and Robin enter the house, James, Wyatt, and I are sitting in the library, pretending to be having a German lesson. Both of them are surprised that James is inside their home, but when they watch him with Wyatt, who is engrossed in the lessons, they don't say much more.

After James leaves, Robin tells me to never invite anyone to the house again when they're not around, and I give her my promise.

Inside my room I lean against the door, panting. Then I sit down on the edge of the bed, going through the photos I took of Robin's journal. There are dozens of them. I want to read through them now, to get into her mind, but I can't do so during the day when she might walk into the room anytime. I have to wait until tonight when everyone's sleeping.

I would like to leave the photos on my phone, but I think it's risky since I carry it with me all day. Instead, I send them to myself by email, then delete them from the phone. It's always better to be safe rather than sorry.

TWENTY-TWO

CHRISTA

I settle in bed and, with trembling hands, open my laptop. The eerie blue-green light that spills from the screen merges with the soft light of the bedside lamp, enveloping me. A heavy weight presses down on my chest as I struggle with the decision to read Robin's journals. But I must if I ever want to get my son back from them. No matter how uncomfortable I am, I have no other option.

I'm not even sure that Wyatt would be given to me if they take him away from the Mayers, considering that I don't have the most stable living situation. I don't even have my own place, and once the Mayers are out of his life they will be out of mine as well... as employers. But if they're arrested and tried for Eva's murder he will be taken back into care, and it won't be long before he's old enough to make his own decisions. He might want to spend time with the only person who has truly cared for him in the last few years, someone different from his adoptive parents who rarely communicate with him.

What if?

What if there's a reason for them wanting to avoid him? Could it be because he knows their secret?

I shudder at the thought that Wyatt might have seen them commit murder, that he experienced their dark side firsthand. It would certainly explain his odd behavior when they walk into the room, and why the atmosphere turns icy cold each time. The thought makes me sick to my stomach, and I'm scared to even consider the possibility. But now that the seed has been planted inside my mind, I can't shake it.

I hope I find the evidence I need in these journals or elsewhere because I don't want to ask Wyatt what he knows, to put him through the trauma of having to relive that event once again. Something like that can really mess up a child.

I inhale deeply, then exhale, and start scrolling through the various journal entries that I photographed. Given that I'm running out of time, I decide to pick random entries and piece things together that way. The only thing I do is divide the two journals into two separate folders—2015 and 2021. I have no idea how far back I need to go in order to figure out this mystery, so I start with one of the entries from 2021.

Before reading, I quickly skim the entry looking for any reference to Eva or anything that will give me a clue as to what happened, something that would lead me closer to the truth.

Then, with a deep breath, I dive into Robin's memories.

TWENTY-THREE

ROBIN

April, 2021

It has finally happened. Today's a day I cannot put into words: the day I found out I'm going to be a mother, although I won't get to hold my little one in my arms until many months from now. When the two red lines appeared on the pregnancy test a week ago, it was like a miracle had happened and today my doctor confirmed it. My miracle is real and it's growing within me.

As I write these words, the feelings of joy and excitement I feel are so overwhelming that I can barely contain them. I'm overcome with emotion at the thought of welcoming my own child into this world... a feeling that cannot be matched.

From the outside, everyone already refers to me as a mother, Wyatt's mother. Legally, he is my son. During the adoption process, I was desperate to have him. Paul and I did everything that was required, going above and beyond to make sure he was ours. The day the papers were signed was one of the happiest days of my life. I could not wait to give him a life he would otherwise have been denied. I wanted to love him, to protect him.

We opened our home to him to give him a new start, and from the moment he was placed in my arms, I fell head over heels in love. His eyes, so large and the color of honey, seemed to understand who I was to him. When he smiled, my heart felt like it was an inch from exploding. His small hands would reach for my face and I'd respond by giving him a kiss on each one.

Despite the sleep deprivation that comes with being a new parent, I chose never to hire a babysitter as I couldn't stand to be apart from my little boy. Nights became our favorite time together. After a long but wonderful day, I'd go sit in the rocking chair with him until he drifted off to sleep.

I was content, but as the years passed, moments of wanting my biological child grew more frequent. During those times, sorrow would come over me and I could feel myself pushing Wyatt away. I'd make up for those moments, giving him more hugs and kisses so he wouldn't feel neglected. Even when he was young, he could sense my distance. His clinginess was palpable, as was his frustration during temper tantrums when I didn't give him enough attention, no matter how much I gave.

I did my best to be there for him, to show him he was loved, but it was never enough. He started wanting more than I could give and looked for ways to please me, to seek my approval. After a while, it all became too much and I found myself pulling away even more, and the more he tried to bridge the gap between us, the further apart we grew.

The distance between us kept growing until, one night, something inside me broke, and it hit me hard that the love I had for the little boy was gone and I felt nothing for him. Initially, I felt guilty and ashamed of my emotions, but there was nothing I could do to shift them. No one knows this, not even Paul. It's a weight I have carried alone all these years in silent shame.

Hard as I try, I can no longer feel any maternal feelings toward him. I tried hard to get it back, the mother-son bond we once shared, but I can't. When I stopped loving him, he became nothing but a reminder of what could have been, of my unfulfilled dreams of having a baby of our own.

Today, Paul told Wyatt that he will soon become a big brother. It was not hard to see the hurt in his eyes. And the rest of the day, I watched him physically withdraw into himself, becoming distressed and sad. But I couldn't think about how he felt. All my affection was centered around the baby inside of me and there was none left for him. My heart is saving all my love for my own baby.

If anyone knew this is how I felt about the boy, they would think I'm coldhearted, but no one will ever understand, not unless they are in my shoes.

No, I'm not coldhearted. I'm just human and I have the right to choose who to love.

At this moment, I choose to love my own child, even before it's born. And that means I must divert my love away from someone else's child. No matter how painful it may be for Wyatt, I will never apologize for doing what comes naturally.

When Paul found out we were going to be real parents, I saw a change in his eyes. It almost seemed like he was feeling the same way I was, choosing to direct his love where it belongs. I noticed how instead of spending time with Wyatt, and doing the things they loved to do together, he stayed with me instead, cradling my flat stomach, talking to our baby.

The birth of this child will undoubtedly alter our lives significantly. We'll have to keep this little one our priority and give it everything it deserves.

Go ahead and criticize me, call me anything you want, but you won't be able to alter my feelings. Nobody can force a heart to love someone it's not meant to love. My heart is already full of love for my biological child and there isn't room for anyone else, not anymore.

But I can only hold myself accountable for what happened. I had been so convinced that adoption was our only alternative. Now I deeply regret that choice, giving up too soon and going for the second option.

Maybe other people find it easy to love someone else's child as well as their own. For a while I thought I was that person, but I was wrong. I'm certain that there are parents out there who feel the same way I do, who have made the mistake of adopting and now regret it—but they won't admit it to anyone, not even to themselves.

If only I could turn back the clock, to undo what has been done. I've been so foolish, so gullible. Adopting a child has taught me an invaluable lesson: Listen to your heart and trust your instinct. I should have followed my gut.

Although I feel guilty and ashamed at times, I have come to understand that it's all right to change your mind. We can make decisions and then things happen, and we realize later on that what we thought we wanted is not right for us. We shouldn't beat ourselves up for wanting something until we get it.

All I know right now is that I don't have the energy to look after Wyatt as well as take care of myself. With every ounce of energy I possess, I need to concentrate solely on ensuring my baby is born healthy and strong.

It's a relief that we have the resources to hire nannies who can take on the task of Wyatt's mother since I'm not willing to. My only comfort is that he's fourteen now. There are only a few years left before he's old enough to be responsible for his own life. I cannot wait to have him out of this house, so that me, my husband, and our child can be a real family without the dark shadow of a mistake hovering over us.

But do I really have the strength to wait until he's eighteen? A single day in his presence feels like an eternity, and every day he's with us I feel like I'm losing a piece of myself. He's a leech, his presence draining the life out of me.

I don't understand why he won't be content with the basics of life—a roof over his head and food on the table. Why does he always have to want more? After all, I give him more than his own, absent, unknown mother ever did. Yet he still isn't grateful for what he has.

All that I can do is continue to ignore him until he stops wanting more from me, from us. But even then, can I ever really be free from him? As long as he carries our name, and as long as my signature is on the adoption papers, I'll never be fully rid of him.

The mistakes of my past will remain.

TWENTY-FOUR

CHRISTA

Robin's confession hits me like a ton of bricks, sending shockwaves through my body. My hands curl into fists as I read her diary entry, my vision blurring with emotion. Once I've read the last word, I slam the laptop shut, my heart pounding in my chest, and shove it away from me so hard it almost topples off the bed. My arms shake when I reach out to catch it, gritting my teeth as I resist the urge to fling it across the room.

I've known all along that Wyatt is adopted, that he's the boy I had been searching for, for many years, while babysitting other children to fill the void that losing my son had left behind.

The day I found him changed my life forever, and it took a drastic turn. Any plans I had made were instantly canceled, any dreams were put on hold, or left to wilt and die for good. I had only one goal in mind and that was to be close to my son and make sure he was okay. I could never think of taking him away from the family he had probably grown to love, to disrupt his life in any way, yet I was not willing to stay away either. It was like an impossible dilemma: How could any mother choose one over the other?

For months, I stalked him and his family. I couldn't stay

away, not after finding him, and so I applied for jobs in the neighborhood where they lived, all so I could keep an eye on him and his family without having to directly interfere. I also attended weekly nanny and housekeeper meetups to gather all the news and gossip about people in the area, including Wyatt's family. Back then I never thought he would need me as much as I needed him. I never anticipated this is where we would end up.

Squeezing the sheets between my fingers, I bite down on my lower lip until the salty tang of blood hits my tongue. My heart is pounding in my throat and the rushing in my ears mutes any noises from outside my body. Even though Robin has long proven to be an unfit mother in my eyes, I'm still appalled to the core by the coldhearted way she spoke about a boy she welcomed into her home and promised to care for, both physically and emotionally. How could she say such horrible things? How could she allow herself to even think them? How could any person with a heart be so cruel?

Driven by rage I jump out of bed and charge to the door, but then I stop. My blood boils with anger and I have to force myself not to run out of the room and confront her. It would be pointless. What good could come out of me revealing what I have read? I can't do that without her knowing that I invaded her privacy. That would never end well.

Besides, the journal entry won't be enough to get Wyatt taken away from them. The law would only be looking for physical signs of abuse, and I haven't seen any yet. Without visible marks on his body, nothing would probably change.

But I know better: Emotional harm runs much deeper than surface wounds.

My body trembles as I press my forehead against the door, a battle raging inside my head between the desire to stay put and to leave the room. Whatever I do next needs to be done with care. I need to think things through and stay calm. But I can't manage that by myself, so I make my way back to the bed and call James.

He's just as stunned as I am, understanding the anguish I'm experiencing as Wyatt's mom after finding out what I just did.

"You're right." His voice is laden with revulsion. "That's a crummy and unforgivable way to talk about a kid, any kid."

I clench my eyes shut. "I don't know what to do now. How can I allow her to get away with such a thing?"

"Christa," he says in a stern voice, "whatever you do, you cannot let your emotions get the better of you."

My eyes fly open. "But it's my son she was insulting. She despises him."

"I am aware of that, darling. It hurts." He pauses for a moment. "I think the best thing for you to do right now is to get out of there, first thing tomorrow morning. Come to my place for a couple of hours."

"No way," I respond, feeling apprehensive about leaving Wyatt in Robin's care. "I don't have a good excuse to take him out of here. Our next lesson is in two days."

"I know," James says, "but there must be a way to still get you and Wyatt out for a few hours. Why don't you tell them that I have to travel out of town the day after tomorrow and want to do the lesson before I go?"

"Okay, that sounds like a good plan. I'll bring it up with Robin tomorrow."

In the morning, I pass on the message, and Robin surprisingly doesn't object.

"But, Christa, it has to be the last lesson since we are leaving Austria soon anyway. I don't think there's any point in continuing."

Freezing up, I remember that if I don't act fast, it'll be too late for me to get the necessary answers. But I try to maintain a neutral expression as I agree with her. I clench and unclench my jaw. "Sure, I'll let James know."

It's killing me inside to pretend I don't feel pure, undiluted hate for her, that I'm not seething inside, that I don't want to grab her and slam her against the wall behind her, to hurt her like she's hurting my son, like she's hurting me.

Fortunately, she also agrees to us leaving right after breakfast. When the time comes, Wyatt and I hop onto our bikes. The crisp morning air is a stark contrast to the sweltering heat of the day before. I welcome the refreshing breeze on my skin, but it's unable to soothe my inner turmoil. As Wyatt cycles ahead of me, he keeps glancing back in my direction. We're connected enough for him to sense that something is wrong, that my mood has shifted.

If only I could tell him that it has to do with him. But I can't, not yet. He cannot find out that I'm his mother, not until the time is right. So, I manage a smile and give him a small wave, my hair floating behind me in the breeze.

We don't go directly to James's. He called and suggested I take Wyatt over to Simon's house so they can spend some time together, and we can talk privately without him hearing what we have to say, or seeing me get upset. Agreeing with him, I follow Wyatt to Simon's house and carry on alone to James's place.

As soon as I drop my bike to the ground and James's arms are wrapped around me, a torrent of emotions breaks loose and I crumble in his embrace. The hiccupping and sobbing eventually subside and he places a gentle kiss on my lips.

"Let me get you that chai tea you love so much, and then we'll figure out what to do, okay?"

I give him a weak smile and nod, then I watch him disappear into the kitchen. I slowly get up from the couch and go about searching for tissues for my runny nose. On my way to the bathroom, I remember having seen a box of tissues on the guest room table, just across from James's bedroom.

Inside the room, I'm about to pick up the entire box and take it with me to the living room, when I notice that one of the two drawers of the table is open a crack.

Something inside me can't stand doors, cupboards, or drawers that aren't properly closed. Out of habit, I grab hold of the drawer knob and push it closed. But just as quickly as it begins to close, my curiosity gets the best of me and I pull it open again. At the bottom of the drawer, something had caught my eye.

The drawer is covered with papers, but on top of them is a photograph of a woman standing in front of a fountain. Her black hair is blowing in the wind, the strands dancing around her pale face. She's dressed in a cream, lacy midi-dress, and her face is illuminated by the soft light of the setting sun. Her dark eyes meet my gaze and I feel something stirring in my heart.

She's not just any woman, and the man behind her is not just any man.

The smiling woman looking up at me with James behind her, kissing her neck, is Eva. On her finger is what looks like an engagement ring that she's happily showing off.

TWENTY-FIVE

CHRISTA

I ring the bell, and James's sister, Angela, opens it. She's on the short side with tight blonde curls, and her eyes resemble blue marbles. There's no resemblance whatsoever to her tall, dark-haired brother. She smiles at me, displaying bright white teeth.

"Oh, you're here to take Wyatt already?" She twists a strand of hair around her finger. "The boys just sat down to watch an action movie."

"I apologize." I peer over my shoulder. "There's been an emergency, and we need to leave."

She places a hand on her chest. "Is everything okay?" She gazes past me. No doubt she's expecting James to be right behind me.

We need to leave now in case he shows up.

"Not sure," I murmur, my words tasting sour on my tongue. "I apologize that Wyatt won't be able to stay. We really must be going."

"It's okay," she replies, gesturing for me to come in.

I shake my head, staying put. "That's all right. I'll wait out here."

She opens her mouth to argue, but then she gives in with a

smile and a nod. "I'll have him out in a second." As soon as she disappears inside, leaving the door open, she calls up the stairs for Wyatt.

Moments later, he stands before me, an expression of confusion on his face. "We just arrived," he protests.

Simon lingers behind, slumped against the banister rail, evidently disappointed.

"I know. I'm really sorry, honey. But we need to go." I want to make a promise to both the boys that I'll bring Wyatt another time, but I can't guarantee that. It may be the last time they'll ever see each other.

After trying and failing to persuade me to change my mind, Wyatt eventually gives up and gets on his bike.

This time as we ride home, he doesn't look back at me every so often, and he's pedaling his bike faster than I would have liked. But he's an excellent cyclist, so I tell myself not to worry about him.

The person I need to worry about is myself because my focus is elsewhere. I'm pretty sure James is calling my phone nonstop. It was a good idea to switch it off.

I can't bring myself to talk to him yet. I need time to make sense of what I saw: Eva with a smile on her lips, happily looking at the camera as James kissed her. The ring on her finger. All this time James had acted like he barely knew her. I explicitly remember him saying so the day he told me her name without meaning to.

A part of me is telling me I must be wrong, that it can't be her. But it is. The woman in the picture is the same one from the flyer. Dark, long, wavy hair cascading down her shoulders, mesmerizing eyes that seem to see into your soul, and full, perfectly formed lips.

What does this all mean and where do we go from here? He lied to me. Does he really want to protect me and Wyatt, or was this all a ruse to get into the house? To get revenge?

We find Robin in the kitchen making a cocktail even though it's barely eleven o'clock.

"You're back so soon?" She looks at the clock on the wall next to the kitchen door.

Without saying a word to me or Robin, Wyatt runs up the stairs, still mad at me for cutting his fun short. I can't bear to look Robin in the eye. I'm still flaming with anger from what I read last night.

"James mixed up the dates. He thought he was leaving for his trip tomorrow, but he's actually leaving today."

I'm not sure whether she believes me or not, and I don't really care.

"I see," she murmurs, turning her attention back to making her cocktail in the blender—pouring rum and cream on top of what's already inside. As soon as the appliance starts whirring, I take this as my cue and leave the kitchen.

Over the next few hours, I busy myself with tidying up the lived-in part of the house, including Robin and Paul's bathroom, which is in disarray. I find towels, clothes, bottles of lotion, and even long strands of hair all over the floor. I'm not certain if Robin did it deliberately to give me more work, but I don't think about that. I have no choice but to clean every nook and cranny until my palms hurt. I need to decide what to do now that I know James lied to me. Without his help, I'm on my own.

How can I ever trust him again after this?

At the end of the day, I take a shower and get into bed, switching on my phone after hours of it being off. Twenty missed calls and numerous messages from James appear.

Not long after, a call comes in from him. As the phone vibrates in my hand, my finger hovers over the off button, but instead I find myself pressing the green button to accept the call and bring it to my ear. My jaw clenches as I speak.

"You said you didn't know her that well."

I don't have time for him to skirt around the issue. He needs to know that I know because I'm not in the mood for him to waste my time. I need to know the truth.

The line is completely silent for what feels like an eternity. He's probably weighing his options and seeing how much he can get away with without getting in trouble.

"Christa, are you okay?" He ignores what I said entirely. "Why did you take off without saying anything?"

"No, everything is not okay, James," I snap back. "You lied to me... about her."

"What are you talking about?" He continues to pretend he doesn't understand, making a fool of me.

"Do I really have to say her name? Please, don't belittle my intelligence. I was in your guest room and found a photograph of her in the drawer. Imagine my shock when I saw you in the same picture. It's quite obvious that you two were quite close."

He's silent again, carefully choosing his words, probably cooking up the perfect lie. Then he clears his throat. "I'm really sorry. I didn't mean to keep it from you. I promise I was going to tell you."

"You said you only knew her from the gossip around town and the flyers, but it turns out that wasn't true. You made me believe your lies all this time, James." I take a moment before I continue. "I thought I could trust you, that I could tell you my secrets."

"I didn't know how to tell you. I didn't want you to misinterpret things."

I walk away from the bed and head to the window, my fingers brushing over the glass, gazing out into the night sky, studying the silhouettes of the far-off mountains. "What's there to misinterpret? You knew her, and she was your fiancée, right?"

"Yes, Eva was... she was my fiancée." His voice quivers with emotion so much that I can feel the pain radiating from his words. "I proposed to her a week before she disappeared. That was two days after she told me she was pregnant."

I struggle to find the right words. I don't know how to react. I don't know whether I should offer him comfort or cling to my anger. I'm at a total loss.

I sit down on the bed again. "Why didn't you tell me, James?" I feel for him and acknowledge the sorrow he must have experienced, losing his fiancée and their unborn child, yet at the same time I'm feeling betrayed. I'm starting to question if what we had was even real.

Without allowing him to answer, I continue. "You should have told me. You made a fool out of me." I bite my lower lip hard, then ask him the one question that matters most. "Why exactly did you start a relationship with me? Was it because you liked me or because you wanted to get close to information concerning the Mayers, information I was closest to? Don't you dare lie to me!"

I suddenly recall the day he was at the house when he knew exactly which room was the master bedroom. It's becoming apparent now that he had been here before. Perhaps Eva had invited him over. For all I know, after waiting for years to exact his revenge, he found out that the Mayers were back in town. What if our meeting at the grocery store was not a coincidence? What if it was all part of the plan? What if he had been following me?

"Initially, I only wanted to get information, but I ended up... liking you."

"What you're telling me is that you took advantage of me? Is that right?"

He doesn't respond, and that's a good enough answer for me.

TWENTY-SIX

CHRISTA

A silvery stream of sunlight creeps in through the half-drawn curtains, causing me to blink my eyes several times to adjust to the morning light. Yawning, I check the clock on the nightstand.

8.30 a.m.? My head reels back in shock. I can't remember the last time I woke up this late.

I slowly peel back the covers, my body aching as if a wall of bricks fell on me while I was asleep. How could I have overslept? The last few days, even if I didn't go out for a morning jog, I still woke up at the usual time.

As I massage my temples, there's a loud knocking at the door that sends pain reverberating through my head. It must be Robin, wondering why I haven't brought her breakfast yet. Since she knows I'm an early riser, she now insists on having her breakfast delivered to their room at seven on the dot.

I stagger out of bed, grab a robe, and head to the door instead of telling her to enter. It's the only thing right now that makes me feel in control.

Instead of Robin, Paul is standing in the hallway, all ready for work in a dark-blue velvet suit and white tie.

"Hi, Paul," I say, surprised because he has never knocked on my door before.

"Robin has been waiting for her breakfast for over an hour." He doesn't even bother to hide the hint of annoyance in his voice.

It's heartbreaking that he's more concerned about Robin than Wyatt. For some parents, their children take the top spot on the priority list. If the situation were reversed, my son would have been the first thing on my mind when I woke up.

"I apologize," I say as I rub my weary eyes. "I overslept."

"It's obvious." He stares at me with a piercing gaze. "This cannot happen again."

Something like this has never happened before and this is his reaction?

"I'll get started on breakfast right away. Where's Wyatt?"

"Robin wants croissants. You'll have to go to the bakery."

My eyes widen in surprise as I cinch the bathrobe tighter around my body. "The bakery?"

"There's only one bakery in town; you must have noticed it before."

"Yes, I'm familiar with it," I say. What surprises me is the fact that they want to send me out of the house. What happened to them not wanting me to interact with the locals? "Can I take Wyatt with me? He might enjoy a stroll around the village."

"You're not going for a walk, Christa. Just go and buy the croissants. Wyatt stays here." He shoves his fists into his pockets. "Don't be too long."

Before he walks away, I ask if I can take one of their cars. If I drove, I could make it to the village and back in no time, to prevent Wyatt being alone with them for longer than necessary.

"No," he responds without turning to look at me.

Anxiety pounds in my chest. Before I leave, I stop in the doorway to Wyatt's room and watch him make his bed.

"Hi, Christa," he says when he notices me, and smiles widely.

The tension in my shoulders melts away. He has forgiven me. "I'm so sorry again about yesterday," I say, closing the door.

"It's fine." He starts to fluff out his pillows. "I can understand why you wanted to leave. You had a fight with James, didn't you?"

I stare at him, my mouth agape. How does he know that James and I had an argument? Is it a guess or had he perhaps walked past my bedroom last night and overheard us on the phone? Panic claws at my chest. What if someone else heard my conversation as well?

Instead of pursuing the topic, I just smile. "I'm heading to the bakery. I'll be back soon, then we can have breakfast together."

"Sounds good," he says.

I leave the house on a mission, cycling like a mad person. It promises to be a hot day today. Even though it's quite early in the morning, the wind is already warm against my face.

By the time I reach the village, twenty minutes have passed. Not a long time, but to me, it feels like a lifetime. Inside the small bakery, I grab everything I need, but before I can leave, Robin calls to give me a list of things she also wants me to buy at the grocery store across the street. I do as I'm told, but quite a few of the items are, apparently, hardly ever in stock. Does Robin know that? Did she send me here just to waste my time, to punish me for something? I call her back to let her know I can't find what she asked for, but the phone goes to voicemail.

Feeling a heaviness in my chest, I run to my bicycle and cycle back to the house. Something is going on. I don't know what it is, but my throat feels like it's closing, blocking my air supply.

After being on the road for about ten minutes, the little

basket propped up at the front of the bike detaches itself and falls to the ground, and the croissants slide out into the dirt.

"Damn," I murmur as I come to a stop.

I pick up the pastries, but there are still pieces of grass and debris stuck to the surface. I consider whether I should go back to the village to get more croissants or just take them home and brush them off, pretending nothing ever happened.

I choose the latter. I need to get back home to Wyatt.

I put them back in the bag and, this time, instead of putting them back in the basket, I push my hand through the handle of the plastic bag.

When I'm halfway home, my thighs start to burn and my legs feel like lead. I'm finding it hard to cycle any faster, but I keep going until I finally arrive.

Something is different. The driveway is empty. Before I left, both cars were parked outside.

My heart thudding, I get off the bike and run into the house, straight to Wyatt's room. He's not there, and when I call all their names, no one responds.

Nobody is home.

Robin and Paul took Wyatt somewhere without telling me. Did they send me to the shops on purpose? Do they know I don't like leaving Wyatt alone with them and thought it would be the only way to separate us?

Exactly what do they know about me?

I continue to search the house, calling loudly, becoming hysterical by the second. They're nowhere to be found. Dropping the croissants on the floor, I grab my phone from my pocket and call Robin, but just like last time the call goes straight to the mailbox. There's no way of knowing where they went and when they will be back. They have never gone away together before. Perhaps they didn't want to leave Wyatt with me in case I take him to the village without their permission.

The next person I call is James. We may have our differences, but I don't know who else to reach out to. I spent all of last night thinking about him and Eva, and came to the conclusion that when we started our friendship, I was keeping a secret from him as well and he did not judge me. And there are still some things he doesn't know. Even though I still feel betrayed by him, he's the only person I know in this town, the only person who could possibly help me.

He answers on the first ring. "I'm really sorry," he says immediately. "I should have told you."

"It's okay," I say quickly. "Wyatt is gone. Robin and Paul... They sent me out to buy croissants and when I came back, they were gone."

"What do you mean gone?" he asks, concern tainting his voice.

"Just gone. While I was out, they left."

"And you have no idea where they went?"

"All I know is that they took my son."

What if they left for good? What if they don't come back? No, I tell myself to stop going crazy. This is their house. They won't just abandon it.

"I'm afraid, James. What if they do something to him? If they really killed Eva, what if they kill my son too? Robin despises him."

"I want you to stop thinking like that," he says. "I need you to calm down and wait for me. I'm on my way."

TWENTY-SEVEN

CHRISTA

I've had many cold showers in my life and hardly ever flinched. But now I'm cold, frozen without being touched by a drop of freezing water. I'm pacing around the living room, on the verge of a meltdown, beside myself with worry as I wait for James to arrive.

Maybe I'm jumping to conclusions. Since both Robin and Paul's cars are gone, they may have different plans, with one taking Wyatt out while the other is somewhere else. Could Paul have taken Wyatt to see his grandmother, and there's nothing for me to worry about?

Perhaps, but my gut is telling me otherwise. I can't shake the feeling that something is seriously wrong as my mind races with all kinds of scenarios, each one more terrifying than the last.

Gripping my phone in my hand, I redial Robin's number and it again goes to the mailbox. The moment her recorded nasal voice fills the line, my stomach turns over and I end the call. I have also tried Paul's phone several times, but he doesn't answer.

Not knowing where they took my son is driving me insane. I need to know what they want to do with him.

Feeling completely helpless, I toss the phone onto the couch and bury my hands in my hair, gripping the strands in my fists, hurting my scalp but not giving a damn because what's inside of me hurts so much more than what's outside. What if, somehow, they found out that Wyatt is my son? What if they took him away from me because of what I know about them? What if they're returning to the US and planning to disappear so I can never find them?

They hardly ever took him out before, never acted like a family, not around me at least. Why now?

As a heavy weight settles in the pit of my stomach, I feel suddenly nauseous. Racing for the bathroom, I make it just in time to throw up and retch over and over again, bringing up nothing, which is no surprise—I haven't eaten anything today.

I don't know how to do this, how to make it through this ordeal.

I run to the window, to see if James has arrived, but the driveway is still empty. So I remain standing by the window, hoping for Robin and Paul to show up, for their cars to appear from the distance, but nothing.

Finally, I see James's car appear on the horizon. My heart lightens just a little as I run out of the living room and yank open the door so hard it slams into the wall behind it. I wrap my arms around my body as tears stream down my cheeks, trailing their way down my neck until they're sucked up by the collar of my t-shirt. Even though we had a disagreement, even though I found out his secret, I'm still glad James dropped everything to come and help me. Right now, there's no anger left in me reserved for him.

As soon as he exits the car, he runs to me, pulling me into his arms. "It's going to be okay," he whispers into my hair, his hand cupping the back of my head.

I'm still unsure exactly what it is he feels for me, but at this point I don't care. I'm relieved to have somebody on my side, to be assured that I'm not completely alone.

Finally, we make our way into the house.

"What if they return soon and find my car in the driveway?" he asks. "Should I park somewhere else?"

I shake my head. "I don't care."

Even if they showed up now, they already know that James is my friend and surely I am allowed visitors. The only problem is that I told Robin he was leaving for Vienna yesterday, but I'll work something out if I need to.

"I need to get back my child," I say as soon as the front door is shut. "But I don't know what to do." I pace around the living room, fresh tears stinging my eyes.

"Come and sit down," James says.

It takes a while for me to heed his advice, but, finally, I'm sitting next to him.

His expression is serious as he studies my face. "This doesn't have to be a bad thing. We could use the time to find what we need."

"How could you say that it's not a bad thing?" I'm growing annoyed with how calm he is in this situation, despite the fact that calm is exactly what I need right now. "They took my son and didn't say a word to me."

"Christa, I don't think they know that Wyatt is your son. For all we know, they just went out as a family."

His words are interrupted by a text message coming into my phone.

"It's from her," I say between gritted teeth.

"It's Robin?" James asks.

Busy reading the text, I don't respond.

Christa, we are on our way to Salzburg to stay with friends. We'll be back in two days.

Robin

I try to call her again, not sure exactly what I want to tell her, but her phone has been switched off again. She clearly does not want to speak to me.

"What did she say?" James scoots closer.

"They drove to Salzburg to visit friends." I'm not sure whether to feel relieved or continue to hold on to my anger. "They'll be back in two days." I swallow down the bitter taste at the back of my throat. "James, they must have sent me out so they could sneak off, and I don't understand why."

"Or maybe not. Perhaps there was some kind of emergency and they had to leave immediately. Either way, them being gone is a good thing. While they're gone, we have enough time to search this house again, to find the evidence we need to take to the cops." He pauses, out of breath because he's clearly excited about this new opportunity. "When they return, hopefully, we'll have something concrete to get them arrested, so you can have your son back."

We both know it's not going to be as easy as that, but I find comfort in his words all the same.

"Maybe you're right." I drop my head into my hands. "I hope we find something." I take a breath and look up again.

James gazes around. "If they have anything at all to do with Eva's death, the evidence has to be here somewhere. We just need to find it. And now there's no rush."

Nodding, I get to my feet, but my head spins. Swaying, I sink back onto the couch and lean against the armrest, unable to stand.

James sits by my side and puts a hand on my arm. "Get some rest. I can get started if you like."

"No, I'm fine." As much as I want to find the evidence, and as grateful as I am that James is here, part of me is still finding it hard to trust him again completely. To be honest, I'm still struggling to understand his motivations. Whatever we are doing, we are doing together.

"I'm really sorry I didn't tell you about Eva," he croaks, removing his hand from my arm. "I just didn't know how to. But I promise you I *was* going to do it. It was just a matter of finding the right time. And then when we started... it got complicated."

"It's fine." I don't have the energy to argue. And I kind of understand why he didn't tell me. I would have reacted the same way I'm reacting right now. But I know one thing is for sure; if I had known he was linked to the missing nanny, I would not have allowed myself to get that close to him.

"But I do like you," he continues. "I like you a lot."

I wish I could say it back, but after everything that's happened, the only person on my mind right now is Wyatt. I cannot allow myself to be distracted by anything or anyone else. He is my priority and getting him back safe is the only thing I'm concerned about.

I cannot see James and me continuing where we left off. There will always be the shadow of Eva standing between us. After this is over, there will no longer be an us. Next week, I will be leaving the country anyway, and we may never see each other again. I don't see myself ever returning to Ruddel. The only reason I came here was for Wyatt.

"It doesn't matter, James," I reply. "Our feelings for each other don't matter right now."

I take a deep breath and force myself to my feet again. This time I stand strong, ready to do anything that will help me get my son back, ready to fight.

James is right. This could be my only chance to get what I want.

TWENTY-EIGHT

CHRISTA

We plan to go through every single room in the house, even the rooms Robin told me to stay away from. Especially those.

Before we search any room, James looks around to see if there are any cameras or other surveillance devices. He assures me that he knows what he's doing. This is actually something he should have done last time we searched the house, but I don't say anything.

Once he finishes combing through the rooms I'll be searching and finds nothing, he goes to the other wing of the house.

I'm not quite sure exactly what we're looking for, but I keep hoping to stumble on a snippet of evidence that could lead us to more answers.

Though Eva has been gone or potentially killed for seven years, this house may still hold secrets. If James is right, and Paul and Robin really did something to her, we might find a murder weapon or maybe a piece of Eva's clothing or other belongings that could implicate them. Or, even better, we might stumble upon Eva's remains. The thought makes my stomach turn, but I know we have to keep looking.

The villa has ten bedrooms in total and after searching through two that are not in the main house, I enter the one that looks lived in. I have been in this room before but it looked totally different then. This time there isn't a speck of dust in sight and the furniture isn't covered with plastic anymore. There's even a cup of coffee on the nightstand with a bit of the liquid at the bottom that hasn't dried out.

The gray, soft plush carpet on the floor swallows my feet as I walk across it. My guess is this is a room that Paul or Robin sleeps in late at night after a fight. Maybe Robin slept here the other night when I saw her leaving the house after their argument.

I step into the small walk-in closet and search it from top to bottom. Despite the signs that someone must have occupied the room recently, there are no clothes hanging from the velvet hangers, and no shoes at the bottom. Every drawer in the room is empty except for one, where I find a remote for the flatscreen TV that's propped on the wall opposite the bed. Unsure of where else to look, I remove the midnight-blue and silver bedding from the bed and flip over the mattress. Still nothing.

Disheartened, I sink onto the edge of the bed to catch my breath, my chest rising and falling as I try to keep calm.

"Have you found anything?" James calls from somewhere in the house.

I take a breath before responding. "No."

"Me neither," he answers back.

I get up. This cannot be it. James is convinced that Eva was murdered, and if this is the place where she died, then there must be something hidden here.

Before leaving the room, I remake the bed to leave it exactly as it was before. I'm dragging my feet to the door when I look back to check that everything is in its place. That's when I notice the door to the ensuite bathroom.

It's a small bathroom, shared by two guest rooms with doors

leading into the individual bedrooms. I have already searched the other room. There's really nothing to see at first sight, but I'm not done. I stand in the middle of the bathroom and turn around, looking from side to side, looking up at the ceiling and down at the floor. Then I start opening and closing drawers, running my hands through them one after the other. Aside from being filled with towels and cosmetics, there's nothing suspicious.

Now there's only one cabinet beneath the sink that I haven't checked. For a second I wonder if I should even bother since I've been disappointed so many times, but I look anyway, finding nothing but cleaning supplies.

As with the other room, I also look underneath and behind the cabinet itself. This time, my fingers come into contact with something and my heart starts beating fast. Before I can stop myself, I yank the cabinet away from the wall and something that was tucked into the small space behind it falls to the floor.

A brown, snakeskin handbag with a long handle.

I know instantly that something is not right. Why would anyone hide a handbag behind a bathroom cabinet?

I drop to my knees and pick up the bag, wiping off the dust with my hands. I get to my feet again and sit on the edge of the claw-footed tub.

There is something inside the bag.

With trembling fingers I unzip it and push my hand inside. I find a strawberry-scented lip gloss and a black phone with a shattered screen. It's switched off. I put them aside and take out the wallet, flipping it open.

A photo is staring back at me from an ID card. It's her. Her hair is shorter, just above her shoulders, but her eyes are wide and bright just as they are in the other photos.

Bingo.

"Where are you?" James asks from inside one of the bedrooms connected to the bathroom.

I can barely speak as I continue to stare at Eva. "In... in here." My fingers clutch the wallet, frozen.

I only move when one of the doors opens and James enters the bathroom. His eyes land on the bag that I dropped to the floor.

His mouth falls open. "It's..." He drops to his knees and pulls the bag to him, holding it to his chest as he heaves, crying like a wounded animal.

I finally understand why he did what he did, why he got close to me and used me to get information. He loved her; he loved this woman so much he was willing to do anything to avenge her death. It's pretty clear now that she did not just disappear.

"I'm sorry," I croak.

I know how it feels to lose someone you love. I thought I had lost Wyatt and, as a result, I felt as though I had lost myself for many years. Lucky for me, I found him, but from the looks of it, James might never get Eva back. Why would her handbag be here with the ID card still inside it if she's still alive?

He buries his face into the handbag and continues to cry, his shoulders shaking, his voice loud and broken. "They killed her," he keeps repeating. "They killed her."

Unsure of what else to do, I go to him, to comfort him the way he has tried to comfort me before. I put my arms around him and rock him until the crying subsides, but it's soon followed by another wave that lasts several minutes. When he finally looks up at me, his eyes are red and swollen and his face is rumpled. He then looks down again and sees the wallet I threw to the floor when I came to him. As though in slow motion, he picks it up and brings it to his face, pulling out the identity card.

"They're monsters," he whispers. This time his voice is not broken, but firm, strong, and loaded with rage.

"Yes," I say, moving back to the bathtub. "They deserve to

be punished for what they did. They cannot get away with this."

James stares at the ID card for a long time, unable to look away from his fiancée's face. "We were so happy together. We talked about the future. I was ecstatic when she told me she was pregnant."

I say nothing. I don't think he wants to hear from me or anyone else. I feel as though he's just talking to himself.

"We need to find more," I say eventually. "I have a feeling there's more stuff hidden in this house that we haven't found yet."

Of course, we could take the handbag straight to the police. But if the police are friends of the Mayers, that may not be enough. They might not even believe we found the bag at the villa. James was Eva's fiancé. Who's to say she hadn't left it at his place? Or worse, what if they think he has something to do with what happened to her?

We can't give up. We have to use every single minute we have to make sure we sweep the entire place. We search the basement, even though we did so last time. Not surprisingly, we don't find anything new.

"What if this is it?" I wring my hands. "What if there's nothing more to find?"

"There must be." Still holding on to Eva's handbag, James exits the house and charges into the garden, his eyes sweeping the grounds.

I know exactly what he's looking for. This is a very remote part of town. What if they killed her and buried her right here on the property? No one would have seen anything.

We walk around the garden and look inside the shed, but nothing stands out. Then James starts tearing at a flower bed. My heart races as I watch him stop and return to the shed. He comes out a few minutes later carrying a shovel. At the same flower bed, he starts digging, dumping broken flowers, grass, and dirt everywhere. It triggers the panic button inside me. I worry about how we're going to explain why we dug up part of the garden.

James soon tosses the shovel aside and continues with his hands, clawing into the earth. I pick up the shovel and start digging in another flowerbed, one filled with daisies. I know what we're doing is crazy and could get us into a whole lot of trouble, but right now my desire to find out if Eva is buried beneath the soil is suddenly burning inside of me like an uncontainable fire. If we find what we're looking for, when Robin and Paul return they won't get a chance to be pissed about their dug-up garden. Instead, they will be more concerned about going to prison.

But we find nothing. Whatever else they are hiding, it's not where we're looking.

Letting go of the shovel, I straighten up and massage the back of my neck to release tension. As I do so, my gaze sweeps the rest of the grounds. Where did they hide her body? If they killed her, they have to have disposed of her somewhere. But the grounds are massive. My eyes drift to the trees lining the property, and the mountains. If this is where Eva is buried, James and I will not be able to find her body on our own. But where does that leave us? Where do we go from here? Can we really prove the Mayers are guilty of murder with only a handbag and no corpse?

TWENTY-NINE

ROBIN

I so desperately wanted to believe it was over. I thought he had changed and left behind his old ways. That's what he made me believe. But I'm not blind. I can see how he's watching the neonatal nurse, especially when she bends down to check on my friend Jane's baby. The nurse's uniform is scandalously short, and it seems like she's purposely trying to get his attention.

But it's not really the nurse's fault. It's Paul's. He promised. After what happened last time, he promised me that we could start over, that it would never happen again.

Yet it feels as if it's happening again—as if no time has passed. I feel the same familiar anger boiling up inside me, the same toxic burn in the pit of my stomach, swirling like liquid lava and making its way up my throat. Betrayal and pain consume me just as they did seven years ago.

Everywhere we go I always feel his eyes roaming, lusting after other women, so I try to avoid that kind of humiliation.

If I had my way, I would not have come to Salzburg, but Jane, an American married to an Austrian, was my closest friend during our time living here and remained so after we returned to the States.

Coming to Salzburg today was unplanned. Jane's delivery date was a week away, but she called me early this morning to let me know the baby came last night via emergency C-section. I jumped at the chance to see her and the little one before we fly back to New York in a few days.

Perhaps I should have come without Paul, who has not so much as glanced in my direction since our arrival. We had been arguing before we left Ruddel and that's why we decided to drive separately. Then at the hotel, when Paul couldn't keep his eyes off the woman behind the counter with her breasts showing from her tight tank top and blazer, things blew up.

After Paul leaves the hospital room, giving us privacy, I sit by Jane's bed and stroke her baby's cheek.

"Is something on your mind?" Jane asks while staring lovingly at her daughter instead of at me.

I don't want to dampen my friend's joy so I nod and say, "Let's talk about your precious little one here."

"No, let's talk about you. I can tell there's something on your mind. What is it?" She looks up with a serious expression. "Come on, talk to me."

For someone who gave birth last night and must be exhausted, she looks beautiful and refreshed, her China-blue eyes bright and her skin more radiant than ever. Even in a hospital bed, she has put on makeup and her auburn hair is pulled into a perfect bun.

My vision blurs as a tear rolls down my cheek. I close my eyes, and the weight of my worries force air from my lungs. "It's just that... Paul... I think he might be cheating again."

Jane's eyebrows inch higher as she gapes at me. "Cheating... again? You can't be serious." She reaches for my hand and squeezes.

I swallow hard and blink, trying to keep more tears from spilling down my face. "I just have this feeling that something isn't right and I'm scared it's happening again."

"Are you sure?" She tightens her grip on my hand and her face softens with concern. "What makes you think that? I thought things had changed since—"

"So did I." I drop my gaze to the floor and wave a dismissive hand, attempting to brush off the topic. "You know what? Let's not dwell on this. It's my problem and you should focus on recovering, taking care of yourself and the baby. I'll be fine."

"But you don't look fine, honey." Jane studies my face, her brow furrowed.

"I will be." I attempt a giggle, but it comes out more like a squeak. "Maybe I'm just imagining things." I massage my right temple with my free hand. "I have a splitting headache right now."

"You know what, you've been here for a while. You should get back to the hotel. Get some rest or talk to Paul about this."

"Maybe I should," I say, but I'm not convinced because a talk like this always ends up in a fight, and we have been having too many of those lately. I kiss my friend and her baby on their foreheads. Having lost my baby, I have to admit it's hard to see Jane with a newborn, but I do my best to focus on her joy and be happy for her. "I'll come back to see you again early in the morning."

Jane smiles and waves. "I'll see you tomorrow."

I'm not surprised to find Paul at the nurse's station, throwing his head back as he laughs out loud. I can't remember the last time I heard him laugh like that with me.

When he turns around and sees me, the smile melts from his face and the mask reserved for me slips back into place. "We're leaving already?" he asks with a smirk that doesn't fool me. We have been at the hospital for two hours and he's been asking to leave every few minutes. But now he has obviously found something to entertain him.

Instead of answering, I walk past him toward the revolving doors. Before walking through, a giggle erupts from behind me, but I don't turn around.

In the car, I don't say anything as Paul drives. I shouldn't have left the other car at the hotel. Being in the same space as him is unbearable.

He's the one to speak first, just as I expect him to. He's one of those people who are uncomfortable with silence.

"Are you okay?" he asks me.

"Why shouldn't I be?" I fold my arms across my chest.

"I know it must have been hard being around Jane and the baby. Is that what's bothering you?"

I take a deep breath and let it out slowly. "I'm okay on that front," I whisper, wrapping my arms tighter around myself. "I'm more concerned about other things."

"What do you mean? What things, Robin? What's going on here?"

"You, Paul. I'm concerned that you're cheating again." The anger in my voice is unmistakable.

The few seconds that pass with him gripping the wheel as if his whole life depends on it feel like a lifetime. Those few seconds say a lot more than words.

"I can't believe you're bringing that up again," he says.

"I wish I didn't have to," I bark. "But when I saw you flirting with the nurses and ogling them—"

"What are you talking about? I told you that it's over. I'm not that kind of man anymore."

"I'm finding that very hard to believe," I say, then stare out the window at the city of Salzburg.

"So what if I sometimes look at other women? I'm not blind."

"Damn you!" I punch him in the arm, not caring that he's driving. "Damn you for making a fool of me."

The fight continues until we reach the hotel.

I don't even bother to look for Wyatt when we return. We instructed him to stay in his room. He probably spent the entire time watching TV or playing one of his violent games. I just didn't want him to stay in Ruddel with Christa, who could have snuck him into the village without our permission. Who knows who might talk to him?

Inside our suite, I sit down on the bed and start to cry. "I can't believe you're doing this to me again," I weep, my shoulders shaking. "And don't you dare lie to me. For all I know you're having an affair with Christa as well."

Paul drops onto the bed next to me. "I'm not." He grabs me by the shoulders and turns me to face him. "What happened with Eva was a mistake. How many times do I need to tell you that?"

"A mistake that happened several times and ended in pregnancy."

Instead of responding, Paul stands and goes to the bathroom to hide his shame.

But I'm not about to let him off the hook. I jump up from the bed and go after him. "What were you thinking, sleeping with her in... in our bed?"

He turns to me with blazing eyes. "What are you thinking bringing this up again after seven years?"

"This is not only about her, Paul. This is about you hardly spending any time with me because you're too busy with work, or so you say. You broke my trust and I don't think you can ever get it back."

"So what do you want? What do you want from me right now?"

"I want to return to Ruddel tomorrow morning."

"But you wanted to stay for two days."

"I want to go back, Paul... in the morning." I want to lock myself in my room, to bury myself under the covers, and hide from the world. I also want him to be away from all those nurses. There's no way I'm going back to the hospital with him. I hate it when he works all the time, but maybe it's better for him to be inside his office all day. At least he cannot smell or touch the women on the screen.

THIRTY

CHRISTA

At seven in the morning, the sounds of cars pulling into the driveway make their way through the walls. Racing to the window, I snatch open the blinds and see them. I step back and bend forward with my hands on my knees, releasing a sigh of relief. They're back already.

James and I didn't make any headway in terms of finding more evidence, and we could have done with more time to do so, but my son is back and that's all that matters to me right now.

I want to run out of the room and go and hug Wyatt, but that would be strange, so I stay standing in the middle of my room, pretending not to have noticed their arrival. I listen to their voices coming from below, seeping through the cracks around my bedroom door. I hear Paul's deep voice and Robin's nasal one, but I don't hear anything from Wyatt—which is not surprising since he hardly says a word in their presence.

I'm not sure what to do. Should I go out and welcome them? I'm afraid if Robin sees my face, she'll know something is up. My thoughts are still lingering on the image of Eva's handbag and what it all means. Now that I'm certain they're guilty of something, I'm not sure how to hide my true feelings.

Just as I'm trying to psyche myself up to face them, there's a knock on my door. The second I open it my heart is flooded with emotion when I see Wyatt standing before me, beaming.

Not even caring if Paul or Robin are watching, I envelop him with my arms. Even at fifteen, he clings to me like a little boy, and I'm overcome with love for him. There are no words needed. He feels the same way I do. He feels the love I feel for him. He must know deep down that we're connected.

"I missed having you around, big boy," I say when we finally let go of each other.

"Same here." At first, he looks a little embarrassed, perhaps for showing his emotions, but then a large grin takes over his face.

"So where did you all go?" I ask.

"We went to Salzburg to visit my mom's friend who just had a baby." He darts a glance toward the stairs before continuing in a hushed voice. "I really didn't want to go."

"Ah," I reply and give him another hug before quickly releasing him when I see Robin climbing the stairs. She doesn't even acknowledge me as she strides past us and into her bedroom with her carryall bag.

"Is she all right?" I mouth at Wyatt. It's obvious Robin is upset. Though I don't like her very much, it must have been hard to see her friend's baby after she lost hers. My heart goes out to her, but not enough to want to comfort her.

Wyatt shrugs, makes a face, then scurries off to his room.

Thirty minutes after their arrival, Paul gets back into his car and leaves without having said a word to me. And Robin still hasn't left her room. Unsure of what else to do, I eventually knock on her door.

"I need to be alone," she says from the other side.

I'm relieved to hear it. I spend the next hour doing cross-word puzzles with Wyatt and doing my chores. I also check that all the items James and I moved during our search are back in place.

As I'm about to go back to the kitchen, it dawns on me that James was meant to come over this evening to look around some more. I rush to my bedroom to call him and cancel the search.

"They're back," I whisper. "Please don't come."

"Crap," he grunts. "What do we do now?"

"Don't worry. I'll keep looking. I'll also talk to Wyatt to see if he might know something."

"That's a good idea. But you need to be careful. You don't want him to go telling them you've been asking questions about Eva."

"True, but I think we can trust him."

Maybe I could tell him some of what is going on without giving away the entire story. It's obvious to me that in the short time that we have known each other and spent time together, Wyatt has proved to be more loyal to me than his adoptive parents. The plan is to try to get as much information from him as I can. The hug he gave me earlier gives me the courage to trust him.

"Good," James says. "I'll wait to hear from you."

"Okay." I clear my throat. "I know you said it wasn't a good idea, but maybe you should just take the bag to the police."

"No. We talked about this. It would be too risky. I'd have to tell them where I found the bag, and they might reach out to the Mayers. We have to wait for more evidence to make sure there's no chance of them getting away with it."

I take in a long breath. "Right. I'll do my best to find something more." A short pause. "But, James, if it doesn't work out, I'll have to come up with another plan."

"I hope you're not thinking what I think you are, Christa."

"Yes, I am." I rub my nose. "I will have to take my son and run."

"If you do that," he cautions me, "you'll be the one going to prison. Are you aware of that?"

I feel a hard knot form in my throat when I realize he's right. Not only would I be locked up, but they might give Wyatt back to Robin and Paul, who could easily get a restraining order against me to keep me away from my son.

"Christa, don't do anything reckless," James pleads. "It won't end well."

"I'll try," I reply hesitantly, not trusting my emotions. Too many thoughts are clouding my judgment; I can't decide what is best right now. I know the one thing I need to do is tell Wyatt the truth about who I really am, but I decide not to tell this to James for fear he may try to talk me out of it. My mind is made up.

"By the way," he asks, "did you find out anything more from her journals?"

"Not much. All she's been writing about so far is her pregnancy, but I'll read more tonight and see if I come across something useful."

We hang up and since Robin is still in her room, I figure this is the perfect time to talk to Wyatt. I ask him to come with me to the office and shut the door behind us.

"What are we doing here?" He throws himself onto the couch with a groan. "Don't tell me we're studying German. I'm not in the mood. A game of Monopoly, now that's something I'd be up for."

"No, we're not learning German." I take a seat next to him. "I thought it would be nice if we had a chat." My eyes flit to the door, and I'm suddenly filled with unease. Maybe the office is not the safest place for me to talk about this after all. The last thing I need is Robin standing behind the door, eavesdropping. Since I'm allowed to take Wyatt for short walks around the property, it might be best for us to just get out of the house entirely.

"Okay," Wyatt says, propping his feet up on the coffee table. "What should we talk about?"

"How about we go for a walk while we talk?" I suggest.

"To the village? Can we pass by Simon's house?" His face brightens at the idea.

"No, I'm sorry, but your mom... Robin will want us to stay home. How about we go to the river instead? It's still better than being stuck inside."

"Fine," he begrudgingly agrees and gets to his feet.

Before we leave, just to be sure we're not breaking any rules, I decide to ask Robin's permission to take Wyatt out. I don't want to upset her and risk us having to fly back to the US even earlier. She's in the middle of the large bed when I enter, crumpled tissues all around her. Her eyes are puffy and bloodshot, her skin so pale it's almost colorless. She looks as if she has been crying for hours. She agrees to let us go, too distracted, I imagine, by her thoughts to argue with me and I exit quickly.

I wait until we're sitting on a bench by the river before I say anything to Wyatt.

"There's something I need to tell you," I say over the background noise of running water. I make sure to keep my voice low, even though no one is around.

"Sounds serious," he quips, flicking a pebble into the river.

I grasp his hand and he gazes at me with wide eyes.

"You're not leaving, are you?"

"Never," I vow. "I'll never leave you."

"So, what is it? Why do you look so... strange?"

"Wyatt, I've been wanting to tell you this for a really long time, but..." I close my eyes for a second, praying for courage. "I'm your mother, Wyatt. Your biological mother."

Time seems to stop while he stares at me with a stunned expression, then he pulls his hand away and stands.

"You're lying," he says finally, his face a mask of rage.

Immediately I regret telling him. What if he turns on me

and runs to Robin or Paul, telling them my secret? It would be disastrous. But it's too late to take back what I said, so I have to urge him to understand that he must keep it a secret.

I get to my feet so our eyes are level. "I am," I say. "I'm really your birth mother. I wanted you to know. But you can't let anyone else find out."

He takes a step away from me. "You're not my mother. My birth mother didn't want me, otherwise she wouldn't have left me in some orphanage when I was a baby, like a piece of garbage."

The lump in my throat nearly suffocates me. Did Robin tell him this? "No, Wyatt, I'm telling you the truth," I say quickly, wanting to touch him but not daring to. "I am really your mother, and I didn't give you away by choice. It's just that I couldn't... It's complicated. I promise I will explain everything to you. But please..." My voice softens and I clasp my hands together in front of me, pleading with him. "Please... don't tell your parents."

I've made a mistake. I've been naïve, assumed our relationship was strong enough for me to tell him anything. But what did I really expect? Of course he's upset that he was given away. Of course he's angry. I should have waited to tell him. I should have been more careful. Now I've probably ruined everything.

Desperate to make things right, I put my hand gently on his shoulder. But he flinches and moves away, too upset to be consoled.

"I understand you're feeling betrayed and angry," I say, my voice trembling with emotion. "And I am so sorry for that. But I'm asking you to keep this a secret—for my sake, for your—"

"You're not my mother," he says, more to himself than to me. Then he shoves his hands into his pockets and walks away from me. I watch as he kicks away a rock in frustration, and my heart aches with sadness and regret.

Worried that he might go straight to Robin and tell her

everything, I run after him, pleading for him to let me explain, but he doesn't stop, doesn't look back until he walks into the house.

I should have been more careful. This is my fault. What have I done?

THIRTY-ONE

CHRISTA

For the remainder of the day, both Wyatt and Robin stay in their rooms. Wyatt only reappears at 7 p.m. to look for something to eat before retreating to his bedroom. Robin refuses to eat anything and Paul has yet to return home. I'm starting to think that he and Robin had some kind of argument. It would explain her low mood. But I don't care about them or their problems. All I care about is what I did and how that might have driven a huge wedge between me and Wyatt.

As the sun sets, I give James a call.

"I messed up," I admit, tears flowing from my eyes.

"What did you do?" he asks in a panicked voice. "You didn't try to talk to them about the purse, did you?"

I shake my head. "No. I said something to Wyatt."

"That his adoptive parents are murderers? Why would you do that?"

I hide my face in my palm. "No, not that. I told him the truth—that I'm his mother."

An eternity of silence passes. I need to break it because it's becoming uncomfortable.

"James, are you there?"

He clears his throat. "I'm here. How did he react to the news?"

"He was angry. He *is* angry. He thinks his mother didn't care about him enough to keep him. I guess it's a fairly normal reaction after all these years of not knowing why he was put up for adoption. He's probably spent years struggling with abandonment issues." I let out a sigh and shut my eyes. "I don't know what to do to make his pain go away,"

What he doesn't know is that I would have done anything at all to keep him, but the decision was out of my hands. The day I lost him I felt as if my world had been torn apart, and I've never been able to put the pieces back together since.

"You must talk to him. If he tells Robin or Paul about what you said to him, you could both be in real danger. You don't think he's spoken to them already, do you?"

"I don't think so," I answer uncertainly. To my knowledge, as soon as Wyatt entered the house earlier, he headed straight to his room and hasn't spoken to Robin the whole day.

Is it possible he could have said something without me knowing? No, that's highly unlikely. I was lingering around his door most of the day, wishing I could talk to him and clarify things, but lacking the guts to do so.

"You need to keep it that way," James says. "They can never find out. If they do, they will probably take him to the States immediately. And you need to continue searching for evidence. We need to get them arrested fast."

"Okay. I'm going to read through the rest of the journal photos and see what I can uncover."

I end the call and flip open my computer. I look through more diary entries; they're mostly centered around Robin's pregnancy. She noted every detail, from the kinds of food she ate and how they made her feel to actual letters to her unborn baby. Each time I read her entries my stomach churns with acid. Here was a woman, pouring all her love onto those pages for an unborn child, yet at the same time she was not willing to accept mine—a boy who hadn't been forced into her life.

Just then, a toilet flushes from down the hallway. I get up, knowing Wyatt doesn't have a restroom in his room, so it has to be him. It's probably a bad idea to go out there and try to talk to him again while Robin is home. And I'm nervous about her overhearing our conversation and discovering the truth. But I can't stop myself.

As soon as he exits the bathroom, a flood of light spills into the dark hallway. He turns to face me and I hold my breath in anticipation. He looks upset and angry, and I can tell he's been crying. I'm scared he might say something out loud for Robin to hear. I place a finger to my lips, my eyes pleading with him.

Rather than saying anything, he turns and shuffles back to his room.

It's too early. He's still hurting. I want to give him the required time to heal, but that might not be an option. I'm worried there isn't enough time left.

What if I do everything in my power to get him away from her, and he still rejects me, convinced I treated him like unwanted trash? The thought is like a sharp blade stuck in my stomach. I take several steps back into my room, shutting the door behind me, then let my body fall to the floor. I bury my face in my palms. My head is hurting as though someone is slamming hammers into my temples over and over again, inflicting more and more pain until I cannot bear it any longer.

I'm startled when someone taps against the door lightly, and I jump up, my hands sweating. It's him. He's ready to talk.

I open the door quickly but it's not him I see.

Robin's eyes are still bloodshot as she stands there in pink silk pajamas and velvet slippers. "I'm hungry," she murmurs before walking off.

Not sure whether to laugh or cry, I follow her downstairs to the kitchen, the trail of her lily perfume lingering in her wake.

She should be able to get herself something to eat. I had offered her dinner earlier, but she'd refused, so I'd said I'd store it in the refrigerator for her to reheat later. But clearly, she's not capable of doing that. Or maybe she just wants to exercise her power over me.

Not saying one word, I head straight to the fridge and remove the rice and steak that I prepared. Steeling my nerves, I place the food in the microwave, counting the seconds until it's warm while listening to her pull out a stool at the island. Although I never minded it before, this time my senses are on high alert and the noise makes my skin crawl. It reminds me of chalk being scraped against a blackboard. Clenching my fists, I refuse to face her, but I can almost feel her eyes searing the back of my head.

When the timer on the microwave beeps, I place the warm food in front of her. She pushes it away without even looking at it.

"I want something freshly cooked," she demands, her voice a low, angry growl. "I don't want leftovers."

My patience with her is growing thin and it's all I can do not to scream and shout. But I won't give her the satisfaction. Resisting the urge, I calmly speak to her as if she's a child. "This is pretty fresh, Robin." I try to keep the exasperation out of my voice. "I cooked it not long ago."

"I don't feel like rice today." This time, a soft smile plays on her lips.

What's she doing? What does she know? What does she suspect?

I take a deep breath, pushing down my mounting anger. "What do you feel like eating?" I have no choice but to play her game. If she's trying to break me, she'll have to try a lot harder.

She requests lasagna and a green salad. I agree, even though it will take some time, and scurry to the pantry, remaining in there for a few minutes to collect myself before I lose my temper. The hum of the fridge seems to amplify while I'm in the pantry, or maybe it's just my heightened senses.

"What's taking you so long in there?" she calls.

Even with the wall between us, I can feel her aura like a heatwave around my body. I grab a box of lasagna sheets, then arch my neck backward to stretch it. The crack is so satisfying that I close my eyes to savor the feeling. Still looking toward the ceiling, when I open my eyes, I notice something strange in one corner of the pantry: a small, red, blinking light that I've never seen before.

Robin calls for me again and I forget about the light and step out of the pantry.

It dawns on me that although James and I searched much of the house, we skipped over the pantry. I'm in here a lot and feel I would have noticed anything strange. But I make a mental note to come back later when Robin isn't watching me so closely.

As I go about preparing her dinner, she continues to watch me, pretending to read a cookbook. The pages crackle and stir in the silence.

I start with the lasagna sauce, frying up garlic and onions before adding cream, tomatoes, chili powder, and other ingredients. When the sauce is simmering, the aroma fills the kitchen and soothes me in a way, allowing me to focus on what I have to do and nothing else. When the sauce is finished, I move on to the salad, then I finish assembling the lasagna and put it in the oven.

As I close the oven door, Robin snaps the cookbook shut and looks up at me with her arms folded on the table. "Christa, what have you done to the flowers in our garden?" she asks.

My heart stops. Forcing myself to look at her with the little confidence I can muster, I tell her what James and I agreed on.

"When you were away, I didn't know what to do with

myself. I was bored, so I decided to... I thought I could just plant some new flowers for you. I thought it might cheer you up."

It was James's idea. We had tried to replant the flowers we had destroyed, but everything was broken and wilted. So he'd driven into the village and come back with new flowers.

"I don't need cheering up," she scolds. "Please don't do anything else in this house without my permission." Then she leaves the kitchen without waiting for me to respond.

She returns when her food is ready and I serve it to her. To my horror and disgust, she only takes three bites before deciding she's had enough and leaves the kitchen again. She doesn't even give me a thank you. It dawns on me that she wasn't even hungry, just looking for an opportunity to torment me.

When a door closes in the distance, I slump onto a stool, desperate not to break down. My forehead presses against the cold marble countertop. My heart is pounding in my ears and my throat is aching with words I wish I had said to her.

And then I hear a voice.

"I'll eat the rest," Wyatt says.

Shaking off the oncoming tears, I look up, surprised to see him there, that he's talking to me. We don't exchange any words as he polishes off the lasagna. I wait for him to say something, anything. But then I realize that his just being here is a big step for both of us—perhaps that's enough for now.

Once he's done eating, instead of giving me the plate to wash, he rinses it off himself and puts it in the dishwasher. Does that mean he no longer sees me as the help? Has he accepted that I am his mother? Maybe I shouldn't read too much into it.

"Thanks," he says, before leaving. "Goodnight."

"Goodnight, Wyatt," I say after him, my heart feeling just a little lighter.

When he disappears through the door, I decide that the moment we just shared was definitely enough.

When I'm done clearing up the kitchen it's ten o'clock. As

soon as I get back to my room, I open my laptop again to look for a diary entry that will give me something to hold on to. I come across one of the entries from the summer of 2015, the year Eva disappeared. After the way Robin treated me, I'm even more desperate to get myself and my son away from her. I have a feeling the behavior she showed me tonight won't be the last of her attempts to make my life a living hell.

THIRTY-TWO

ROBIN

August, 2015

They think I'm naïve and blind, but I see everything. I've been watching them every day, and I'm well aware of what's happening behind my back.

It's only been three weeks since she started working here and I can tell that things have changed. For one, Paul no longer spends much time in his office. Instead, he pretends to make himself useful around the house, doing tasks he never used to do before, like working in the garden and fixing things. Who is he trying to fool? He's no handyman. Instead of fixing things, he's actually making it worse, breaking them, just like he's breaking me.

I asked him today if there's something going on between him and Eva. His reaction? Anger, as usual. It's always like that when I confront him. He accused me of being paranoid, of only seeing what I want to see. He was so defensive, I immediately knew I was right, that my intuition is not lying to me. I've seen the way he behaves when we go out, how he smiles differently at other women. He thinks I'm in the dark, but I'm well aware of everything that's going on underneath our roof.

In hindsight, I should have refused to hire Eva. I had combed through a few applications and I had already interviewed other candidates before her and even shortlisted a few. I had instantly ruled her out as soon as I met her, but the one mistake I made was not tearing up her application and CV. Paul had noticed them in the bin and asked why I wasn't giving her a chance when she was far more experienced than the other applicants. How could I have explained to him that I felt she was too attractive for the job without coming off as an insecure spouse? I'd wanted to prove to him that I was secure in my marriage, and sure my husband would never cross the line. He'd never actually cheated before, though he was always quick to notice beauty when it presented itself.

The only reason I finally agreed to hire Eva was due to a rumor that she was in a relationship. It's easy to find information around this town if one asks the right people the right questions. I should have known that a committed relationship means nothing to a weak-willed person when they are tempted. I foolishly thought that she was only a flirt and was loyal to her boyfriend. But no, she's greedy; she wants my man.

I made the mistake of letting the temptation into my own home. She would wear inappropriate clothes and laugh loudly at his jokes, even if they weren't funny, and he would douse himself in cologne, even when he had nowhere to go. All the signs of betrayal were there, every single one of them.

They had been having an affair long before I even knew it had begun, not that I can pinpoint the exact moment it started. But today I caught them red-handed. I saw my husband in bed with her, in our bedroom. He assumed I was out getting my hair done in the village, and Wyatt hardly ever leaves his room, which meant they were free to sneak around. Perhaps he was too intoxicated by the illicit pleasure to think about being caught. Or maybe he secretly wanted me to catch them. Maybe that was his plan all along. What if he wants to leave me for her? There's no way I'll let him leave me.

Before him, I was always attracted to men who were not as attracted to me, men who used me as a placeholder until they found the next best thing. I really thought Paul was different. I was so in love when he asked me to be his wife that I blindly signed a prenup that could very well leave me penniless if we get divorced. But the lifestyle I've become accustomed to is not something I'm willing to give up.

I must put a stop to this before it's too late. Eva wants something that's mine and I'm not letting her take more than she has already taken from me.

I won't tolerate their behavior. They could have done this anywhere else, but they chose to do it in our home. This just goes to show how little respect they have for me.

It's over between them. It has already gone on long enough.

People say that revenge is a dish best enjoyed cold, but I prefer to serve mine piping hot.

THIRTY-THREE

CHRISTA

As I press the power button and the laptop's screen goes dark, my stomach contracts with nausea. My heart is racing, my mouth is dry, and I can feel heat radiating from my face as I push myself up into a sitting position. The dizzying thoughts whirling around in my mind are like a hurricane.

This is what we've been searching for. I feel it in my bones. The police won't be able to deny this evidence, not with the handbag to back it up. Surely what I read provides enough proof to put Robin behind bars.

I sit on the edge of the bed and massage my temples. A negative thought pops into my head that discourages me, claiming that this isn't enough. The journal entry doesn't explicitly say she murdered Eva. Stopping her might not mean erasing her from the world, even if that's what my logic tells me. The police might think otherwise, especially if they're friendly with the Mayers.

I'm not certain who was responsible for this heinous act, but I'm confident either Robin or Paul is the murderer, and I'm certain there's something in this house that will confirm my suspicions. Where did they hide the corpse if not here?

My stomach churns at the thought of Eva accepting James's proposal while she was unfaithful to him with Paul. How depraved can someone be? Then I recall that Eva was pregnant when she died. What if the baby was Paul's and not James's? Wouldn't that be a motive for murder? For either Paul or Robin? What if Eva wanted to expose the details of her affair with Paul, and what if one of them was prepared to do whatever it took to stop her? What if Eva wanted to tell Robin—not knowing she already knew—and Paul flipped and strangled her like Robin described in her journal, this time crossing the line of no return?

It's possible Paul acted to keep his indiscretions a secret, or maybe Robin's revenge at the prospect of her husband leaving her was the driver. Who could blame a woman for going insane with rage after witnessing her husband in bed with another? Not everyone is driven to murder, of course, but someone clearly was on this occasion.

The big question remains: Where is the body? We searched everywhere. Or did we?

A memory comes to me of standing in the pantry earlier, a place I walk in and out of almost every day. The red flashing light. What was that? I wonder if it could be a hidden camera. If so, why just the pantry and not any other room in the house? Unless there's something in there that someone wants to keep hidden.

There was also that strange humming noise, a different kind of sound, something I never really paid attention to until tonight. Initially, I had assumed it to be the sound of the fridge, but it sounded unnaturally loud this time.

I can't stop myself, even though I know the risks. I must figure out what's happening before it's too late, especially now that Wyatt knows I'm his mom. I have to get him away from these people and back with me.

I turn the handle slowly and inch my bedroom door open,

careful not to make a sound as I tiptoe toward the staircase, avoiding parts of the steps that I know have a tendency to creak. My palm is slick against the railing as I continue my journey in the dark.

With each step I consider how James will respond to the affair. He will be devastated when he finds out. He's seeking justice for the woman he loved, unaware that she had been deceitful, that all along she was keeping a secret from him. She accepted his proposal knowing full well what she was doing behind his back. And she was possibly pregnant with another man's baby. How in the world can I break that news to him?

I shake my head and push the thought away so I can focus. I can't afford to make a mistake; this might be my only opportunity. I cannot think of any other place in the house where anything else will be hidden.

I exhale heavily once my feet hit the bottom of the stairs, glancing up to check if anyone's watching. The moonlight spilling through the windows is just enough to give some light to the hallway, and I don't spot anyone. I'm in the clear.

I tiptoe into the kitchen and quickly close the door behind me. I then pause to consider my safety. I do not want to be stuck inside the pantry with no way to defend myself.

I reach into the drawer of knives but take my hand away before grabbing one. The thought of stabbing someone with a blade makes me physically ill, so instead I reach for a broom that's leaning against the wall.

I enter the pantry and close the door behind me to muffle any noise that might escape.

Looking up, I see the tiny red light, blinking from a corner of the room. My heart races as I approach it, wondering if someone can see me right now. If it is a camera, I hope that Robin and Paul are sleeping, and will only be able to see the footage when it is too late. If I find something in here tonight, the police will show up at their doorstep in a matter of minutes.

Still paranoid, I lean the broom against the wall and go back into the kitchen. From the junk drawer, I remove a roll of duct tape and cut off a piece. Grabbing a chair, I bring it back to the pantry and climb up to reach the camera. With shaking hands, I press the duct tape over the red light, hoping it will be enough to hide me from prying eyes.

I take a moment to calm down, steadying my breathing before getting back down and scanning the room.

It's so spacious it could be mistaken for someone's bedroom. Floor-to-ceiling shelves are filled to bursting with cans, jars, and packages of food as if the Mayers are preparing for a coming disaster. I stand in the center and close my eyes, listening for any noise. Sure enough, the hum is still there. I open the door again and immediately hear the hum of the kitchen fridge, but when I close it again, that sound is gone, separated from the other that seems to be trapped inside the pantry. There are no electronic appliances in the room that could explain the sound, and definitely no other fridge around.

As I try to figure out where the sound is coming from, another unsettling thought enters my mind.

What if I'm wrong? What if it wasn't Paul or Robin who committed the crime? What if it was James? Could he have been the one out for revenge? What if he knew what Eva did and committed a crime of passion? What if he is the one I should be scared of, the man I have been spending so much time with, the man I have come to trust? Could he be a murderer?

A chill runs down my back and I hold onto one of the cabinets for support. It just doesn't seem right. It doesn't add up. If James is the actual murderer, why would he be so intent on finding evidence that the Mayers are responsible for his fiancée's death when, after seven years, the case has pretty much gone cold?

My thoughts are a jumbled mess, chaotic questions clashing

against the interior walls of my skull, and making my head throb. I can't make sense of anything right now. But I need to start somewhere, and this room is as good a place as any. Then I can work out where to go from here.

I strain my ears for any sound that reaches me. The hum seems to be growing in intensity, or maybe I'm just paying more attention to it now. I decide to search the pantry from top to bottom, hoping all the while that I don't get caught. My plan is that if Robin shows up, I'll pretend I couldn't sleep, so I thought of reorganizing the pantry. I pray she'll believe me.

I begin with the tins, filled with beans, corn, and an array of vegetables and purees. I move aside the jars of pickles and place the boxes of cereal in a pile on the floor. I clear shelf after shelf to expose the walls behind them. I'm unsure what I'm searching for; all I know is that I need to find the source of the sound.

Then another noise catches my attention and I pause, straining my ears to listen. It seems to be coming from a distance, and is like something creaking. I stand still, listening closely and wishing I had a way to lock the door. But then there's silence again and I continue sorting until every last can and box lies at my feet, leaving the shelves completely bare.

I survey every shelf, spinning around to assess every corner of the room. The walls are a dazzling white, masking any secrets save for one, the wall opposite the door. It has a small, round, white circle in its center, almost like a decal. Someone could easily overlook it if they didn't take an extra good look.

I take a deep breath and cautiously touch the circle on the wall. It's slightly elevated and silky beneath my fingertip. The decal is just a cover with a button hidden underneath. With my heart racing, I press it and pause, counting each beat. One, two, three.

There's a soft click, followed by the wall shifting out of place to reveal another room. It's slightly smaller in size, a wine cellar from the looks of it. I stand in the doorway, mouth open, staring at the towering shelves of wine bottles.

A secret wine cellar.

Being in the wine business, it *does* make sense the Mayer family has a wine cellar, but it could also be the ideal place to hide something from prying eyes. A shudder runs through me as I step inside and my gaze is automatically drawn to a large, white upright freezer. My heart pounds as I make my way to it. I can now hear its hum loud and clear.

As my fingers encircle the handle, my head starts to spin even more and I feel as if I'm on the verge of fainting. But I cannot faint. I need to stay strong. This could be what I'm looking for. Eva's corpse could be inside the freezer.

I take a deep breath, close my eyes, and tug the handle. When I open my eyes I see multiple bags of ice, and at first I feel a sense of relief wash over me. But, as I lift them, I see something that turns my stomach and stops my breath—Eva's lifeless body. She's in the fetal position, her limbs contorted at unnatural angles.

Her icy pale skin and glassy eyes gaze back at me, and I bite back a scream. I quickly step back, trying not to vomit, but desperate to look again. I need to make sure what I'm seeing is real. When I do, my entire body shivers with fear and disgust, and I struggle to catch my breath. Heaving, I stagger back and lean against the wall as bile rises in my throat and tears prick at the corners of my eyes. This is what I thought I might find in this house, but I still hoped James was wrong. I hoped that Eva was safe somewhere, that she had just run away and didn't want to be found. But now it's clear that she never went anywhere. She was murdered.

Before I can stop it, vomit bubbles up my throat and spews onto the floor. I hastily wipe my mouth with the back of my hand and take several deep breaths to steady myself.

The stench of vomit and the sight of Eva's body in the freezer overwhelms me and I can't stop shaking and crying.

But I can't dwell on my reaction for long. I need to act. My mind races as I try to figure out what to do next.

An idea forms in my mind. I can take a photo on my phone so James can take it to the police. I turn around to go back to the pantry to retrieve my phone, and that's when I see Robin, standing in the doorway looking right at me, and holding the largest kitchen knife she owns.

"You," I murmur.

My fear, like nothing I'd ever known before, slices through me. But with it comes anger and a determination that floods my body with adrenaline, prompting me to reach for the broom I brought in with me.

"So you know," she hisses, trapping us both in the pantry by shutting the door behind her. Even though it's not actually locked, she stands in the way, barring my escape.

I'm trapped in a room with a monster that would do anything to keep its dark secrets hidden. If I don't act fast and fight for my life, she might murder me and stuff my body into the freezer, right next to Eva's remains.

THIRTY-FOUR

CHRISTA

I won't give in. I won't let this be how my story ends. Robin won't be allowed to do to me what she did to Eva. I refuse to be another face pasted on a bulletin board with the word "missing" in bold letters above my head. I will not become another statistic.

The look in Robin's eyes is lethal and their dark color appears to be blazing with fury.

"You killed her," I mumble, taking a step away from her, but staying in the entryway to the other room because I do not want to be even more distanced from the outside world. "You murdered Eva, the nanny that worked for you seven years ago."

"What makes you think I did it?"

The sudden chill in the air and the cold expression on her face make me take another step back. Still holding the knife next to her, her gaze darts past my shoulder to the freezer where her hidden secret has been dormant for seven years.

"I know the truth, Robin. I know all your secrets. I know that Paul was having an affair with Eva and that you wanted to get rid of her. Now get out of my way, I'm going to the police."

"You're wrong," she hisses, brandishing the blade. "You have no idea what you're talking about."

Without giving her the opportunity to launch another attack, I swing the broom handle directly at her hand that's gripping the knife. It clatters to the ground. Not stopping there, I swing again, this time connecting with her left leg, causing an immediate scream of pain that reverberates off the walls.

"You're making a huge mistake," she croaks as she slides to the floor and tries to crawl toward the knife that's slid beneath one of the shelves. "You don't understand."

"I understand perfectly," I say, my jaw tightly clenched. "You are a murderer and you will be locked up."

When I lift the broomstick to hit her again, Robin abandons her attempts to retrieve the knife and scrambles away before the broom slams into the floor so hard it fractures in two. The next instant, she's on her feet heading for the pantry door. She grabs the handle and tries to slam the door shut in an attempt to trap me inside, but I yank it open and the handle slips from her grip.

"You won't get away with this, Robin," I say.

Undeterred, she limps toward the knife drawer and grabs another weapon, her knuckles white as she points it at me with chilling desperation. Her voice quavers as she stares me down. "You have no idea what you're getting yourself into," she hisses through gritted teeth.

I dash across the kitchen. As I run, I feel a searing pain in my left shoulder blade, but I don't halt my stride until I reach the kitchen door. Then I come to an abrupt stop as it swings open and Paul stands there, pointing a gun directly at me.

"What's going on here?" His voice is low and loaded like the gun in his hand.

"Paul, thank goodness you're here," Robin cries out. "She's trying to kill me. I think she broke my leg. This woman is dangerous."

"No." I look Robin in the eye, standing tall despite trembling inside, and the pain in my shoulder radiating like wildfire. "You are the disturbed and dangerous one," I say firmly. "You killed Eva and held her corpse here, in this house, for seven years. The police need to know what happened. Her family needs to know she's been stuffed into a freezer by a deranged woman like some food item." I can't stop my tears at this point, and I'm talking so loudly that if Wyatt is anywhere near the stairs, he will have heard everything by now. He will know exactly what his adoptive parents have done.

Paul looks stunned, while Robin yells at me to stop telling lies, denying the crime I'm accusing her of.

In an instant, something shifts in the air. Paul takes a step back, the gun dangling at his side. His gaze is no longer directed toward me, but at his wife. The look on his face is one of shock and anguish. "What... What is she saying?" His voice is choked with emotion as he speaks to Robin.

She shakes her head in silence, tears spilling from her eyes. "That woman is a liar," she cries out, her voice muffled by her sobs. "Don't you see? She's trying to ruin us. You were right. Hiring her was a mistake."

Before I can stop her, she lunges for me with a wild look in her eyes, thrusting the knife out in front of her. I drop to the floor and roll out of the way, and to my relief the knife falls and skitters from her grasp. We grapple on the kitchen tiles, our limbs entwined as Paul watches in stunned silence, his face pale with shock at what he has just heard.

He doesn't know about this. This is all Robin.

Soon after, I see him sprint past us. I suspect he's going to the pantry to verify if I'm telling the truth. Furious, Robin grabs my hair and tries to slam my head into the floor, but I shove her away and she falls hard onto her back. She lets out a forceful breath upon impact, but she's quite strong and it doesn't take long for her to overpower me again. Letting out a guttural roar, she forces her hands around my throat, each of her fingers like an iron grip pressed against my skin.

I push back with all my might, but she has the advantage of strength and size. I feel my airway slowly constricting, leaving me desperate for air. Through the ringing in my ears, I detect a loud pop, followed by another. Robin's fingers loosen for a second and we both turn to stare at the door.

In a flash, I see a figure appear in the doorway. It's James, his face twisted by rage and his arm outstretched, pointing a gun directly at us.

"You murdered her," he cries, his voice hoarse and raw as he locks eyes with Robin. Tears stream down his face, and his shaking hands choke the gun.

Before Robin has a chance to deny the accusation, he pulls the trigger, the sound of gunfire echoing off the walls.

Robin's eyes widen in shock, then her body slides off me.

James steadies his grip and fires one more shot for good measure.

His hands quivering, the gun still in his grip, I momentarily worry that he's going to shoot me too.

"Don't," I plead, shaking my head as I crawl to a sitting position and take in the sight of Paul's body on the floor close to the pantry door. Then I remember the two popping sounds I heard while fighting with Robin. That was Paul being shot.

"James, don't." I bring my hands together, begging.

He blinks several times and then his arm falls to his side, letting the gun drop to the ground. He decided to take matters into his own hands and kill those who he believed had murdered his fiancée, instead of leaving it up to the authorities. I feel sorry for him, but right now all I can think of is that I'm standing in front of a killer. Fear pulsing in my veins, I scoot away from him.

My gaze shifts away from James to the hallway. Wyatt is

standing there, his eyes bulging out of their sockets. Did he see it? Did he see James kill his adoptive parents?

Acting on instinct, I rush toward my son. I'm no longer afraid of James. The only thought in my mind is that I need to protect Wyatt, to wrap my arms around him and make it all better.

"It's all right, sweetheart," I say as Wyatt begins to sob, his arms tight around me. "They were... They were horrible people."

He doesn't resist as I embrace him, nor do I feel any push-back when I rock him back and forth. He's just as tormented as I am by what has happened.

Over his shoulder I watch James slump to the ground, fishing his phone out of his pocket. His fingers wildly press the keys and he raises it to his ear and speaks hurriedly in German. I only understand a few words but enough to know he's informing the police about what has happened and that they should come.

After ending the call, he lifts his head and his glistening eyes connect with mine. "You're free to go," he utters in a soft whisper, then drops his gaze to the floor.

He got what he wanted in terms of revenge, and he doesn't seem concerned that he may now face jail time. Maybe he doesn't believe life is worth living without Eva. I think about telling him what I know about her, and what she did to him, but I can't bring myself to hurt him further than he already has been, and it's possible he already knows. Perhaps he heard me and Robin talking in the pantry. He must have been lurking around this huge house for a while for him to appear so suddenly.

I close my eyes and lay my chin on the top of Wyatt's shoulder as we wait for the officers to arrive. I'm not sure what will happen from here, where they will take him, but I want to spend a few last moments with him, feeling his warmth.

I didn't do anything wrong, I only acted in self-defense, but what if the police see it differently? What if they deem it a premeditated plan between me and James? The thing that troubles me most is that Paul didn't seem to know about Eva's murder. If that's true, then James might have killed an innocent man, and there's a chance I could be seen as his accomplice.

THIRTY-FIVE

CHRISTA

When I first stepped foot in Austria, I never imagined that my trip would end with Robin and Paul dead.

When the police officers arrive, they document the situation by taking pictures of the body, securing any evidence, and interviewing us. I'm asked to give a brief recount of the events, which I do with steady eyes and no emotion in my voice. I vividly recall every single moment of what happened, leaving nothing out as I have nothing to hide about what occurred tonight.

Then, a woman who is not a police officer arrives. She's dressed in a suit and her hair is tied back in a neat bun. She has what one would call a baby face, but her dark hair has gray streaks in it, hinting at the fact that she's older than she appears, perhaps in her late fifties. She introduces herself as Heidi Fischer from child protective services.

My heart drops into my stomach before she even says the words. "No," I say, shaking my head. "You're not taking him." I glance at Wyatt then back at the woman.

"I'm afraid he has to come with me." I'm not surprised that

she's fluent in English. The cops must have informed her over the phone that Wyatt and I don't speak German.

"No, you can't. He's my son, he belongs with me!" I plead with the officers and Heidi, tears streaming down my face.

I quickly explain my situation as fast as I can and, at first, she seems confused, but when one of the officers say something to her in German, she glances at me and shakes her head. "We understand your plea, but for the safety of the boy and everyone else involved, we must take him away until we can arrange a more suitable living situation," she replies. "I'm really sorry."

"Just do a DNA test," I choke out, my hands clasped together. "You'll see he's my son. He's safer with me than with strangers." From the corner of my eye, I spot Wyatt cowering in the corner, looking scared and confused. I can't let them take him away from me.

"I'm sorry," Heidi repeats, "but he needs to stay in our custody until this case is fully resolved." Perhaps seeing the despair in my eyes, she offers to give me more time to say goodbye to Wyatt.

Left with no other choice, I step forward, wrap my arms around him and squeeze him tight.

"It's all right, Wyatt," I whisper softly. "No matter what happens, I love you and I will never stop fighting for you." I pause to look at Heidi. "Can I help him pack, please?"

Heidi nods, her gaze softening. "Yes, you can, but don't be long."

Even though I wanted a moment alone with Wyatt, a police officer follows us upstairs and hovers in the doorway.

"I don't want to go. Please, don't let them take me away," Wyatt tearfully pleads. His eyes beg me to do something even though there's nothing I can do.

I can feel my heart breaking into tiny pieces, and my throat tightens as the reality of the situation sinks in.

In a few minutes I fill a suitcase with some of his clothes, the PlayStation, and some books. Then I look at my son and try to form a smile. "You're going to stay with a very nice family until this is all sorted out. I'm sure we'll be together again very soon. I will do everything I can to make sure you come back to me." I squeeze his shoulders then leave the room, returning with a passport photo of me. I press it into his hand. "So you don't forget me. I'll never forget you."

He looks at the photo, then wraps his fingers tightly around it. He doesn't let it go, not even when he steps out the front door a few minutes later followed by Heidi and one of the police officers. Even though he's fifteen, he looks like a scared little boy, and I feel my heart breaking for him, and for me.

As the door closes behind them, I'm filled with a deep sadness that I cannot even begin to put into words. I know he's safe now, but I can't help but feel like a part of me has been ripped away. I have no idea exactly where they're taking him, but I'm comforted to know he will no longer be staying with Robin and Paul. But who will he end up with? Will they be worse than his adoptive parents? I'm his mother, the only person who could truly love him and protect him.

I have no clue where they have taken James for questioning. It's possible he's already at the police station, already being held in a cell. If I fail to provide the right answers, I might find myself there too.

Fortunately, the female police officer sitting beside me is competent in English, enough to comprehend my answers and ask me their questions. Her name is Officer Wagner, and she has short blonde hair that's made even shorter by her black police hat. For a woman, she's muscular and towers over me by a good foot. However, I can faintly detect a kind-heartedness in her cobalt-blue eyes.

"Walk me through the events one more time," she instructs, getting ready to write it all down again.

THIRTY-SIX

CHRISTA

Officer Wagner is sitting facing me in the living room, writing down my answers and glancing up every now and then, watching my face for any signs of lies.

I bite my lip and take a deep breath, forcing my face to stay calm to avoid any negative judgment. I've already gone over the details, but it's typical for the police to look for any discrepancies.

I'm about to answer her when two men emerge from the kitchen, bringing my attention away from her question. Before Wyatt was taken away, Eva's body was removed from the house by the same men—who are dressed in white uniforms, medical masks, and gloves—ending the years of searching for her.

I glance over at Officer Wagner and explain everything with heartbreaking intensity, every emotion and detail I can recall.

"I just wanted to work for the Mayers because my son was here. I wanted to be close to him."

"And then you discovered that the last nanny disappeared?"

"Yes." I feel a lump form in my throat. "I heard it in town and decided to investigate it."

"With the help of Mr. James Brooks?"

"Yes. We wanted to find out what happened... for different reasons. He was engaged to Eva and I just... I wanted some assurance that the family taking care of my son wasn't dangerous."

"How did you figure out the body was in the pantry freezer?"

"I didn't. I searched the entire house and didn't find anything. Then I heard a weird sound in there—a hum—I wondered if there was something I wasn't seeing."

"Are you saying it was your gut instinct that led you to the hidden wine cellar?"

"No. I also saw a red light, and I suspected it was a hidden camera. I didn't see cameras anywhere else in the house." I clasp my hands together. "Please, Officer, help me get my son back."

She narrows her eyes, her pen hovering over her notepad. "Please explain to me why you never told Robin and Paul Mayer that Wyatt Mayer is your son."

It's a stupid question, to be honest, because the answer is so obvious. "Because they never would have allowed me to get close to him. No adoptive parents would agree to that."

The officer runs a hand through her curly hair and exchanges a few words in German with one of her male colleagues. After he responds to her, she returns her focus to me. "Is there a way to show that Wyatt is your son without a DNA test?"

"Um... He's the spitting image of his father."

"Unfortunately, that won't be enough evidence, Miss Rogers. Anything written that could prove what you're saying is true?"

"No. Please just do a DNA test if you don't believe me. That would prove it."

A few more words are exchanged between her and the other officer, who then reaches for his phone and makes a call.

The questioning goes on for another half hour and I'm then moved to the station.

The interrogation room is tiny, the white walls so close I can reach out and touch them. A dim lightbulb barely illuminates the room, and there are only two chairs and a small, metal table between me and Officer Wagner. The smells of sweat, fear, and desperation hang heavy in the air, causing my stomach to lurch. I can't help but think of the many people who have sat in this chair before me.

The sound of a ticking clock in the background forces me back to the present and I focus on the officer. I'm asked the same questions again and again until I'm totally drained and worried I might say the wrong things.

"What happened to James Brooks?" I ask when I'm given a short break. "Where is he?"

"He's being held in custody," Officer Wagner replies. "We found evidence inside his house showing that he had been planning the Mayers's murder for quite some time."

My hands fly to my face and I erupt into tears from sheer fatigue and sorrow.

"Miss Rogers," the officer says after giving me less than a minute to cry, "I need to ask you a few questions about yourself."

My heart jumps to my throat and I look up with wet eyes. "What... what about me?"

"Before you started working for the Mayers, where were you employed?"

"I worked as a babysitter for several families." I avert my gaze to focus on a small crack in the wall and sniffle. "I had a few other jobs too, but babysitting was what I did mostly."

"In the United States?"

I nod.

She scribbles something on her paper, then looks up at me. "Can you give me the name of your previous employer?"

I could give her a fake name, but she's a cop, and will likely figure out I'm lying. "Amanda and Mark Golden from New York," I say, swallowing my fear. "They had a two-year-old son named Dylan."

I doubt she's going to call them up and ask them questions about me, and even if she does, I never said much about myself to them anyway.

"Are you originally from New York?" she asks, putting the pen down as if to signal that we are friends now and we're just having a good old chat.

I won't let her fool me, though. She's just trying to get me to let my guard down. Instead of answering immediately, I wait a few heartbeats, trying to weigh the consequences of a truthful answer versus a lie. Once again, I decide to go with the truth... the harmless version of it.

"No, I'm originally from Kentucky," I say, looking down and praying she won't ask more questions.

"Where in Kentucky?" She picks up her pen again and writes something down.

I can feel every drop of sweat forming on my forehead. "Bluefort. It's a very small town."

Perhaps it would have been smarter to give her the name of a different town, but if she later finds out I'm lying, she might wonder why and dig into my past to find out what I'm hiding. If they ever find out I was once institutionalized because I was considered a danger to my baby, I will never be considered stable enough to get custody.

She's quiet for such a long time that I look up to read her expression. Instead of asking me more questions, she calls her colleague in and they whisper a few words to each other in German.

"Excuse us." They both step out of the room and Officer Wagner returns fifteen minutes later and sits back down. "When you said you came from Bluefort, the name sounded familiar, so I went to look it up. There were some headlines a few years back, am I right? Something about a cult."

I don't understand why she's asking me these questions. It's obvious that she knows the answers from searching online. If she's looking for a reaction, she won't be getting one.

I can feel my heart in my throat, and it's hard for me to form any words. So I just keep staring at her. Maybe it's better for me to say nothing.

Officer Wagner stares back for a few seconds, then stands up. "I think that's all for now. I'm sure we'll have a few more questions for you, but for now, you're free to go."

I breathe a sigh of relief and stand up, rushing past the cop before she can change her mind. Outside, I exhale a deep breath as I try to calm my racing heart. I may have slipped up, but I'm not in trouble.

I book a room in a hotel, planning to stay in Austria as long as it takes to make sure Wyatt is okay, but there's no way I'm returning to the scene of the crime. The police mentioned he would be sent back to the United States, being a US citizen, but they don't know when exactly. I won't go anywhere until I know what will happen to him.

Early the next morning, I receive a call requesting that I come in for a DNA test. When I arrive at the hospital, Wyatt is already inside a small, white room where they collect samples. He throws himself into my arms, like a little boy desperate for his mother. He looks like he hasn't slept for a long time.

"Please don't leave me." He clings to me. "I want to stay with you."

"I won't leave you," I promise him. "I'll do whatever it takes for us to be together, but first they need to prove that you're my son."

After the tests, back at the hotel, I call Emily and tell her everything that has happened.

"Goodness, Christa. Just what did you do? Why didn't you tell me what you were up to all this time?"

"I didn't think you would support it."

"Without a doubt, I wouldn't have approved. What you did is insane. You could have gotten hurt. From what you're telling me, those people sounded really dangerous. I knew this scheme was a terrible one from the beginning. I should have talked you out of going."

I don't tell her that Robin managed to cut my shoulder with the knife. It's only a minor wound, so there's no reason to make her worried.

"I'm really okay. Just waiting for the results to prove that Wyatt is my son. Then we can come back home."

"It could be much more complex than that... you get that don't you? Under the law, he was their child. Before their death they could have appointed someone, maybe a family member, to be his guardian. Just because you're the biological mother doesn't mean... And with everything in your past—"

"I'm choosing to be positive," I cut her off. "Everything will work out in the end. I'm just happy that he's no longer with those people."

Those people. I'm still finding it hard to believe that both Robin and Paul no longer exist in the world, that they're dead, that I will never have to see them again.

"Do you know when you're coming home?" Emily asks, her voice tinged with worry.

"I don't know. I'm not allowed to leave just yet. And even if I were, I'm not leaving without Wyatt."

"Okay," she says, sighing. "I'm so sorry for everything that happened." Her voice is heavy with sympathy. "Please keep me updated, okay? And if you need me to come there, just let me know."

* * *

Four days after we give our samples, I get a call from the police station asking me to come in. The idea that they might have the DNA results drives me out of the hotel room, and I hurry to the station. I can hardly breathe as I walk into the gray building that resembles a small fortress, my heart thundering.

Officer Wagner meets me at the reception and escorts me to the same interrogation room I was in days ago.

"Do you have the results?" I ask as I drop into the chair. I don't even mind being inside the stifling room, all I care about is finally proving to them that Wyatt is my son.

"Not yet." She sits down opposite me. "But we have some new developments you might be interested in."

Before I can respond, another officer walks in with a stack of papers that she hands to Officer Wagner before leaving the room again.

Officer Wagner spreads the papers on the table between us. "Were you aware that Robin Mayer kept a journal?"

"Hmm... yes." Hot blood rushes to my face when I remember the first journal entry I read.

"Has she ever, by any chance, told you about the things she wrote about?"

"I'm not sure what you mean. Keeping a journal is a private task. People write about things they don't necessarily tell anyone, even their closest friends."

"So you never discussed the content?"

"No." I'm not going to tell her about the entries I read. If I reveal that, I would have to also reveal how I got them. I wouldn't want to give her a single reason not to trust me.

She slides one of the pages closer to me, but far enough to make sure I can't read it. "We found these on her phone. There are quite a number of entries that mention Wyatt, and they're quite troubling."

"What about Wyatt?" I clench my fists under the table. The room is deathly silent, so quiet I can hear my heart beating.

Officer Wagner stares at me, her eyes expressionless. Then she pulls the paper toward her again and lowers her gaze to it. "This entry is from last year, in June," she says, and starts to read.

It makes me nauseous the way Wyatt tries to worm his way into my heart, desperate for my love and affection. He'd wander into the room and then sit next to me, beginning a conversation I would rather not be a part of. He'd bring me tea, or offer to help me wash the dishes or do random chores around the house, even though the maid does these things already.

But the closer he gets, the more he tries to get me to love him, the more I want to push him away. The revulsion that builds in my throat every time he nears me grows every day.

I don't want him near my baby. I don't want him near me. His presence is like a lingering poison that seeps through the walls, sapping away at my strength, courage, and sanity.

I must continue to keep him away from me.

On the outside, I will go on pretending to be his mother, but behind closed doors there's nothing between us.

I will do only what's absolutely necessary to fool the world into believing he's my son and I care about him. But it's only on paper. I'm no longer able to offer him what a real mother should, anything beyond material things is off limits.

I keep waiting for the day I can finally be free of him, the boy I used to love and have now come to hate.

THIRTY-SEVEN

ROBIN

July, 2021

Before I open my eyes, I send up a silent prayer that today will be an easy one, and that I'll be strong enough to overcome whatever comes my way. But anxiety is already swirling in my stomach as it does every day, never giving me a moment's peace.

I always dread it when Paul is away on extended work trips because it means I'm trapped inside a house with Wyatt alone. Paul has no idea what kind of monster he is. Wyatt is a completely different person in front of him and everyone else who meets him. Normally it's not so bad when Sophia, our housekeeper, is around, but she doesn't live-in, and currently she's visiting her parents in Florida. I had tried to convince her to change her travels to the next week, when Paul is back, but Sophia said there was a family emergency and she wouldn't be able to change her plans.

Yawning, my eyes still closed, I stretch out my arms under the covers, drawing them back toward my body when I touch something warm. Paul's side of the bed should be empty and cold. But it's not.

My eyes fly open and I almost scream when I see the person in bed next to me. "Wyatt," I croak, jumping out of bed. "What are you doing here? How did you get in?" I'm certain I locked the door last night.

"Morning, Mom," Wyatt says, yawning as he sits up in bed. Then he grins.

I ball my fists. "I asked what you're doing here."

He tilts his head to one side. "Do I need a reason to sleep in my mother's bed?"

"I'm not your..." I swallow hard and lick my bottom lip, preventing myself from saying the words I so desperately want to say, the words I want the whole world to know. "Please, get out." I point a finger to the door.

"Why?" He has the nerve to look hurt. "Mom, I just thought we should spend a little more time together. You never have time to hang out."

"You're not a baby anymore." I wrap a hand around my neck, which feels hot. "You're fourteen years old and perfectly capable of being on your own." I stomp to the door, yanking it open. "I don't want you to ever come in our room again without permission, is that clear?"

Saying nothing, he gets out of bed. When he nears the door, I step away from him. Being in close proximity to him makes my skin crawl.

"You don't have to be afraid of me, Mommy," he whispers. "I'm your child." The corners of his lips curl up in a smile that's clearly meant to taunt me.

I want to remind him that he is adopted. When he turned thirteen, Paul and I told him. I wanted him to know that we were not related by blood, to put another wall of separation between me and him. I thought that this would make him stay away from me, to keep a distance. In reality, it had the opposite effect: he sought even more of my affection and did whatever he could to get close, so close it made me uncomfortable.

While he stands by the door, I return to the bed, a protective hand on my belly as I distance myself.

"Sometimes I think you're afraid of me," Wyatt says, feigning disappointment. "I wonder why."

"Wyatt, please... I just need to be alone," I say in a more patient voice. I don't want to trigger him.

As I watch him, I can't help wondering when he came into our bedroom and how long he has been next to me in our bed. I fold my arms across my chest, and I can feel my throat tighten with fear and rage.

Before he walks out of the room, he gives me another one of his twisted grins and says, "I love you, Mom. I'll see you around."

I stopped telling him I love him a long time ago, but that doesn't stop him from saying it to me, hoping that one day I'll respond. But that's never going to happen.

"See you later," I say instead.

As soon as he's gone, I decide that, after taking a shower, I'll get out of the house. Wyatt is just too unpredictable and I have no idea what he could do next. I need to protect myself.

Half an hour after I kick him out of the room, I go down to the kitchen for a glass of orange juice before leaving the house to spend the day with a friend. I find the kitchen in disarray. All the cups, glasses, plates, and everything else that's normally in the cabinets has been taken out and spread out across the counters and even the floor. Not only that, but they're all covered in chocolate sauce and maple syrup, dripped on them to make it hard to remove.

He did it on purpose. He knows Sophia is not here to help me clean up, and he wanted to punish me for pushing him away. He finds a way to punish me every time I refuse to show him affection.

I glance at the plates on the floor to see that some of the syrup and chocolate sauce has been smeared all over the place, including the tiles, walls, and many of the cabinets. My heart sinks when I spot more of it on the tall windows. The sticky stuff is everywhere. It will be a nightmare to clean.

Tears fill my eyes and the back of my throat, like a flood threatening to choke me.

Even though I could temporarily hire someone to come and clean up, it's best to take care of the mess myself because people around this neighborhood talk way too much. I know for a fact that the nannies and housekeepers on our street have regular meetups that are spent gossiping about their employers. I can only imagine what they would say about the state of my kitchen. If I had a small child in the house, it would be easy to explain away, but at fourteen, Wyatt is big enough not to create such a mess.

My face is hot with rage and the heat is quickly spreading to the rest of my body. I could go and confront Wyatt right this minute, but I know from experience that it would not end well. He will just find another creative way to taunt me, and, being pregnant, this is not a battle I want to fight. I already live in constant fear that the stress will harm my baby.

I fill a bucket with warm, soapy water and get to my hands and knees to scrub the tiles. I blame myself for letting it come this far. The truth is, Wyatt knows something terrible about me that no one else does. Maybe I should have told Paul, just confessed everything to him, so Wyatt would not be able to hold my secret over my head. But it's too late now. The only thing I have the power to do is suck it up and pray for time to fly by until Wyatt is grown up and is out of the house and on his own. But I have a feeling he will continue to taunt me from a distance.

Even though I'm not behind bars for the crime I committed, I might as well be in handcuffs, handcuffs that connect me to Wyatt, the key thrown away.

I dip the sponge into the warm water and as I squeeze it, the hairs at the back of my neck rise and bristle. I turn to see him standing in the doorway watching me.

"Why did you do this?" I ask then continue to scrub.

"I didn't, Mom," he replies in a voice that doesn't sound like that of a child. "You did it to yourself."

He's right. Eva's death is what started this whole nightmare, the one thing that allows Wyatt to act with impunity because he knows there's nothing I can do about his behavior.

After all, the worst punishment he could serve me is to report me to the authorities for what I did.

THIRTY-EIGHT

ROBIN

August, 2015

A week after catching my husband in bed with Eva, I see them again, not in the bed we share, but the laundry room on the far side of the villa where hardly anyone goes. I had told Paul that I was driving to Salzburg to spend a day with Jane, and I did intend to do it, but halfway through the journey, I changed my mind.

One of the reasons I had wanted to go away was because I couldn't bear the sight of my husband, to remember what he did to me. I needed a break from him. But on my drive to Salzburg, it occurred to me that by running away, even if just for a day, I was giving him the opportunity to hurt me even more, to continue with his extracurricular activities without fear of being caught.

After seeing them in the laundry room, I go back outside and get into the car. Instead of driving away from the house and going on the search for a place to lick my wounds in private, I drive the car into the barely used garage. If Paul comes out of the house right now, he will not know that I've returned, unless of course Wyatt has seen the car from inside the house and decides to tell him. I just want some time alone before I have to face them.

I exit the car and hurry to another room that's only three doors down from the laundry room, a guest room that hasn't been lived in for some time. I lock the door and sit on the bed. My hands clutching my knees, I rock myself back and forth, warm tears streaming from my eyes and dripping onto my arms.

I'm not exactly sure how long I stay inside the room. I forgot my phone in the car, so I can't check the time. After a while, the sound of a car engine comes to life and I open the curtains a crack to peer outside.

It's Paul in the car, and he's driving off. My guess is that it's around 6 p.m. and Eva should be heading off in a few minutes as well, after doing more work than she's paid for.

Since Paul is going to God knows where, maybe it's best I talk to Eva first, to let her know that she no longer has a job with us, something I should have done the first time I saw her sleeping with my husband.

When I'm sure Paul is long gone, I leave the room and head to the main wing, finding Eva wiping down the counter in the kitchen.

The moment she sees me, she jumps back, eyes wide. "Mrs. Mayer!" she breathes, her voice quavering as if each word is an effort. "I had no idea you were still here—I thought you had left for Salzburg."

"Yes, that had been the plan," I reply icily, my gaze blazing into hers. "But I changed my mind."

She watches me for a long time, and I wonder if she can see the tears in my eyes.

"Okay," she says and gets back to work. "I'm just about to finish up here, then I'll be heading home. I'm running a little late."

I just stare, watching her with my hands clenched at my

sides, forcing myself to say something, to fire her on the spot. Finally, I say the words burning in my throat. "Your work here is done."

Eva slowly turns to face me, her expression unreadable. "Yes, I'll just take out the garbage."

I nod and dip my head to one side. "Did you tidy up the laundry room today? The one in the other wing, I mean. When I checked a few minutes ago, it was filthy."

Eva visibly stiffens, then she starts to twist the rag in her hands. She knows that I know what happened in that room.

"I didn't... No," she stammers, her voice cracking under the pressure.

"I know everything, Eva," I say, my words slicing through the air like a sharp blade. "I saw you. You're sleeping with my husband, aren't you?"

Eva drops the rag in the sink and picks up her phone from the counter, where she always keeps it so she can listen to music while she works. As she fiddles with it, she turns away from me.

Something breaks inside me in that moment, and it ignites a fire in my chest. "You can't even look at me?" My anger is at boiling point as I stride forward, closing the gap between me and the other woman. Before I'm even aware of what I'm doing, my hand is gripping her shoulder and yanking her around to look me in the eye, to see what she did to me.

Eva's phone falls from her hand and lands with a crash on the floor. The screen splinters but doesn't shatter.

"What did you do?" She drops to her knees and picks up her damaged phone. Furious, she gets to her feet again and comes close to me, her eyes filled with rage. "You broke my phone," she says between clenched teeth, spittle flying from her mouth.

"And you broke my marriage," I hiss. "I gave you a job and this is how you repay me?"

Eva flicks her long hair over her shoulder and lets out a

raucous laugh. Then she steps closer, the intensity of her gaze burning into my very soul. "It's not my fault that you're unable to satisfy your husband's needs." A cruel smirk plays on her lips as she rubs her belly. "Has he told you our two-week-old little secret? I wonder if it's a boy."

Anger pumping in my veins, I lunge forward, my hand colliding with her jaw in an explosion of rage.

Shocked by what I just did, my head snaps back while Eva stands tall, her nostrils flaring and her eyes blazing like wildfire. Then she puts her phone behind her on the counter and faces me, her shoulders pushed back, a look of satisfaction on her face.

"I understand why you're upset. I gave your husband what you couldn't."

"Get out of this house now," I demand with a shaky voice, motioning to the door with a finger. "And stay away from my husband—or else."

"Or else what?" Eva raises an eyebrow, both hands on her hips. "Will you hit me again or something worse? I know how powerful jealousy can be. It makes people do crazy things."

"In that case, yes." My hand shaking with fury, I yank open the cutlery drawer and grab a hold of the sharpest knife. I grip the handle so tight my knuckles turn white. But I don't pull it out. "If I ever see you near my husband again, I will kill you."

Eva laughs mockingly, and my boiling anger reaches a tipping point. With a fierce roar, I grab the nearest object—a heavy glass bowl—and bring it crashing hard against the side of her head. I scream again with an all-consuming rage and swing it at the other side with such force that it shatters.

Eva falls to the floor in a heap of blood and broken glass. Her eyes are wide with terror as she grasps both sides of her head and screams in agony, blood spurting from the wounds I inflicted.

Trembling, I collapse to my knees, the blood from Eva's

wounds staining my hands. "I'm so sorry," I whisper, though it's no use.

Eva doesn't respond and her eyes have gone blank. In a desperate attempt to save her, I press a dishcloth against the wound on one side of her head, trying to stop the bleeding. But the blood seeps through my fingers too fast and soon her head rolls forward and hits her chest.

I scramble to check for a pulse. There's one, but it's weak, and her breathing is becoming slow and labored.

With my heart in my throat, I jump to my feet, sprinting out of the kitchen to get my phone from the car.

But once I have it, I can't make myself dial for help. If I call, I'll have to tell the police what I did.

I gasp for air and stumble back into the house, running into the kitchen, my feet skidding on the tiles until I come to a stop in the doorway. My gaze immediately falls on the gruesome sight in front of me.

Instead of just Eva in there, slumped against the wall with blood trickling from her wounds, Wyatt, our eight-year-old son, is sitting next to her with a bloody knife in his hand. My heart stutters when my gaze takes in a round red circle on Eva's stomach, an expanding circle of ruby red.

"Wyatt." My lips tremble as I watch the boy I adopted as a beautiful and innocent baby grinning up at me. "What did you do?"

"I did it for you, Mommy." Still holding the knife, he gets to his feet.

To my horror, he comes to me and wraps his arms around my body. I'm too frozen to push him away. My phone drops at the same time as the knife falls from Wyatt's hand and hits the floor with a loud clang.

I finally detangle myself from his embrace. "What did you do, Wyatt?"

He shrugs as he looks at Eva's lifeless body. "She was

already dead, Mommy. You killed her. I wanted her not to wake up anymore."

I stumble to the sink and throw up. I want to scream, but all I can do is choke on my sobs. Then I face the body in my kitchen, trying to comprehend what just happened.

It can't be. I can't have killed Eva. When I left her, she was still breathing. Now here she is, a lifeless body, her blood spilling out across the kitchen floor.

Who really killed her, me or my son?

THIRTY-NINE

ROBIN

August, 2021

Six years later, not a day has gone by without me regretting what happened. That night, Wyatt insisted that Eva was already dead when he found her, and although a part of me doubted his words, what could I do about it? I was guilty of bringing Eva to death's door by hitting her over the head with that bowl, a deadly blow that had the potential to kill someone.

If the case ever went to court, who would believe me over an eight-year-old boy anyway?

To be on the safe side, I never told him where I hid the body.

The day after Eva died, I convinced Paul that I wanted to renovate the kitchen to make it more comfortable for us, and also to keep me busy. Paul thought it was a good idea and left me to my own devices.

Though I did make the kitchen more modern, my main focus was on the pantry, which I divided into two. Since it was large enough to be someone's bedroom, I removed a section of it and had it converted into a secret room, which only I knew about.

Wyatt promised to never tell anyone what I did, but although he kept his promise, he uses every opportunity to remind me of it, especially when we're alone at home, like today when Paul has gone on one of his business trips.

On the outside, my adopted son is like any normal fourteen-year-old boy, albeit withdrawn. Sometimes we even manage to put on a show that fools people into believing we have an ordinary mother-and-son relationship. No one would ever guess he has a mean streak because only I get to see that side of him. And he knows I won't tell anyone or send him away because an unseen force ties us together, a secret so dark and menacing that it could devastate if it were ever revealed. Our connection is inescapable and indestructible, a hidden burden that haunts me with its reminder of that fateful day.

It was all my fault. If I hadn't been so foolish, I wouldn't be linked to him in this way. I wouldn't owe him a debt that can never be repaid.

When we're alone, he enjoys tormenting me in various ways, such as calling my phone over and over again just to whisper my name, and playing scary pranks on me. Now that he knows I'm pregnant, he has become even more cruel.

But tonight, he has gone too far. An hour ago, I walked into the broom closet to get a mop and some cleaning supplies when Wyatt locked the door, trapping me inside the dark room I'm unable to light up as the light switch is on the outside. Since I was a child, I was always terrified of the dark and never slept without a night-light. It's a phobia I still haven't overcome. Laying on the cold floor, cradling my pregnant belly and gasping for air, I have no idea how long Wyatt will keep me trapped inside this room. I'm terrified that he might only let me out in the morning, shortly before the housekeeper arrives.

With no window, the room is dark and airless, and the only

sound I can hear is that of my own breathing. Sweat and tears stream down my face as I battle the darkness.

A faint light pierces the darkness from beneath the door, where a thin sliver of illumination reveals what I think is Wyatt's silhouette. Even with a door between us, the air is thick with his anger, an invisible force that permeates the walls and leaves me breathless.

The minutes pass slowly as my fear and uncertainty mount.

"Wyatt," I call, "please don't do this. I'm begging you. I'll do anything you want, just let me out."

Silence is his answer, a deafening confirmation that he will not release me any time soon.

From a distance, my phone starts ringing. I had left it in the living room. It must be Paul calling to check up on me. He has been especially caring since I became pregnant, and when he's home he treats me like I'm a porcelain doll, something to be handled with care.

The ringing eventually stops, and so does my hope of getting out of the broom closet. A tear cascades down my cheek, knowing that my husband will never know what dark games Wyatt is playing with me. I can never tell him, otherwise he will discover what his wife is capable of. Wyatt is a child, and he would probably get away with the part he played in the murder, but I could go to prison.

The mere thought of being behind bars, inside a locked cell, causes me to shake with fear. My only solace is the image of my unborn baby, soothing me with the assurance that things will be all right.

When I sense a movement outside again, I call for Wyatt, who still doesn't respond. Suddenly I'm lightheaded and dizzy and black dots swim in my vision. I slowly get up from my spot on the floor and reach for the door handle. When it doesn't budge, I sink down again, and wrap my arms around my legs.

With my forehead on my knees, I rock back and forth, soothing both me and my baby.

I must survive the darkness for my baby's sake.

What seems like hours pass and I eventually fall asleep only to be woken up by a sharp pain in my belly.

"No," I mutter.

I cannot lose this child only halfway into my pregnancy. Crouching down in pain, I whisper a prayer for my baby to be safe and healthy and for me to find a way out of my prison.

Desperate, I bang my fist on the door and cry for Wyatt to let me out. "I'm in pain. Please... it hurts. I need to go to the hospital."

When Wyatt does not open the door, I realize that this might be exactly what he wants, for something to happen to the baby. Since he's so desperate for my love, he would not want me to give that love to someone else, especially not my own flesh and blood.

Desperate to save my child, I scream out until my voice breaks from fatigue and exhaustion. The pain is even worse now, and I can feel moisture seeping through the thick layers of my dress, but the door remains shut.

I collapse in a corner and close my eyes. Then I take a deep breath and whisper a silent prayer, but it's not answered. As I had feared, Wyatt only unlocks the door in the morning.

As soon as I stumble out of the room, I see the blood trickling down my leg.

* * *

Forty-eight hours after I lose my baby, I return home late at night, my heart in pieces. Our neighbor, Paloma, who lives a few blocks down the street, never left my side since the moment I called to beg her to drive me to the hospital. After the medical assessment confirmed the miscarriage, she took me to her house to care for me. But Paul is returning tonight and I want to be home.

Another friend of mine, who also has a son about Wyatt's age, had offered to take him for the weekend. I'd gladly accepted because I couldn't bear to even look at him.

"Exactly what happened, Robin?" Paloma asks as she parks the car. "I still don't understand."

I peer out the window and respond with the first lie that comes to me. "I don't know. The pain came out of nowhere."

Paloma, whose brother happens to be a cop, cannot know the truth; it would lead to much darker truths.

"I'm so sorry," she whispers and gives me a hug.

I manage a soft smile and unbuckle my seatbelt.

Paloma runs a hand through her freshly cut bob. "Are you sure you'll be okay until Paul arrives?"

"He'll be here within the hour. I'll be fine," I reply and get out of the car.

Inside the house, I go straight to the broom closet and open the door. The blood is gone, so is my urine, all washed away by the housekeeper, but I can still see it in my mind's eye, still sniff the metallic scent of the blood.

I collapse, sobbing into the rug as I remember the baby I never got to hold, the child Wyatt killed. My heart breaks as I think of all I had hoped for my child, the dreams I had for its future. All that had been taken away in a single moment of torment.

I finally stand and drag myself up the stairs, my mind still processing the magnitude of what has happened. In the bedroom, I carefully lie down on the bed, my body aching and my heart crushed. I lie silent and motionless, as I come to terms with the loss I suffered. I think of Wyatt and the pain he has caused me, how he has taken away something I had so desperately wanted and needed.

I can never tell anyone what he did, but from now on I will

avoid being completely alone with him. He killed my baby. What would stop him from killing me?

Paul has always been against having stay-in help, but since he's not always here, I need the extra protection. Having someone around all the time would prevent Wyatt from tormenting me again. And I will do everything possible not to be in the same room as him.

I know what darkness lurks within his heart and so I must keep watch, my senses sharp and my wits quick, forever prepared to protect myself.

It's an endless game of cat and mouse. Until the day I can finally be free of him, I will continue to lead a double life. A life I never wanted, but one that I must accept. I will hide the truth for as long as I can. After all, I don't have any other choice.

The phone rings and even though I can see it's Paul, I'm too weak to answer. Instead, I lie there and listen until the call ends and the silence of the room sets in once more.

When he finally gets home, after picking up Wyatt from his friend's house, I can barely look him in the eye as I hug him tight and weep, grateful for the warmth and comfort of his embrace.

When I open my eyes again, I see Wyatt standing in our bedroom doorway, leaning against the doorframe, his face contorted into a sneer, his eyes dark and menacing. I shiver and close my eyes, unable to endure the sight of him.

Since the day Eva died, he's made every attempt to get me to love him again. But I can now say with absolute certainty that, instead of love, all I feel for him is unadulterated hatred, and I will never be sorry for it.

From now on we will be strangers living in the same house. And for as long as he's living with us, I will no longer have keys in the locks of any door. I never want to give him a chance to do what he did again, to imprison me inside my own home.

FORTY

CHRISTA

Officer Wagner drops the papers onto the table and meets my eyes. "As you heard, in some of these journal entries, Robin Mayer suspected that it was not she who killed Eva, but that it was really Wyatt, her adopted son."

"My son," I mutter and drop my head into my hands. "He didn't. He didn't do that." How could a child of mine, or any child, commit such violence? I don't believe it.

Officer Wagner places a hand on my back and I look up, but I can barely see her through my blurry eyes.

"Miss Rogers, we are still investigating the case. We don't know yet if Mrs. Mayer's claims are true. But based on these entries, we need to speak to Wyatt, and we will let you know if he may be involved in any way."

It's a long time before I can respond. When I do, it's barely a whisper. "Okay."

When I rise from the chair, I feel like I'm floating toward the door.

As I make my way down the silent hallway my feet feel heavy, my steps echoing. Unable to breathe, I stop walking and stare at a criminal in handcuffs, a disheveled-looking man in his mid-twenties, who's being led away by police officers.

Suddenly, I see Wyatt's face on that man, and I'm slammed with emotion. I take a deep breath and continue down the hallway, my mind spinning with worry. I don't know what to think.

Could Robin be right? Is there a chance my son is a killer?

No, I won't believe it. He can't be. Wyatt is innocent and Robin hated him so much she wanted to blame him for something he didn't do, in case she got caught.

Back in my hotel room, I break down in tears. I can hear my heart pounding in my chest and the walls seems to press in on me from all sides. I hug my arms tightly around myself and squeeze my eyes shut, trying and failing to make sense of everything. Eventually, my tears subside and I fall asleep, dreaming of a time when a mother doesn't have to fear for her son's future.

* * *

I spend the next forty-eight hours in a daze, unable to focus or eat. My mind is a jumble of thoughts, worries, and fears as I await a call from the station. I do reach out to them several times, but they repeatedly tell me that they need time to investigate Robin's claims and they will get back to me as soon as they have something more concrete.

On the third day, instead of a call, I receive a visit at the hotel from Officer Wagner.

My stomach clenched tight with nerves, I show her to a lumpy couch in a color that reminds me of vomit. I lower myself into one of the chairs and she hands me a white envelope, which I rip open to find a single sheet of paper. With trembling hands, I scan it. DNA test results.

Officer Wagner comes to stand next to me and translates the text for me. "It says there that Wyatt is not your son," she says.

Shock waves pulse through me and tears prick my eyes. "Oh, my God," I whisper as I weep uncontrollably. I was so sure I had found my baby. Maybe I should be relieved that a boy who is thought to have killed someone is not my son, but the fact that he isn't leaves a gaping hole in my chest and the same big question that has followed me for many years: If it's not him, where is my child?

I think back to the files I saw at a private adoption agency in Lexington, where I spent a month working as a cleaner to gain access to their archives. After snooping around, I came across a file of a baby boy born in Bluefort, which was unusual because Bluefort is a small town and rarely had any babies put up for adoption.

The boy's parents were unknown, and there was a note attached stating that he was found abandoned in a dumpster behind a gas station. The agency had given him the name Wyatt and he was adopted by Robin and Paul Mayer from out of state.

It was the only lead I had and it had led me to New York, where I finally found Wyatt, or so I thought. I had followed him and his family for months, watching him from afar and imagining what our reunion would be like. But now, with the DNA test results in my hands, it's painfully clear that I had been wrong all along. I had been so eager to believe that I had finally found my son that I ignored my better judgment and pursued a dead end, when I could have found a way to do a cheek swab.

Officer Wagner gives me the time I need to grieve and process the new information. When I'm able to speak again, I pull myself together and ask the only question that remains.

"Does Wyatt know?" I feel terrible for telling him I was his mother even though I had no evidence to support it. I wish I could take back those words and spare him the pain of losing the mother he thought he had found.

Officer Wagner nods. "He was told, yes."

"And how did he... How did he react to the news?" My heart is heavy with guilt.

"He didn't say anything," Officer Wagner replies, her expression filled with sympathy. "But he was withdrawn and cold afterward. I think it's safe to say that he took the news pretty hard."

I nod as tears prick the corners of my eyes. "What will happen to him?"

She shrugs. "We have spoken to him and he denied the accusations."

"So what happens next?" I wrap my arms around my body, feeling suddenly cold.

"As it stands, journals are hearsay and so there is not enough evidence to convict Wyatt." She pauses and leans back. "But we did get hold of Eva Weber's phone, and as it turns out, she recorded the last few minutes of her life. In those recordings, it's clear that Robin and Eva did have a heated argument, and that Robin hurt her in some way, but we can't be sure to what extent."

"So Robin could have killed her?"

The officer nods. "It is a possibility."

FORTY-ONE

CHRISTA

The plane lifts into the sky above Austria, but I don't see its beauty through the small window. My view is obscured by the emotions that are raging through me, emotions I don't know how to turn off, how to stop them from choking me. I'm seated at the window and have a perfect view, but I can't find it in me to appreciate the scenery, to see the mountains, the rivers, or the beautiful, ancient castles.

I feel nothing, nothing but emptiness as the officer's words repeat inside my head over and over like a tornado destroying everything in its path.

Wyatt is not your son.

I close my eyes to try to block out the agonizing truth, but it doesn't help. As much as I'm determined to shut my mind off, it's just as determined to scream louder and harsher, to plunge the knife deeper.

Wyatt isn't my son. Wyatt isn't my son. Wyatt isn't my son.

The boy I spent so much time chasing, watching, trying to protect. The boy I dedicated my life to, and gave up everything for. He's not my son. He is someone else's child.

Maybe deep down I suspected he wasn't mine, but refused

to accept it. I didn't want to believe it. For years, I truly believed that they had stolen my baby and given him up for adoption without my consent because they didn't trust me to keep him. So I made it my life's mission to find him, to bring him back to me. And I thought I had. I thought Wyatt was the little boy I had been dreaming of for many years. He looked just like his father, a man I never want to see again, though I was willing to live with his reflection.

Two weeks ago, when Officer Wagner brought me the DNA results, I was devastated, crushed beyond repair. Hearing he could be a killer had been painful enough. I didn't want to believe any of it. Just like fifteen years ago when I didn't want to believe my baby was dead.

A flight attendant walks past and beams at me and the person sitting beside me, an old man with a long beard braided to the tip. I don't smile back because there's nothing for me to be happy about. It already takes up so much energy just to keep myself from crumbling, to keep going forward.

The past few days were dark, and I was unable to get out of bed for a whole week except when the police showed up to ask me questions they had already asked me dozens of times. Since they could not prove Wyatt's involvement, they relied more on Eva's phone recording and thought it to be strong enough evidence to prove Robin could have killed her. She'd had a strong enough motive.

There was no evidence found to prove that Paul was involved in any way. He'd cheated on his wife, but it doesn't seem as though he was a murderer.

This, of course, makes things very complicated for James. I spoke to him last week at the jail and he was not the man I met a few weeks ago. His eyes were dead and there was really not much left to say between us. He had accepted his fate and though I urged him to still fight for his freedom, he didn't seem interested. I guess to him, being in prison is a small price to pay.

"I got what I wanted," he said to me. "I wanted them to pay for what they did." He admitted to me that the police found evidence in his home that he had been planning to kill them for years. That he had been waiting for the Mayers to return to Austria so he could get his revenge.

"I'm okay with prison," he said. "Without Eva in my life, I'm not interested in living."

"You really loved her, didn't you?" I asked.

"She was the love of my life." His eyes suddenly flashed with rage. "And that bastard... he took advantage of her."

I reeled back in shock. "You knew about—"

"The affair?" He nodded lightly and looked away. "That's why I did it."

I suddenly understood. Robin died because she killed Eva, and Paul died because he cheated with her. In James's eyes, they were both guilty of a crime.

We said goodbye and I had tears in my eyes as I walked away from the man I almost fell in love with. A man I had really come to care for and trusted for a minute. A man who could never give his heart to me even if he wanted to.

I told James I would write to him, to keep in touch, but he told me it might be best not to. He's probably right. After everything that happened, exactly what would we talk about? There would always be a dark cloud looming over us, reminding us of what he did and the mistakes I made. Maybe it's best to leave it all behind and start over.

Start over. What would that even look like for me? Where would I start? I've lost the life I knew before meeting Wyatt, and I feel lost now because I don't have anything to work toward, anything to hope for. No goals, no plans, just me and my pain. How does one get back from what's happened to me? How does one recover from this?

For years, everything I did was to get my son back. Now I'm returning to the US empty-handed. No job, no child, no hope.

The only thing I carry inside my heart is pain, more pain than I had before I left the United States, before I walked into Robin and Paul's lives. Pain that will follow me for the rest of my life.

And if I dare forget, the nightmares will remind me of that night inside the pantry.

Emily said I should be thankful that I'm still alive, that I get to start over, but I don't see it that way. All I feel is dead inside. Even though Paul or Robin did not take my life, I feel like they did.

Like James, I can't find any reason to keep fighting.

FORTY-TWO
CHRISTA

Life has changed drastically since I left Austria five months ago, but, at the same time, some things have remained the same. The pain I left with is still inside my chest, haunting me in moments of stillness. But I managed to pick up the pieces that I could.

Instead of looking after other people's children, which would feel like pouring salt into an open wound, now I waitress at night and clean hotel rooms during the day. I work myself to the bone so I don't have to think too much, so that I don't have to remember. But it's a futile effort, of course—I can't outrun my thoughts. All the same, I need to keep doing something.

I have stopped looking for my son, no longer believing he's still out there, alive and well, waiting for me to find him. Now I've started imagining a different scene, images of him lying with his eyes closed in my arms as I kiss his forehead goodbye. I hold onto that image night after night, day after day.

I still think about Wyatt, still wondering if he's doing okay, still guilty for not getting my facts straight before telling him I was his mother.

I've been in the US almost as long as he has and I know that he's living with a foster family in Cove Haven, Vermont.

I tracked him down some time ago, not for the purpose of disrupting his life again, as that wouldn't be fair on him, but to make sure he was doing all right. I was relieved to learn that he was living with a foster family and not in an orphanage. After the trauma he has been through, he deserves the love and care of a family and a comforting home in which he can start to heal. I prayed every day that he ended up with good people.

I never expected to see him again. Then two weeks ago, I received an email from Judy Adams, his foster mother, who told me that Wyatt had fallen into a state of despondency and therapy had not been of use. She asked if I would talk to him, but he refused to come to the phone. The next day, the phone rang again. It was Wyatt and all he said was that he wanted to see me, that I should come to Cove Haven because he had something important to tell me and he wanted to do it in person.

At first, I didn't think it was a good idea for him to see me again since it might open up old wounds. But he was really persistent. I told him I would think about it and we hung up.

After days of mulling it over, I decided that maybe it wouldn't be such a bad idea. Since we did not say goodbye to each other properly in Austria, maybe seeing me again would give him closure, and I'd get a chance to apologize for the hurt I caused him.

When I called Judy to ask if I have the permission to come and see Wyatt, she thought it would be a good idea.

She suggested that I surprise him by picking him up from his school, and we arranged for me to meet her for a drink before so she could give me the address and directions.

It's a week later, and an hour and a half ago, I arrived in Cove Haven and immediately met Judy at a local bar. After chatting for a while and her giving me the address of the school, I book a room in a hotel only a few blocks away. I only ask for one night because I don't expect to stay longer.

I remain awake most of the night, rehearsing what I would say to Wyatt when I see him again.

* * *

When I wake up in the morning, it's too early to head to the high school, so I have a cold shower and take my time getting dressed. At 7 a.m., I eat breakfast at the hotel restaurant, which tastes like cardboard, but I don't mind. I'm too focused on the conversation I need to have with Wyatt.

It takes me about ten minutes to find the high school, and I'm relieved to find kids already arriving. The school is small and quaint, like the town. The building is one story, painted a light blue, with a row of bicycles lined up against the wall. On the other side of the courtyard, I can see a basketball hoop and a playground.

I park my car and walk nervously toward the school's entrance, but I don't get close enough for anyone to notice me, someone who's neither a teacher nor a parent. I watch from afar as the children enter the building and try to locate Wyatt among them. But I don't see him.

I wait until 8 a.m. and there's still no sign of Wyatt. One option would be to go straight into the school and see if he's in attendance and ask to speak to him, but I wouldn't want to surprise him in front of his class. I know I can't stay here much longer, so I decide to go back to the hotel and come back at the end of the school day.

I spend the day walking around town, distracting myself with watching the locals going about their everyday life. I feel a strange mixture of dread, guilt, and longing for the boy I haven't seen in months.

I end up at the town's library in the mid-afternoon and spend a few hours reading about the town's history. When I'm walking out, I remember my visit with Wyatt to the bookstore in Ruddel, how the shopkeeper claimed to have seen me before.

She was right. I've been keeping another secret. Desiring to be around Wyatt, I did visit Ruddel for the first time seven years ago, the summer Eva was killed. I could never tell James or anyone else that I followed Eva and Wyatt around the village for several days until she spotted me and confronted me, threatening to go to the police if I didn't stop following them. That was the last time I saw her. Nervous that she might spot me again, I stayed away from the villa. Maybe if I hadn't done that, I might have witnessed her murder.

I return to the school before 3 p.m. As I arrive, the bell rings and children pour out of the building. I struggle to spot Wyatt among the crowd. But then I see him, his head down and moving quickly, not stopping to chat with anyone. He's wearing a brown shirt with a black backpack on his shoulder. He looks a little different to how I remember him; he seems thinner and his hair is slightly longer. But it's definitely Wyatt.

He spots me and his face turns to shock, and he just stands there motionless. My heart skips a beat and I can feel the tears pricking my eyes as I watch him, wishing I could draw him into a hug. He had asked me to come see him, but he doesn't look like he was expecting me to actually show up.

We stay like that, staring at each other and not speaking for what feels like an eternity. Finally, I break the silence.

"Wyatt, it's me," I say softly. "You wanted me to come and see you. I wanted to surprise you." I pause. "I'm so sorry I haven't called after returning to the US. A lot has been going on."

My words seem to break the spell. Wyatt hesitantly takes a few steps toward me, his face growing serious. "I'm sure it has." He lowers his gaze to my belly with an expression of what I can only call disgust. "You're pregnant."

It was six weeks after arriving in the US when I started

having constant nausea and thought it was because of my unstable mental health and the horrifying nightmares. I went to the doctor for sleeping pills and that's when he told me the news.

I may not have the child I gave birth to fifteen years ago, but there's another one growing inside of me. The only souvenir I got from my time in Austria. And since James was the only person I've been with in two years, he is the father.

After going over it for many nights, I wrote him a letter. I told him the truth because I don't want him going through what I did, never knowing that he has a child out there. I haven't received any response, but at least I was able to do the right thing and let him know. I hope it was the right thing. I guess I will never know. After all, he said not to contact him, which I did anyway. But I made him a promise that if he chose not to get involved, I'd understand, and I'd love our child enough for both of us.

I read about his case on the internet and followed the trial closely. I am aware that he has been sentenced to life in prison. My heart ached for him as I read the verdict, but I was somewhat relieved that when I saw him he had seemed to accept his fate. It would have been much tougher if he had been hoping for a different outcome.

I lay a protective hand over my belly and smile at Wyatt. "It was a surprise. How are you?" I need to change the subject because he doesn't exactly look overjoyed about my pregnancy.

"I didn't think you would come," he says, still staring at my belly.

"You said it was important." I swallow hard. I don't know why, but he looks more angry than happy about me being here. "Should we maybe go and sit somewhere? I could take you out for something to eat and then drive you home."

"I heard you're not my mother," he says, ignoring my invitation.

"No, I'm not. I'm sorry. I wanted to apologize to you, to reach out, but I didn't want to make things worse." I pause. "I was wrong. I thought—"

"Save your breath. It doesn't matter." His voice is not the voice of the child I used to know, the child I still care so deeply about. This one is tainted by hatred. Is this why he called me here, to show me how angry he is?

"You're just like her. You never cared about me."

"Robin? You think I'm like her?" My chest tightens at the mere thought.

"Yeah. She never wanted me. She never even bothered to hide it. You saw how she was. She never wanted to be around me, even after everything I did for her. Not even a thank you."

"What, Wyatt? What did you do for her?" I glance at the kids walking past us. "Look, let's go and have a seat somewhere. We can talk."

"Oh, don't worry. What I have to say won't take long." He moves close enough to whisper in my ear. "I did it."

I shake my head, not trusting myself to speak.

His chuckle sends a shiver down my spine. "You don't know what I mean, do you?"

"I... no. What are you saying?"

He draws in a long breath, then he blows out. "What I wanted to tell you in person is that it was me. I did it because she was too much of a coward to do it herself. I did what she couldn't do."

He doesn't put it into words, but the meaning is clear. *No.* It can't be. Robin can't have been telling the truth.

"That's not true, Wyatt. Stop saying things like that." I reach out to him, but he pulls away.

He continues, telling me things I never ever wanted to hear. "I thought she would love me more if I finished what she started. But instead, she hated me more. Then she got pregnant with that stupid brat and continued to treat me like I didn't exist. I'm glad it's dead. I guess karma really is a bitch, huh?"

I don't want to believe him, but something deep inside tells me to be wary. All I can do is stare into his eyes, trying to read the truth in them. What I see leaves me cold.

"You're lying. You're not a... you didn't do it."

"*Ich bin kein Lügner.*" He smiles, winks, then walks away. "*Auf Wiedersehen Christa. Sei vorsichtig,*" he says over his shoulder in a perfect German accent.

I'm left standing alone, still trying to make sense of what just happened.

Everything I believed was wrong.

Wyatt could be the person who left me the note the day I arrived in Austria. Even if he only said two words, I could tell that his German was fluent. Had he just been pretending to us all that he didn't speak German?

What hurts and terrifies me the most is that he may not have said it in words, but he has confessed to being a murderer.

EPILOGUE
CHRISTA

Giving birth to my daughter was supposed to be one of the happiest days of my life. The last nine months, I fell in love with the little life growing inside of me and couldn't wait to meet her. I didn't know it would be a girl. I didn't want to know. After the last couple of months, I was in need of a good surprise. And she is the best surprise I could have gotten.

Unfortunately, the day of my delivery did not go as planned. The labor was long and hard, and I had to have a cesarean section, but I was so excited to meet my baby in the end that everything else faded away. Until now.

Two days after giving birth, I'm lying in my hospital bed, my hand inside Heather's basinet, her little fingers wrapped around my finger. But I'm not looking into her face this time, learning her expressions. My eyes are glued to the TV screen above my bed.

As I try to focus on what the reporter is saying, a nurse walks in to check on me. "It would be wise if you got some rest when your little one does," she says quietly.

I ignore her and keep my attention on the tragedy unfolding on the screen. The story, of a woman who lost her life in a house fire three days ago in Cove Haven, hits me hard.

When the nurse leaves, I reach for the remote and crank up the volume, not wanting to miss a word, even as much as I don't want what I'm hearing to be true.

The news anchor reports, "The fire reportedly started in her bedroom, and it spread quickly throughout the entire home. Their neighbors heard screams and were able to alert the fire department, but by the time it was contained, one of the people had already died. It's believed that the fire was started by a candle that was knocked over."

My vision blurs as the photo of the victim appears on the screen, accompanied by her name. Judy Adams, who was apparently a cherished member of the community.

"She and her husband, Lester, were foster parents of six children over the years. We would like to express our condolences to her family and everyone else who was affected by this tragedy."

The picture of Judy slowly fades from the screen and I sit bolt upright in my bed, my heart pounding. I can't shake the feeling that it wasn't an accident.

The sound of a soft cry coming from the bassinet fills the room and I close my eyes as tears stream down my face. Even though I'm scared, I take a deep breath and remove my hand from the baby's basinet, forcing myself to calm down and think it through.

When Heather starts to fuss again, I pick her up and cradle her in my arms, rocking her back and forth, hoping that the movement will lull her to sleep. Then I switch off the TV.

It's frightening to think that someone I was close to could be a murderer, responsible for multiple murders. Though I don't want to, I begin to blame myself for what happened. There are so many things I did wrong. I should have told Wyatt myself that I wasn't his biological mother instead of having someone else do it on my behalf. I should have contacted him sooner after we returned to the US, rather than waiting for months. I should have done a lot of things that I failed to do. I hurt him, and in turn he might have hurt Judy, a woman who had invited him into her home and seemed to care for him.

When Emily comes to the hospital to visit later in the day, I tell her everything that's happened. She holds me while I cry, telling me it's not my fault, but deep down I'm still racked with guilt.

"What will you do?" she asks, her eyes full of worry. She's now standing in front of me in black jeans and a beige tank top, her long dark hair framing her face in waves. "Christa, I don't want to tell you what to do, but I think you need to go to the police."

"I can't do that," I say, my voice heavy with regret. I gaze into her eyes, trying to convey the depth of my feelings. "I know you're saying that it's not my fault, but I feel like it is. He's just a child, a child who's hurting deeply."

"Yes, a child who committed a crime." Emily's eyes flash at me. "And if he does it again, how do you think that will make you feel in the future? You need to do the right thing because what if he comes after you or Heather?"

Her words chill me to the bone. I know she's right, and I need to go to the police, but the idea of turning in a child is something I can't wrap my head around. However, the thought of Heather and me being in danger is something I can't bear to think about.

"I'll call the police in the morning," I finally say, the weight of the decision heavy on my shoulders.

"No." Emily takes my hand in hers. "I know how hard this is for you. How about I do it? I can handle it. You just focus on yourself and Heather. The police will probably want to talk to you eventually, but I can take care of the initial report."

I look at her with gratitude, feeling relieved that someone

else will take the burden of contacting the police off my shoulders. "Thank you," I whisper, feeling the guilt slowly subsiding.

After she leaves, I take a short nap. When I wake up, I find Heather's basinet empty.

Fear floods my heart as I get out of the hospital bed, panicking and searching every corner of the room before bursting out into the hallway, my stitches pulling painfully with each step. I press a hand to my abdomen, trying to ease the pain, and call out Heather's name, even though I feel ridiculous for expecting a baby to answer.

But suddenly, a familiar sensation of dread grips me. As I sprint toward the nursery dark thoughts creep into my mind. The same horrors I experienced when I was seventeen and suffered from postpartum depression after my baby was born and they branded me an unfit mother. What if it's happening again and they've taken my child away from me?

Before I can reach the nursery, a panic attack hits me like a freight train causing me to gasp for air and feel dizzy. I slump against the wall, attempting to calm myself down, but it's no use. The memories of the past and the fear for my daughter's safety are consuming me whole. Tears are streaming down my face and I clench my fist, hitting the wall, feeling as helpless and powerless as I did back then.

I think I'm screaming because I can feel the soreness in my throat, but I can't tell for sure because my ears are ringing so loudly. Soon my vision starts to blur, and I feel like I'm drowning. The world goes dark around me, and, for a moment, I think I'll pass out.

Suddenly, a nurse appears and places a hand on my shoulder, her calm voice breaking through my hysteria. But I can't see her face because my vision is still blurred with tears, and I can only hear the soothing tone of her voice.

"Miss Rogers, are you okay?" she asks and, when I don't respond, she grabs my arm gently but firmly, leading me to a small room where she helps me sit down. "Take deep breaths, in and out," she instructs, and I follow her lead, trying to calm my racing heart. "It's okay. You're safe here. You're not alone."

I follow her instructions and take deep breaths, slowly regaining control of my emotions. When my vision clears and my breathing returns to normal, I look at her and try to speak.

"Please help me," I manage to say, my voice small and hoarse. "My baby is gone. Please don't let them take her away." I get to my feet again, but the nurse gently pushes me back down.

"Miss Rogers, your daughter is safe. She's in the nursery, sleeping soundly. She was crying when you were asleep and one of our nurses took her out of the room to calm her down. No one is taking your baby from you."

Relief washes over me like a tidal wave. "Thank you so much," I croak, my voice shaking. "Can I see her? I need to see her."

"No, you need to stay here and calm down. I'll get someone to bring her to you."

As I wait, my mind wanders back to the memories that had consumed me moments before. I never expected to feel that kind of fear again—the kind that squeezes your heart and consumes your mind, making it hard to breathe. The kind that leaves you feeling helpless and powerless.

But it's not just the memories of the past that are consuming me. It's the fear of the future too.

Before now, I was worried about Wyatt doing something to me or Heather, but there may still be other people out there who could hurt me, who could hurt my daughter. People who are capable of anything.

As I sit there, lost in my thoughts, the door opens, and the same nurse walks in, holding my daughter in her arms. I can't help the tears that spill down my cheeks as I reach out to take my daughter into my embrace. She's warm and soft against my chest, and I hold her close, grateful for her safety. But for how long can I keep her safe? How long before the past catches up with me? I push the thought from my mind and focus on the present. I look at my daughter's peaceful face, her small hand wrapped around my finger. She's a reminder of what I have to hold onto, of what's worth fighting for.

But looking into her face I also see something else, an image of her brother, the child I failed to protect. Would I really be able to live with myself knowing he could still be out there and I don't try again to find him? What kind of mother would that make me?

When the nurse leaves the room, I bring my mouth to Heather's ear and whisper, "Thank you, baby. Thank you for reminding me not to give up. We'll find your brother, I promise."

Giving up is not an option. I need to continue looking for my son, to bring him home to his sister, to keep them both safe from evils I know firsthand exist in this world.

A LETTER FROM L.G. DAVIS

Dear Reader,

I'd like to thank you so much for reading *The New Nanny*. It was such a joy to create Christa's character. As I sat down to write, I found myself losing track of time, getting lost in the world she lived in, feeling every emotion that she felt as if it were my own. I hope that you felt the same way too.

Since I live in Austria, it was especially fun to create the fictional, mountainous town of Ruddel as a breathtaking backdrop for Christa's journey.

I look forward to creating more stories and characters like Christa, characters that are full of depth, flaws, and strengths. Characters that you'll fall in love with, root for, and perhaps even shed a tear for.

For now, I want to take a moment to share a little secret with you. This is not the end for Christa and Wyatt. Their story will continue on in the next book that I'm so excited to share with you.

In order to be notified every time I have a new book published, please sign up at the link below. Your email address will never be shared and you can unsubscribe at any time.

www.bookouture.com/l-g-davis

If you enjoyed reading *The New Nanny*, I would be deeply grateful if you let other readers know by posting a review, so they can discover and decide if it's the kind of book that they would enjoy. Your support means the world to me and motivates me to continue creating stories that touch the hearts of readers like you. Thank you in advance for your time.

I love to hear from my readers, so don't hesitate to reach out. My Facebook page, Instagram and Twitter accounts are open for communication. Don't hesitate to contact me with any questions, comments, or just to say hello. I appreciate every message I receive and I make it a point to respond as soon as I can.

Thank you again for taking the time to read *The New Nanny*.

Much love,

Liz xxx

http://www.author-lgdavis.com

 facebook.com/LGDavisBooks
 twitter.com/LGDavisAuthor
 instagram.com/LGDavisAuthor

ACKNOWLEDGMENTS

Writing a book is never a solitary endeavor. It takes a village to bring a story to life, and I am grateful for the support of many people throughout this journey.

First and foremost, I would like to thank my editor, Jennifer Hunt, for her incredible support and guidance throughout the writing process. Without her keen eye and dedication, this book would not be what it is today.

I'm also grateful to the entire team at Bookouture for their encouragement, expertise, and commitment to bringing my book to a wider audience.

To my husband and children, thank you for your unwavering support and encouragement. Your love kept me going during the tough times, and I couldn't have done it without you. Your unwavering support has been a source of comfort and inspiration.

And lastly, I want to express my deepest gratitude to my readers. Your support and love for my stories means more to me than words can express. I'm grateful for every review, comment, and message of support. Thank you for taking the time to read my work and for allowing me to be a part of your lives, even if only for a little while. As I embark on my next writing adventure, I take all of your kindness and support with me, knowing that I have a community of readers and supporters cheering me on.

I love you all, and I can't wait to share my next book with you.